LEE COUNTY
107 Hawki
Sanford, N. C. 27330

SING A SONG OF CYANIDE

The day the Cyanide Man first struck, cub reporter Larry Baker was wondering how he was going to pay off his overdraft on the 150 dollars a month the Shanghai *Daily News* paid him.

But someone up there must have loved him, because within hours they had sent him a highly-unlikely guardian angel in the shape of Mrs. Pym, that battle-axe who, against all expectation, had risen to the rank of detective inspector in the Shanghai Municipal Police.

Called to a block of flats where an exiled Russian dancer won't answer her door, Mrs Pym drags young Baker along. When they arrive the girl is dead. Cause of death: cyanide poisoning. At her insistence, Larry is assigned to the story for the *Daily News*, and it soon becomes clear that sizzling below the surface, ready to boil over, are the political tensions that beset Shanghai in the twenties.

The Cyanide Man might make the headlines, but mention the Hop-Ley Dancers and there's real trouble . . .

SING A SONG OF CYANIDE

A Mrs. Pym Story

Nigel Morland

First published 1953
by
Cassell and Company Limited
This edition 1989 by Chivers Press
published by arrangement with
Macmillan Publishing Company

ISBN 0 86220 757 6

Foreword copyright © Bernard Knight, 1989

British Library Cataloguing in Publication Data available

for the blonde with
the big grey eyes . . .
PAM MORLAND

Printed and bound in Great Britain by
Redwood Burn Limited, Trowbridge, Wiltshire

FOREWORD

It is something of a reviewing cliché to say that a play or book 'operates on several levels', but Nigel Morland's *Sing a Song of Cyanide* has to be described in this way. Primarily, it is a straightforward and rather simple thriller of the old type, owing much to Edgar Wallace, who befriended him in his younger days. In fact, Nigel Morland edited the *Edgar Wallace News Review* for some time.

The Cyanide book is an easy read, good clean fun in *Boy's Own* style, with sharp-edged stereotype characters and a highly improbable story-line. The pace never slows down, there is a murder a minute and the hero races from one crisis to the next with barely time to grab a sandwich or have a snooze.

Yet knowing something of the author gives an insight into the book and illuminates some of the descriptive passages in a way which is not only interesting, but probably gives them some historical value. The book is set in Shanghai in the twenties, in that strange European enclave surrounded by the 'fiendish Chinee', and is in part autobiographical, as the author himself confirms in his preface.

Nigel Morland, whom I knew fairly well through his later interest in forensic medicine, was born in London in 1905 and entered journalism and writing the hard way, being largely self-educated and working up through newspaper packing, as a copy-printer and even a spell as a mortuary attendant! He then went as a young man to Shanghai as a real 'cub-reporter', the sort that used to be featured in boys' stories and strip-cartoons. This is where the relevance to *Sing a Song of Cyanide* appears, as it is obvious that the hero *is* Nigel Morland.

If one sets aside the daft story, the descriptive parts of the book must surely be a fairly accurate account of life in that peculiar island of Europeans which was the International Settlement. He even begins the book with a sketch map and his racy descriptions of hectic car chases are replete with accurate accounts of the geography of the city. Even more interesting are his throw-away vignettes of the politics of the times, with mentions of Mao Tse-tung and Chiang Kai-shek. Some of these even appear as asterisked footnotes, a strange sight in a 'who-dunnit'.

There is a chapter, almost irrelevant to the plot, where the intrepid cub-reporter takes off into the Chinese hinterland and becomes embroiled in a ferocious battle between the war-lords. There is a strong flavour of the authentic about this and I wish I had read this book while Nigel was still alive, so that I could have asked him how deep his involvement really was in this battle.

Nigel wrote prodigiously, under a string of pseudonyms. The best-known were his 'Mrs Palmyra Evangeline Pym' books, about a formidable and highly unlikely female Assistant Commissioner of the Metropolitan Police. She appears to be an amalgam of Margaret Rutherford and James Bond, dressing in country tweeds with a Luger in her handbag, tearing around in a red Bugatti!

Because of the huge success of umpteen Mrs Pym novels, Nigel Morland says that he was asked to explain how this battle-axe began in business, so he seized the opportunity to launch her retrospectively in Shanghai, giving himself latitude to insert some nostalgia and autobiography of his own. *Sing a Song of Cyanide* is thus a total flash-back. Though placed firmly in 1922–23, it was written as late as 1953. It reads strangely in places, because the style and content are so classically nineteen-twenties that one is lulled into feeling that it was written contemporaneously, until one is tripped up now and then by a mention of 'nuclear weapons' and the (Second) World War.

Without giving away the dénouement, one can say that the crux of the story has a forensic medical twist, albeit based on very shaky scientific foundations. Nigel Morland was an accomplished amateur forensic scientist, founding a number of magazines and journals on the subject, such as *The Criminologist*, *The International Journal of Forensic Dentistry* and *Forensic Photography*. He wrote several textbooks on forensic topics, especially criminology and sexual offences. All this was in addition to his huge fiction output of over 300 books, as well as radio and film scripts. One of his novels was made into a film in the 'forties, starring Mary Clare as Mrs. Pym.

Read the story without worrying too much about the plethora of corpses, but take in the atmosphere of that alien city of pre-war Shanghai, with its last gasps of arrogant imperialism and hints of corruption and immorality which Nigel's generation of writers would be too genteel to spell out.

BERNARD KNIGHT

THE BLACK DAGGER CRIME SERIES

The Black Dagger Crime series is a result of a joint effort between Chivers Press and a sub-committee of the Crime Writers' Association, consisting of Marian Babson, Peter Chambers and chaired by John Kennedy Melling. It is designed to select outstanding examples of every type of detective story, so that enthusiasts will have the opportunity to read once more classics that have been scarce for years, while at the same time introducing them to a new generation who have not previously had the chance to enjoy them.

CONTENTS

CHAPTER		PAGE
I.	LADY IN DARKNESS	1
II.	DEATH RIDES SWIFTLY	8
III.	THE LEGEND OF LAFFIN	16
IV.	JADE BY NIGHT	28
V.	THE MAN IN THE RITZ-CARLTON	38
VI.	STILL MORE CYANIDE	53
VII.	HOME OF THE DANCERS	66
VIII.	THE PATHWAYS OF MIDNIGHT	73
IX.	WILD PURSUIT	87
X.	THE FIRE-BUG	100
XI.	BACKGROUND TO FONG	109
XII.	WAR	118
XIII.	THE LITTLE TALL RABBITS	133
XIV.	GARNETT'S HOUSE	145
XV.	THE YELLOW RENAULT	156
XVI.	THE MAN WHO WASN'T THERE	167
XVII.	THE FRONT PAGE	180
XVIII.	SUSPICION	191
XIX.	BOMBSHELL	205
XX.	THE PARADOX	216
XXI.	FANTASTIC STORY	222

PYM, PALMYRA EVANGELINE, Assistant Commissioner, Metropolitan Police ; *b.* Berkshire, 24 June, 1892 ; *o.d.* of late Dr. and Mrs. John Eighteen ; *m.* late Richard Pym, of Shanghai, 1921 ; *educ.* Valley College, Sonning ; St. Hilda's College, Oxford. Reporter on London *Morning Herald*, 1913–14 ; attached Women's Royal Naval Service, 1914–16 ; Chief Secretary to Director of Remounts, China, 1916–19 ; Shanghai Municipal Police, 1920–23 ; Lecturer, Deutsche Forschungsanstalt für Psychiatrie (*Kriminalistische*), 1926 ; Assistant Adviser to N.Y. Police Academy, 1927–30 ; attached to police organizations in Berlin, Stockholm, Rome, Buenos Aires, Madrid and Chicago, 1930–34, in several capacities. Temporarily attached U.S. Dept. of Justice (F.B.I.), 1941 ; temporary official duties, Ministerio de Gobernacion, Madrid, 1943. *Publications :* The Mentality of the Higher Criminality, 1927 ; A System of Palmar Registration, 1930 ; The Prevalence of Religion among Homicides, 1934 ; Observations on the Classification of Eye-Prints, 1937 ; Poroscopy, and the Problem of Classification, 1940 ; An Aspect of the Paranoid Criminal, 1940 ; A National Bureau for Compulsory Fingerprint Registration, 1942 ; The Woman Police Officer, 1947. *Recreations :* Physical culture, reading, criminological research, and writing. *Address :* Denham House, Red Lion Square, London, W.C.1. (*Telephone unlisted.*)

PEOPLE IN THE STORY

LARRY BAKER. Newspaper man.
MRS. PYM. Central Police Station.
SUPERINTENDENT LAYSTALL. Central Police Station.
SERGEANT KELLY. Central Police Station.
DR. FEDOR. Police Surgeon.
SERGEANT CHUM-KWAT. Central Police Station.
GUIDO BARBADORO. Ritz-Carlton.
NATHAN SCHYLER. Lawyer.
CHARLIE LEE. *Daily News* doorman.
LANNY COAGER. City Editor, *Daily News*.
DINTY MOORE. Saloon keeper.
TOBY GARNETT. *Free Press*.
SUNG. House-boy.
'THE CYANIDE MAN.'
CHARLIE VOUCHER. *Voucher's Weekly*.
DAISY TING. Hat-check girl.
'THE BROTHERS HO.' Ritz-Carlton.
HIGHLO' HARRY. Ritz-Carlton.
RICO SANTONELLI. Ritz-Carlton.
MRS. ROTGERS
LORRIE BALA
BENJAMIN CUDWORTH } The Country Club set.
MRS. ERP
PAUL CHANG. Socialite.
JENNIE CHANG. His sister.
DR. WU HSIUNG. Scholar.
ARTHUR KEE. Central Police Station.
LYDIA TSCHENKO. Ritz-Carlton.
MRS. MACNAUGHTON. Landlady.
IRINA ROBERTI. Visitor to the *News*.
ALBERT FONG. Chinese.
YÜAN CHOU. Philosopher.
EDWARD CARTER BOWNE. Chairman, Shanghai Municipal Council.

TUK. Lodging-house keeper.
RANDY McCALLUM. Broker.
ARTHUR FINLAY. Shanghai Light Horse Company.
LEW SCHLESINGER. Shanghai American Company.
SAM HOLLOWAY. Yip Kee Garage.
FANG. Mechanic.
JOHNNY TEE. Doorkeeper.
LT. MA SUNG. Chang Tso-lin's army.

The Dead.

NADIA SHERBINA. Dancer.
LESLIE CHOW. Book-keeper.
LESLIE HO. Ritz-Carlton.
JACOB LAFFIN. Multi-millionaire.

For years now, readers who like Mrs. Pym have asked me at regular intervals for her very first adventure, the story of her initial climb to fame in the years before she came to New Scotland Yard.

A short story on these lines—a sort of kite to test public reaction—was tried in a famous magazine: the results were so pleasing that here it is, Mrs. Pym's bow in the world of detection.

While I make the truthful claim that the story, the characters, the names, are all fictitious, certain real names do appear; they have been qualified by an occasional footnote, showing I have done no more than borrow from history. Finally, I should say that all the *people* and the *incidents* are wholly fictitious: this would not be right. People I knew and loved appear in this novel under false names, but—melancholy thought!—none of them is now living, and, even if they were still in this world, I doubt if they would object, for they have been kindly dealt with.

As to the incidents, I cannot, again, entirely claim the cover of fiction since so much of this narrative is autobiographical, as the reader will rightly suspect.

N. M.

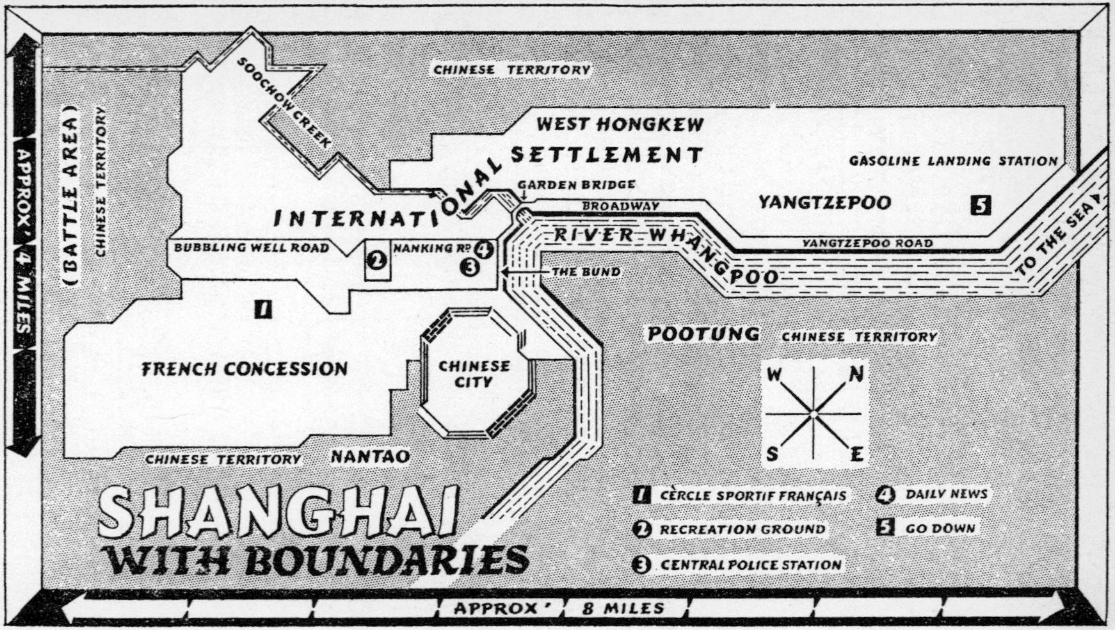
SHANGHAI
WITH BOUNDARIES
CHINESE TERRITORY
(BATTLE AREA)
SOOCHOW CREEK
WEST HONGKEW
INTERNATIONAL SETTLEMENT
GARDEN BRIDGE
BROADWAY
GASOLINE LANDING STATION
YANGTZEPOO
YANGTZEPOO ROAD
RIVER WHANGPOO
TO THE SEA
BUBBLING WELL ROAD
NANKING RD
THE BUND
FRENCH CONCESSION
CHINESE CITY
NANTAO
POOTUNG
W N S E
1 CÈRCLE SPORTIF FRANÇAIS
2 RECREATION GROUND
3 CENTRAL POLICE STATION
4 DAILY NEWS
5 GO DOWN
APPROX' 4 MILES
APPROX' 8 MILES

CHAPTER I

LADY IN DARKNESS

The day the Cyanide Man first struck I came out of the Californian-Oriental Bank doorway into the spring blaze of Nanking Road, wondering how I was going to make my overdraft get into the black.

Waiting on the kerb for a gap in the wild tangle of cars, trucks, rickshaws, and barrows, I had nothing else in mind except that darn overdraft. To really appreciate how I felt, you had to be a kid reporter on the Shanghai *Daily News*, drawing one hundred and fifty dollars a month, and living at the rate of two hundred.

That always was the snag about Shanghai. The classy novelists dub it 'The Paris of the East' or 'The Crossroads of the World.' Believe me, it had only one name, and that was overdraft. Either a man had to stay at home and read improving books, or else he got out into the city, keeping his nose close to the hub of things. A reporter who sat every night in his dreary bed-sitting-room would have been fired in a week.

I didn't know the answer. At twenty-one, a year out from Regina—it was and still is the nicest little city in Canada—I was on my own in Shanghai. Coming there was my own idea, when my mother's uncle left me a legacy of five hundred Canadian dollars. I wanted to see the world and soak myself in the mysterious East. The only mysterious thing about it was how a man made enough to eat and keep in the social run.

Even in those days, when the Cyanide Man was just getting ready to move in, Shanghai was a stinker. The first world war was over, and the great boom of the early 1920's was at its zenith. The city was packed with money, tourists, gangsters, and White Russians—all refugees, so named to distinguish them from the other sort. Apartments cost a fortune; so did everything else except liquor and cigarettes.

And there I was, stuck on a dusty kerb in the International Settlement, with my Overdraft—at twenty-one you spell it with a capital O—sitting squarely on my shoulders. To me Regina and heaven looked about the same, in that order.

I had an hour to fill before I went to lunch with a pal of mine. The best thing I could figure was window-shopping. I did it, hoping an idea might break.

The windows were packed with everything a man needed, priced at rates which shook me. There was a smooth-looking suit of English tweed in Lane Crawford's window that I would have given a lot to possess. I stood and admired it, put it on my reflection in the plate-glass, when the passing traffic showed gaps. On my six-foot of well-muscled body the suit fitted as if it had been made to measure; it even made my tangle of brown hair respectable. I couldn't see my eyes, but guessed they were still blue, so they toned as well.

I was so absorbed in the game that it was some seconds before my eyes focused correctly and I saw a woman standing beside me. She had her hands on her hips, watching me, a solid woman of middle height, with a strong face and a mouth that took no nonsense from anybody. She wore a tough-looking tweed suit with a massive handbag under one arm. Her pile of brown hair was crowned with a hat that must have made even the Chinese laugh—not that such a polite race would have done such a thing.

I swung round, beaming at her.

'Why, Mrs. Pym! I didn't see you.'

'That's what I thought.' She nodded at the suit. 'What's cooking, Larry Baker? Spring gone to your head?'

'No, ma'am. I was admiring the effect on me.'

'That?' She sniffed. 'Stick to quiet browns, son. You'd look like a bookmaker in that thing. Doing anything?'

' No. Just come from the bank and filling in time before I go to tiffin.'

' H'm.' She considered me out of those grey-blue eyes that could either chill you or skin you like a knife : it was usually one or the other. ' You know, Larry, you should go back to Regina and get a job. This city's no place for a nice kid.'

' Thanks, ma'am.' I smiled at her. ' I was thinking on those lines myself. I'm making a hundred and fifty, and spending two hundred. It's not so good.'

' Chits, liquor and women ? '

' Chits. You sign those neat little slips of paper when you order, then the first of the month turns up with the shroffs.* The way the bills total up beats me.'

' That's the size of it.' She knuckled her firm chin. ' You're still a cub on the *Daily News* ? '

' Yes, ma'am.'

' I'll have to look after you, then. I don't like babies running round, broke.' The glare in her eyes made me think I'd said the wrong thing before I'd even opened my mouth. ' No goo, or I'll knock your head off. The rest of the papers will howl if I give you a story : let 'em howl. Get into the car and don't talk.'

Mrs. Pym was using a Bugatti that year, a rollicking job painted scarlet. It looked fast, and it was, or she wouldn't be driving it. I got in the passenger seat and slid down, an eye on that stern profile, as the car eased into the Nanking Road traffic tangle.

She was worth looking at, a hard, rough, grim woman I never quite understood until I knew her better. In these present days of nuclear fission and H-bombs, she is Mrs. Assistant Commissioner Pym, of New Scotland Yard, who makes me welcome when I can get across to London from my Toronto job for a vacation. She was still something new in Shanghai that morning when we met.

She had been there longer than I had, after walking out of the job of Chief Secretary to the Director of Remounts

* Bill collectors.

(War Office, Special Service) in China. She had been stationed in Peking until she quit with that memorable tagline the Outports were still discussing : ' I'm sick of shipping Mongolian ponies to an army that doesn't need them, particularly with the European War over a year back. The whole stunt's a gag to enable favoured civil servants to get China tea on the spot at wholesale rates.'

Behind her was some reporting work on the old London *Morning Herald*, followed by a briefly spectacular career in the Women's Royal Naval Service, until she got everybody so spitting mad she was shipped to China as help for the Director of Remounts. What she did in that position nobody ever fathomed ; her unofficial activities included some snappy detective work in which she cleaned up and exposed several big swindles, broke Li-Fang, who was making a fortune out of remounts no one ever saw, and drove Harry Batcham from Peking and a racket he had run comfortably for twenty years.

Maybe it was her natural flair for detective work that did the trick. Anyhow, she came to Shanghai under her own name of Palmyra Evangeline Eighteen, somehow landing a job in the Municipal Police. She battered her way to a detective sergeant's rank in the C.I.D., quit to marry a retired ironmaster named Richard Pym. He died a few months later (and did the Country Club set go to town on that !). She went back to the S.M.P., raised to a detective inspectorship, her mouth grimmer than ever when people inquired about her private life.

That marriage was, I now think, the only mistake she ever made. What interested her in marriage was a mystery : even after all these years she has never spoken about it. Personally, I think she married because she was sore at herself over something—a woman figuring that way can be crazier than a self-stung scorpion.

There she was, a combination of phenomenon and chain lightning. Half the town hated her and the other half was plain scared, but she knew her job and did it magnificently, without fear or favour. I had gone with her on one or two small assignments. She liked me because I did as I was told, and, to be honest, admired her like hell. There was something about Mrs. Pym you couldn't resist. She wasn't motherly or even kind. She had all the brains in the world and, even then at thirty odd, she gave the impression she was both a battle-axe and hewn granite.

Just the same, behind that violent personality there was a heart, buried deep. You got your head chewed off if you thanked her for anything, yet, once she liked you, you followed along as I did. To-day Superintendent Shott and Dick Loddon, of the *Daily Report*, do just that thing, but don't ask them why.

When a man won her confidence he played things her way and enjoyed himself, in spite of her tongue. It's my contention Francis Drake and the rest of them felt the same about Queen Elizabeth. She was a penny-pincher, wore a red wig, and griped all day, but those toughies thought she was swell.

That sums it. Mrs. Pym, to me, was an outsize in personality and unexpectedness. She was also dead straight, which, in Shanghai, rated her in the halo class.

The intermission for thought on my part had given the Bugatti time to storm its way along Nanking Road to Bubbling Well Road. Mrs. Pym always drove as if she was one minute ahead of death. It took some doing in Shanghai just before lunch. She cut around the back of a grey street car, scared the pants off a chauffeur in a plum and gold Rolls Royce, and braked before a tall apartment building overlooking the Recreation Ground.

I was staring up at it when she dug my ribs.

'Out you get, boy. We're here on business.' She left the car, ramming the door shut, to consider the apartment block as if she hated it. 'Girl named Nadia Sherbina doesn't answer her door or the 'phone. They dug me out to handle it. That's Shanghai. Send a detective inspector along when some White Russian oversleeps. C'm on and shake her out of a hangover.'

The foyer was well equipped and expensive, running to

potted palms, gilt, and plush furniture. This was no dump, but a place reeking with class and money. Five hundred dollars* a month wouldn't have rented living space there. The hall porter was a big, pock-marked Chinese in elegant blue. He saluted Mrs. Pym because she was white; you could see he hated doing it.

'Morning, miss. You wanchee one person?'

'Nadia Sherbina?'

'No have got.'

She glared at the prompt answer—most native servants used it without hesitation—and stumped to the angle where the elevators were. The porter followed.

'No have got.'

'Police.' She snapped into the vernacular and almost took his hide off. 'What-side apartment?'

'Plenty sorrow. My pay you missy chop-chop.' He took off his flat-peaked cap, bowing us into the car. I could see the back of his red neck sweating on the journey to the third floor.

He insisted on leading us along a smart-looking corridor to a door numbered seven in English and Chinese characters. Mrs. Pym stared at him until he saluted again and shuffled back to the elevator.

'Put a coolie in doorman's uniform and you make a monkey out of him.' Her tone was scathing. She banged on the door since it was too exclusive to have a knocker or a bell-push, banging again when nothing happened.

The yale-type lock seemed to interest her. She took an ivorine calling-card from her pocket, bending it smoothly. I leaned over to watch as she pressed the door hard with one hand, making a small gap, slipping the card round the lock. It snicked back.

'Learning, handsome? You'll know what to do when you're locked out.' In the open doorway she listened.

---

* You should get this currency problem clear. People in most organizations were paid in the non-existent tael (a measure of silver). The silver dollar in general use (called Mexican because it came from there) equalled about fifty cents in U.S. money, or around two shillings, English; in the days I am writing about.

The dark hall was silent. There seemed to be nobody home, even when I ripped off a shout to get attention.

Mrs. Pym led the way through the empty rooms, switching on the lights as she moved, rooms furnished in what the American popular press were beginning to dub 'the plush love-nest' style. There was plenty of space, drawn curtains, and a flat air of vitiation.

When we reached the bedroom, lush with fancy tulle and gilt-daubed gimcrack, she put on the light. We stopped in the doorway together, held by the first sight of the handiwork performed by the one who gained me my promotion, the one I dubbed ' The Cyanide Man.'

CHAPTER II

DEATH RIDES SWIFTLY

'Lovely' was not a word that had entered into the currency of superlatives in those days. But blonde, slim, and undoubtedly a lovely, Nadia Sherbina was lying in blue silk sheets and frothy coverings, a Tiffany jewel in a Fifth Avenue setting. She was the sort of girl to fill any man's dreams, if he had those types of dreams.

However, cyanide is not a gentle killer. The fact she had beaten back even that poison's revolting hand showed what sort of woman she was. I said so to Mrs. Pym.

'Romantical cuss, aren't you? I admit it looks like cyanide, and maybe she's prettier than most. Still, she's morgue-meat, but Death doesn't get away with a thing when I'm doing the checking.'

She bent over Nadia, considering her. Delicately, without disturbing anything, she probed through the covers, looked on the floor, then under the bed.

'Nothing, ma'am?'

'Not a thing. She might have taken a capsule, or even chewed the stuff like gum'—she made a grimace of distaste—'assuming she's a suicide.'

'Eh?' That shook me. 'You don't mean *murder*?'

Mrs. Pym's eyes were sardonic. She stood with hands on her hips, frowning at the room.

'Son, there's money in this place. That coat I see beyond the built-in wardrobe door is sable. The workaday job alongside is Kolinsky. And the jewels on that dressing-table would set up the Rickshawmen's Mission for life.'

'Perhaps it's an affair of the heart? She's Russian, isn't she?'

The answering sniff was loud.

'Nonsense ! The Slav temperament's about the same as any other sort of temperament. Girls with what she's got don't up and kill themselves, just because Willie drools after a passing redhead. Girls like Nadia don't even have to hunt : the prey comes running, tongues hanging out.' She began a search through the bedroom, into the other rooms. I stayed at her heels, impressed at the swift, efficient manner she probed every place of concealment. When the job was over, she sat on the edge of a table in the living-room.

'Anything, ma'am ? '

'Not in the sense I want it. Stacks of letters from men : big-time goo and every one of them as good as cash. She's got six thousand dollars in the bank, and a year's contract with the Ritz-Carlton.' That was our show-place, a combination of cinema, restaurant and high-class cabaret. 'Oh, yes, she's having her hair permanently waved at the Astor shop to-morrow.'

'I don't get it.'

'I do. Here's a chit showing she fixed the appointment yesterday afternoon. Women do a lot of funny things, but they don't plan permanents forty-eight hours ahead, and swig cyanide in between.'

'It might've been a sudden shock, surely ? '

'Huh ! Larry, I'll tell you one little thing you haven't learned in your twenty-one years on this earth. When a woman lands in a love-tangle, she broods on it a few days then maybe jumps in the river. She certainly doesn't fix a hairdresser's appointment like that, go home to bed and take a cyanide nightcap.'

'I always thought suicides made a point of planning things ahead, just to fool people.'

'So they do.' Mrs. Pym nearly beamed. 'Nice thinking ! But if you saw what I saw you'd notice she'd cleaned her teeth before she went to bed. She'd taken off her make-up and thrown the used tissues in the bathroom wastebasket. It stacks up.

'If she planned suicide, she'd've gone to bed painted

like a totem pole. A pretty girl like that, even if she were loopy about her mythical Willie, wouldn't stand for the idea of strange men gaping at her the way she sleeps.' She hooked up the telephone receiver, glancing at me over one shoulder. ' It's murder. Settle that in your mind, some man handing out cyanide, betcha ! ' She gave the number of the Central Police Station, looking up at me. ' You don't use this story till I give you a release.'

' No, ma'am. I have to get assigned to it, anyhow.'

' Fine. Leave that to me.' She suddenly blasted the head off the telephone operator in a mixture of English and Shanghai vernacular—the telephone service would have raised the blood-pressure in a saint—and cut this short when she got the station. ' 'Lo, switchboard ? Pym here. Give me Superintendent Laystall in a hurry—'lo, Super ? Pym. I'm at Nadia Sherbina's flat. She's dead. Yes, sudden. Cyanide, and I call it murder. Okay, thanks.' She cradled the receiver, nodding. ' On their way. Go down and see that bossy doorman ; ask him just what made him call us, will you ? Laystall's department had a message from a man—maybe that Chinese admiral—claiming she didn't answer the door or the 'phone.'

I did the chore, talked with the pock-marked porter, and was back in the apartment within ten minutes. Mrs. Pym was in the bedroom, scrutinizing the blonde.

' He didn't call you, ma'am. Been on the downstairs door since eight this morning : we're the first callers he's had.'

' Are we, dammit ! *Don't* tell me we're up against one of those killers who advises the police, like something out of a detective story.'

' That's what he said. He didn't seem to be lying.'

' No ? You never can tell . . . ' She trailed off the sentence, going to the door. Tall, white-haired, gentle-faced Superintendent Laystall was entering the front door, with the vast bulk of Sergeant Kelly at his heels. We've forgotten Mike Kelly to-day. He was caught in Singapore that February morning when the Japs marched in, and died there before the Cricket Club gates with three other Irishmen, and two machine-guns, blasting the yellowbellies to hell. In the bars of the Far East, when Irishmen get together, you can often hear about Mike Kelly, clawing through the Japs with a twelve-inch wrench in one hand, howling his ' *Up* the Rebels ! ' before he was cut down to go to Valhalla with an escort of slain fit for a Viking.

Laystall glanced at Mrs. Pym, then at the corpse.

' Poor little monkey.' He shook his head, that man with the biggest heart in the world. ' Killing a nice little thing like that.'

Mrs. Pym saw Kelly's morose expression, and glowered, sitting heavily on this show of male distress.

' Murder ! ' Her voice was sharp. ' Pretty girls don't end that way of their own accord, even if they have been playing games.'

' You're sure it's murder ? '

' Sure I'm sure.' She answered Laystall's question with her findings, anticipating his glance at me. ' Larry's here because I brought him. Don't worry, he'll keep his mouth sewn up till I say so.'

' I've seen her dance,' Kelly said. ' Her, and the whole Ritz-Carlton chorus. On St. Patrick's Day, it was, she was after performing an Irish jig. Pert as a colleen.'

Mrs. Pym frowned at the enormous, sentimental Irishman.

' Kelly, how you can croon over a White Russian dancing an Irish—aw, mush. Super, am I delegated to this enquiry ? '

' You mean, in charge ? '

' And why not ? She's a woman, I'm a woman ; and even if the whole of the Shanghai Municipal Council would like me dead, I'm still carrying an inspector's warrant.'

' Yes.' Laystall rubbed one ear. He was largely responsible for Mrs. Pym, and the S.M.C., women-haters to a man, had never quite got over it. ' I don't see why not. Could you handle it ? '

' *Huh ?* '

'I mean, there may be trouble.'

'Trouble and I get along.' Her eyes were sardonic. 'Don't tell me you're scared of those old biddies round the Council table?'

'No; they just run things.' Laystall stared at me, wondering if I should be listening. 'Very well, Mrs. Pym. I've believed in you from the beginning.'

She glared. Any personal remarks made her irritable. Kelly stepped in, his red face beaming.

'Whisht and begorra, as the stage Irishman said! You let her handle this, Super, and I'll be helping if Mrs. Pym'll stand for it. Go on, sir. Dig in your heels.'

Laystall smiled. He couldn't resist Kelly, no more than any of us.

'Consider it logged. Now, ma'am, how do we stand?'

'Trouble. White folk don't get murdered in this city— least, not often. Here's a good-looking gal, with money and a flock of men chasing her. Somebody's given her cyanide. Now tell me, just what does this mean?' She produced a folded slip of paper, a telephone message chit. On it were some Russian characters. Below, obviously a translation, was written: 'The Hop-Ley Dancers.'

'They don't exist.' Kelly's voice was dogmatic. He knew Shanghai, the Chinese City, and, come to that, most of China, like men know their own faces. 'Me, I've got a bit of Russian and that word there is *tantsovát*. It's something to do with dancing, I'm sure.'

'Um? Then—what's on your mind, Super?'

Laystall had his eyes on the body, staring thoughtfully.

'You know,' his voice was hesitant, as if he was doubtful. 'When I first came out here, when the Boxers were on the job, I have an idea somebody once mentioned the Hop-Ley Dancers to me, in connection with the Jovial Hearts.'

'Hell!' Mrs. Pym glowered. '*Don't*, for pity's sake, tell me there's a Chinese secret society in this!'

'But the Jovial Hearts were wiped out after the legations in Peking were relieved,' Kelly pointed out. 'The Boxer leaders were mostly hanged, Super.'

Kelly stared, startled at being graded a night-life authority.

'Why, on St. Patrick's Night it would be around four a.m. Regularly, the place closes between two and three.'

'We're getting somewhere. I wonder if there is a night man on duty in the hall?'

'No, ma'am.' I could answer that one. 'The doorman told me he came on around eight. He quit last night at ten, but said there was no one when I asked about the night.'

'Okay. Superintendent, the body can be carted off now. Can I have a man left here till I know what I've got in mind?'

Laystall nodded, sending Kelly to fetch the usual spare man who would have arrived with the fingerprint expert and the photographer.

When the party had broken up Mrs. Pym told me to follow her. We went out of the apartment block into the sun, and four doors along to a European tobacco shop.

She waved me to wait, disappearing into the public telephone booth. When she came back she was nodding.

'That fixes you, son. I talked with Coager, your desk man.'

'Lanny Coager, on the City Desk? But——'

'I said I would fix it. He didn't want you on the story. I didn't tell him what the story was. Now he's biting chunks off the walls with worry.'

'Gosh——'

'Let me talk, will you? I said either you tag along with me and cover the story, or the handout goes to the *North China Post*. If you keep your deadline and it's hot, he swore you'd find another twenty-five in your pay fold.' Her glare was awful when I started to say what I felt. 'Look, you know darned well I hate goo. Hush up and come along to the Ritz-Carlton. I've got work to do.'

It made me feel good. I'd wiped out some of that overdraft, and my cub days were finished. I could have kissed her concrete jaw, but had the good sense not to try it.

'Not all of them you will remember, Kelly. However, perhaps I am wrong.'

'That's what I hope. Did you bring a doctor?' Mrs. Pym's voice was brisk.

The investigation became official after that. Little Dr. Fedor, acting police surgeon, was brought in with the fingerprint men and the photographer. When their work was done, Fedor checked over the body.

'Typical cyanide convulsion,' he told us. 'The mouth is clean, therefore I'd say it was in capsule form. Did you find any vessel?' Mrs. Pym shook her head. 'That confirms it. Do you want her opened?'

Laystall glanced at Mrs. Pym. She nodded.

'Better get a coroner's order. It's murder, I still say. We've got to check everything.'

'Can you get an idea of the time of death?' Laystall asked.

Fedor rubbed his balding head with one hand, blew out a loud breath.

'That question! I can say nothing till I've examined the stomach. Seeing you found her this way, I'd plump for hydrocyanic acid; potassium cyanide symptoms take longer to develop and there is prior sign of gastric irritation, which means the girl could have called a physician in time. It's hard to make a ruling. If you'll all go out of the room for ten minutes, I can give you an idea.'

When Fedor called, we trooped back. He had a thick glass thermometer held before his eyes, and was making calculations on a prescription pad with a pencil.

'Yes.' He looked up at Mrs. Pym. 'Apologize, ma'am. I was thinking of your sensibilities.' Mrs. Pym's loud sniff suggested she was not troubled by such things. 'Well, I have a shy nature, let's say. This is just a rough test, very much subject to the stomach findings. The way I see it, death *could* have occurred somewhere between five and seven this morning.'

'Ah!' Mrs. Pym turned to Kelly. 'What time does the Ritz-Carlton close?'

We were almost level with the Ritz-Carlton, not more than five minutes from Nadia Sherbina's place, when a Sikh policeman walked slap into the Bugatti's route. Mrs. Pym braked and began to say what she thought, frowning at the prompt gathering of curious natives on the kerb.

Her eyes nearly trimmed the cop's great black beard off his chin. I thought, for one moment, she was going to grab his black-and-white painted *lahthi* and whale his hide with it.

'Pardon, Missy Inspector.' He showed all his teeth and tried to bow. 'Office tell me you come along. Please to ask you telephone Central Station, very quick.'

'Oh?' She grumbled an apology, waving him out of the way. 'What're they raving about now?' She went to the Ritz-Carlton, halting and gesturing me out. 'Maybe the S.M.C.'s called a special meeting to have me hauled off. *That* wouldn't astonish me.'

I waited in the foyer of the great building while she found a 'phone booth. When she came stamping back her face was plain mad.

'It's an epidemic!'

'Why, ma'am, something wrong?'

'Something's gone sideways, or we've got a nut loose. Routine call from a rooming house in Kulun Road, Chapei. Chinese sergeant was sent to check on a death. Bird's a ledger clerk in Cathay Oil.'

'You mean . . .?'

'I mean there's a dead fellow named Leslie Chow, and the native sergeant says it's cyanide, and that's where we're going, *khwa-tien*!'

The Bugatti moved like a red streak. I didn't even notice. I had just coined that name for the Cyanide Man, and my mind was hammering at a typewriter, tearing off a newspaperman's dream, an exclusive story that wrote itself.

CHAPTER III

THE LEGEND OF LAFFIN

KULUN ROAD was a brief run. I had got around to looking at the world by the time we were nearing the end of Thibet Road. The Bugatti dodged through the traffic with sure agility, past the gas works and that grim odour, then we were across the Soochow Creek and its tangle of moored boats.

The rooming house was easy to find, a tall, ugly, rundown building, advertising rooms for rent in English and Chinese.

Sergeant Chum-Kwat was waiting in the dirty hallway. I knew him well, an undersized little Cantonese who wore very neat civilian clothes and carried a smile his eyes never shared. He had graduated with honours from the Sun Yat-sen University, and was probably the only Chinese police officer in Shanghai with a doctorate in literature.

'Good morning, ma'am; good morning, Mr. Baker. I am sorry to have bothered you, ma'am.'

Mrs. Pym's nod was affable; she liked Chum-Kwat.

'What's the trouble, Sergeant?'

'The owner of the house, Mr. Li-Chwang, found a lodger dead in bed. Very commendably he sent for assistance. I examined the dead man, and recognized the cyanotic pallor. I can smell no odour in the mouth, but that, Mrs. Pym, is my failing. I am one of those individuals who lack that ability.'

'I see. Where's the body?'

'This way, if you please.'

Chum-Kwat gave her his polite little bobbing bow, leading the way to the low-priced 'third floor back.' The room was cramped and crowded, the habitation of a Europeanized native who wasn't proud of being Chinese and wanted to get away from it.

Mrs. Pym sniffed at the fumed oak furniture, the carefully framed prints from English and American journals, heading for the bed.

The dead man had died more violently than Nadia Sherbina. The body was locked in a last contortion of pain, the eyes staring, and the lips caught in a bow of agony. She bent over the wide mouth.

'You're not the only one.' She nodded to the sergeant. 'I can't detect it. Larry, you try.'

It was not the sort of job I liked, but I did it, closing my eyes when I got close to the staring face.

'Very faint, ma'am, a sort of sweetish smell. Almonds?'

'Cyanide!' The exclamation was angry. 'It's an epidemic, or something. Sergeant, know anything?'

'A little, ma'am. Deceased came in at eleven o'clock last night, going straight to bed. When the boy called him at seven he did not answer. Mr. Li-Chwang was called and found this.'

'Seven? That's hours ago.'

'Yes, ma'am. Mr. Li-Chwang first attended to his duties, then went to relatives for advice, finally communicating with Central Station.' I hid a grin at this; it was so very typical of Chinese caution, which has the English beaten when it comes to considering the step before it's taken. 'I was then sent here, ma'am.'

'Who is the man?'

'Leslie Chow, from Ningpo. A ledger clerk in Cathay Oil for seven years. Respectable, educated, fond of European company. Work very hard to improve himself. Reserved, clean living, pays his bills. Has no father, but send every month money to assist his lady mother.'

Mrs. Pym stared at the dead man, taking the catalogue for granted. It was nothing new in China, where a whole city knows a man and everything about him within twenty-four hours of his arrival. Secret Service is kid stuff compared to Chinese ability in learning all about background.

'Sergeant, is it likely he'd have any connection with Nadia Sherbina, of the Ritz-Carlton?'

'That is the dead Russian lady? I doubt it, ma'am. The Ritz-Carlton would be beyond his means.'

'Probably. What about Cathay Oil?'

'The compradore* spoke highly of him, said he was a good, reliable man.' Chum-Kwat's brown eyes were gently ironic as if he had anticipated the query. 'His books are in perfect order; they have been checked. Even though he's a Ningpo man, it is not near our New Year.'

It made Mrs. Pym's strong mouth purse suspiciously. The joke was so obliquely Chinese that it is worth explaining. In China, when a native is in financial trouble, he usually robs the firm or just runs away in the eve of Chinese New Year, when all debts are supposed to be settled. If he runs, the action is summed up by saying he 'Have go Ningpo-side,' which, to the wise, tells all there is to know. Ningpo was outside Settlement jurisdiction, as Shanghai was then constituted.

'It's got me beat. I wonder what the hell's happening?'

'Shall I handle the investigation, ma'am?'

'You'd better, Sergeant. It's coincidental enough to tie up with Nadia Sherbina. Route your reports through me, will you? We'd better work in parallel.'

'Yes, ma'am.' Chum-Kwat was pleased at this. 'You will stay?'

'Lord, no!' She had no intention of causing him to lose 'face' by remaining there, overseeing him. 'I'll get along to the Ritz-Carlton. Keep this quiet until I say so, Sergeant. I'll be in touch.'

This time we got back to the Ritz-Carlton without any hold-up. At her gesture I trailed along. She by-passed a swooping doorman, leading the way up the red-carpeted stairs to the mezzanine foyer. She might not have professed knowing much about the place; she certainly knew the man she wanted when she walked into a room without

---

* The compradore was a Chinese institution, something like the secretary of a limited liability company, but with more power, a sort of general manager, grandfather, and link between the bosses and the staff in any organization.

knocking on the door, ignoring its terse brass plate : GUIDO
BARBADORO—KEEP OUT.

He was working at his desk, a trim, big, baldish man with
bright brown eyes, and moustaches like those of King Victor
Emmanuel III, who was still sitting safely on the Italian
throne because he had prudently accepted the demand of
the newly-arisen Mussolini that he should run the government. Barbadoro, to his credit, never stood for the Fascists ;
he was a good Royalist, and that type of smoothly urbane
Italian who seems to gravitate naturally to running something to do with hospitality, usually an hotel or a restaurant.

He stood up abruptly, bowing when he recognized Mrs.
Pym.

'*Signora!* I am enchanted, but——'

'You alone?' Mrs. Pym looked round the big room,
then sat in the visitor's chair. 'Take it easy, Barbadoro.
This is official.'

'I am honoured. An aperitif perhaps, *Signora*?' He
glanced at me, wondering who I was.

'Never touch it. This is Larry Baker, of the *News*.
Barbadoro, I'm here about Nadia Sherbina.'

'Nadia?' The brown eyes were suddenly wary. 'What
has the lady done that she should not?'

'Like that, is she?'

'You understand how it is?' Barbadoro made a huge
shrug. 'She is young, perhaps twenty-two. She is jolly,
with much *felicità*. She makes with the cabaret a great
success. Often she drinks, and is so wild. *Incantevole!*'

'You know her well, then?'

'Who can say that of a woman? She was merry and
enjoyed the good time with many men. In Italy we say
bella femmina, che ride vuol dire borsa che piange ; which is to
say that when a beautiful woman smiles, the purse sheds
tears.' He showed his white teeth.

'I'd imagined that.' I could see she was thinking of the
furs in Nadia's wardrobe. 'Tell me something about her.'

The seriousness in Mrs. Pym's voice brought Barbadoro's
head from a furtive glance at a wall clock.

'You wish to know, officially?'

'Exactly.'

'So?' His fingers tapped gently on the desk. He was trying to find out what she had in mind, but even Barbadoro, a man who could read an episode in a glance, got nothing from those steady eyes. 'I tell you what I know. She comes here from Kiev when the dirty *Contadino* government has killed her mother and father. With so many little Russians she comes to Shanghai, *nize* people whose great sin they are gentle and wash the body every day.

'I see she is very pretty, that she dances well and has a voice. Not a great voice, but pleasant, *melodioso*. I put her in my chorus and soon she is advancing. I see she does as she is told, that she is sensible. I advance her and for the New Year celebration I give her a solo. She is a great success. I am very happy.'

'Succinct enough. What about her private life?'

'Ah! You are very serious, I think, Mrs. Pym?' Barbadoro twirled his great white moustache in a worried way. 'I know little. She behave herself, create no scandal. She flirt a little, dally a little—but nothing serious. No, she is not in love, yet. And the men? Ah, they come and go. I know little of them.'

'Any particular men?' Mrs. Pym's expression was austere; she was always a particularly clean-minded woman, and I could see she was not enjoying the conversation.

'Nothing at all; merely friends. She is pleasant to all, to Jacob Laffin she is the jolly miss; to Tom, Dick and Harry also. Even to Nathan Schyler, her lawyer—that is, he is the one who comes in when she makes her contract with us.'

It didn't tell us very much. Laffin was the richest man in the Settlement, a dour old character who went around very little, lived alone and kept to himself. Schyler was respectable enough, a specialist in corporation law well up in the good books of the American Consulate. I'd met him once, a grave and charming man who liked good living.

About his only distinction was an ability to drink any man under the table and never appear drunk himself.

Mrs. Pym seemed disappointed.

' Nobody outstanding ? '

' What can I say of a pretty woman who knows everybody ? '

' Yes.' She gave him the truth bluntly. ' That's why I'm here.'

Barbadoro's expression was shocked. I think he was really upset.

' The little Nadia ? That is most terrible. But why was she killed ? '

' I did not say that ! '

' But what else ? ' He raised his eyebrows. ' Why should a beautiful dancer who has everything in the world kill herself ? It is not natural. There is no lover. She is happy. *Pouf!*—she is murdered, you will see.'

I think it was so close to her own reasoning that Mrs. Pym didn't argue the point.

' Maybe you're right. Barbadoro, this is a serious business. When you are on duty you hear a great deal ? '

' Undoubtedly. People are confidant, you will understand ? '

' That's what I thought.' She stood up. ' This is going to be a sticky business. You keep your ears skinned. If you hear anything you'll advise me ? '

' Instantly. I listen and tell you. In my heart now I am . . . am *doloroso*, but I am also the business man. I must at once prepare. Nadia she has been ; now she has gone. Another must take her place, *presto*.'

That epitaph was Shanghai all over. You built up what you thought was something good and solid, then one tide of events washed it away like so much sand, and the next ebb found someone else building so fast you might never have been at all.

On the way out I told it to Mrs. Pym. Her expression was mildly sardonic.

' Catching up on the way of the world, Larry ? That's

about the only thing this city has. Five years here and you'll learn, ache, and see more than you would with fifty any place else. It's past time for food. Hungry?'

'I had that tiffin date.' I grinned, remembering that friend of mine who had probably gone home long ago. 'I could chew on something, ma'am.'

'The Swedish place is next to Sincere's. Jump to it and we can grab five minutes at the *smorgasbörd*.'

When we came out of Böök's, Mrs. Pym stood with one foot on the running-board of the Bugatti, then jerked down the jacket of her tweed suit, nodding.

'We'll try Schyler first. Lawyers always know the dirt.'

I didn't argue. I was lucky enough, being retained like this, and it didn't worry me at all that the others would have the Sherbina story by now. Mine was going to be good.

We checked Schyler's address in the Hong-list, a very comprehensive local directory, heading there at once.

Schyler was high up in the Glen-Shaw Building on the Bund, right next to the *North China Post* block. A self-service elevator took us to the fifth floor where we found the front section was all rented by the lawyer, which meant he was in a highly successful line of business.

I liked the man and his personal office as soon as we got in to him. Schyler was as good-looking as a motion picture star, a tall, finely-built man with excellent features, kind grey eyes and dead white hair. If anything, the faint pinkness of his nose rather chilled the effect—you can't absorb enough liquor to float in without showing it—but his clothes were so good you forgot about it.

He sat in his big room, furnished in the same good taste, with a notable view across the Whangpoo to the Pootung godowns and the flat, sunny country beyond. He got to his feet, smiling, when his clerk showed us in, coming round the desk with a hand stretched out.

'Mrs. Inspector Pym. It's nice to see you, madam. I've heard a lot about you, of course. And you, Larry Baker; the *News*, isn't it?'

I felt pleased. Schyler had a good American politician's

gift of knowing who you were without introduction, and of being pleased to greet you, an old trick that never fails. It probably explained those expensive offices.

Mrs. Pym accepted a chair.

' You do yourself well, Mr. Schyler.'

' I suppose I shouldn't grumble.' He pushed cigars and cigarettes across the desk. ' I'm always very glad to see you, naturally. Your appointment was something of a sensation in this city ; it gives me great pleasure to welcome you in my own portion of it.'

' Thank you. I believe you're a corporation lawyer ? '

' That is so.' He smiled at us. ' Don't tell me one of my respectable clients is in police trouble ? '

' The question of respectability is one I dare say you can answer.' She condensed the Sherbina murder as pithily as a newspaper man. ' That's why I'm here.'

' Nadia Sherbina ? Poor little kid—you're sure she was murdered ? '

' Perfectly sure.'

' It's unbelievable.' Schyler touched his pink nose, frowning. ' You know, that's just terrible. Why, I was with a party at the Ritz-Carlton last night. She was her usual brilliant self. When she had a drink with us, she seemed as bright as ever.'

' No doubt. Victims aren't usually aware they're to be murdered.'

He could not hide a slight smile at that very dry remark.

' That was silly of me ! It's pretty bad news, isn't it ? Europeans don't get murdered in Shanghai ; in fact, I don't think I can remember the last one, with the exception of the drunken sailor who was shot on Yalu Road last year.'

' Everything's got to start sometime. Mr. Schyler, Barbadoro tells me you acted for Nadia when she signed up with him ? '

' Quite correct. I take it you want to hear how that happened and what I know ? '

' Exactly.'

' There's not much to it. I go to the Ritz-Carlton a

great deal. I first met her just after the New Year at a client's table, Jacob Laffin.'

' Oh, he knew her, then ? '

' Laffin ? Who knows what Laffin knows ? He's a funny old gentleman. If you don't know this, he lives entirely alone in that great house of his, not one single servant. Every now and again he figures on some entertainment, and trails out in a tail suit he must've bought when I was a kid. He always goes to the Ritz-Carlton, to the same table, and drinks one glass of Vichy water.' Schyler laughed. ' It beats me why he does it.

' However, that's his idea and nobody argues with Laffin. He might be eighty ; he's still the biggest man in these parts. Nadia told me he took a fancy to her. Even when she was in the chorus, she had to go and sit at his table when he turned up.

' After she got that solo spot and made a hit, Barbadoro offered her a contract. Laffin was there on the night she had the news, and told me to see she got a fair deal. I just did as I was told. Frankly, I wouldn't be in this suite if it wasn't for Laffin's business, so I wasn't going to up and tell the old gentleman I was a corporation lawyer.'

' Fair enough. That's all you know about her ? '

' I don't know much more. She used to come and have a drink with me when I went to the show. She was a nice little thing. She started out with nothing, and when she got on she naturally dug every man she knew for money. Laffin told me she'd tried to make him buy her things, but so ingenuously that he never took her seriously, not that he'd let a piece of native *cash* get away from him.'

' Oh, yes, he's mean, isn't he ? '

' Mean ? ' Schyler roared. ' When Laffin came here he was just a builder, but he knew Shanghai was on the way up. He put every nickel he could make into real estate. To-day I'd say he owns most of the best business-section blocks. Gossip, and I only quote it, says he's worth a couple of hundred million dollars.

' If I'm not boring you, I'll take you up on thinking him

mean. Years ago, when he was only a multi-millionaire, he used to have a distant relative living in Yangtzepoo.

'One day, at the Bund Club bar, old Laffin was moaning about it, claiming he couldn't afford a dime street-car fare to visit his relative every week as he'd like to. Gorrie Patomar—dead now, but he used to be a broker—told him, for the laugh, that he'd give him a dime. Do you know old Laffin demanded that dime every Thursday for a year to make the visit to his relative, and kept it up till the man died?'

'Informative, not that it helps me with Nadia. She must've known that, anyway.'

'Oh, I daresay she did, but it wouldn't stop a girl trying, would it? I think Laffin liked the artless way she tried to get his money. She never quit trying, but she never dropped the old boy when she didn't get any. I think they got along, and liked each other—Laffin's a nice old boy when he isn't thinking of money. And Nadia? As bright as a new dollar and full of that fun you get in some Russians.'

'You've been very helpful, Mr. Schyler. It's good background, but it doesn't help me much.'

'You have no clues?'

'At the moment I'm stumped.'

'It's queer. May I ask, how was she killed?'

'Certainly you can ask. Poisoned.'

'Poor Nadia! That's a pretty bad thing to do. Darn it, nobody could've hated her enough to murder her, let alone using poison.' Schyler thrust fingers through his white hair. 'I knew her as much as anybody. Mrs. Pym, she just wasn't *involved* enough with anybody for that to happen.'

'You're sure of that?'

'She was frank to me. She considered me her lawyer, and folks talk frankly to lawyers and doctors. She was dead keen to make money, get money, and save money. Then she was going to the States to get herself a big name. Many's the time she told me she wasn't risking any entanglements that might gum up her plans. Maybe you figure her as a good-time, feather-brained blonde? She wasn't that, madam. She was as unsentimental as some Russians can be. If she found a way of making money, she'd do it, but she'd never have risked a man in her life. No, Mrs. Pym, when you dig a little, you'll find Nadia watched her step.'

'Just the same, there's someone in this. We got a tip by telephone that she didn't answer her door or her 'phone. It was an anonymous tip, in a man's voice. Normally we should never have worried about it, but there was that girl in Hongkew who died from an overdose of sleeping draught last month. The desk sergeant was slow in answering a telephone call for help. There was criticism, you remember? Superintendent Laystall pinned up an order that telephone calls, however silly, had to be dealt with at once. Now, who was the man?'

'There's no trace of him?'

'Not a thing. Our operator asked for a name. The man hung up. That's why I'm puzzled.'

'I'll ask around for you. I can tackle Laffin, and one or two of her girl friends. Shall I contact you?'

'Thank you.' Mrs. Pym stood up from the chair, jerking at her jacket. 'I don't need to tell you this is going to make a noise.'

'That's certain. The old biddies at the Country Club will eat it up.'

'That place!' Mrs. Pym made a noise. She had good reason to dislike the Country Club, or, as most of us called it, Gossip Centre. 'Not that it worries me. Should I visit Laffin?'

'He wouldn't answer the door.' Schyler chuckled. 'When I go I have to put a note in his box a week ahead, naming the appointment I want. If he doesn't telephone me to the contrary, I go along and keep it. Treats me like a schoolboy'.

'H'm. Thank you. I'll hope you get news for me.'

When we got down to the Bund again, Mrs. Pym looked at me, then nodded.

'Okay, Larry, this is it. I'm going back to headquarters on desk work. You have a story to write.'

'Ma'am, I don't know how——'

'Larry!'

'Sorry. I forgot. What can I say?'

'As much as you like, but keep Leslie Chow out of it. I don't know where he fits. The news is off the record until I say so. Okay?'

'You bet.'

'And, Larry.' She turned from climbing into the Bugatti. Her eyes were sardonic. 'Don't forget. I'm running the investigation. I like publicity. Got pictures of me?'

'Several. Which one shall we use, ma'am?'

'The one you took of me at my desk in December. Shows the Pym profile—you remember, tough lady looking on her toes? Tell the world I have a dozen clues.'

'Have you, ma'am?'

'What d'you think? It sounds good and Gossip Centre will have something to bite on. Be seeing you.'

She waved and started up the car, dodging dexterously round a loaded produce barrow and its team of 'hi-ya'-ing coolies. I waved back and headed for the office.

The *Daily News* had an old building in Szechuen Road, about a block from Nanking Road, a shabby wreck of a place that shook when the presses in the basement were at work. I liked it in the sentimental way of kids over their first real working home.

Charlie Lee, on the door, gave me his big grin. I checked in the pigeon-holes for any personal mail. There was only a pink slip, a telephone message. It made my head sing:

> Telephone inward. L. Baker. News. 1.18 p.m.
> *Message :* Leave police business to policemen. If you have never heard of the Hop-Ley Dancers, you will do so if you don't get to work on some other story. (No signature or name.)

CHAPTER IV

JADE BY NIGHT

I STREAKED up the creaking stairs for the second floor, across the newsroom, ignoring shouts of greeting, and crashed into Lanny Coager's cramped office, breathing hard.

Lanny was at his desk, wearing the inevitable pink shirt. He's been dead for years now, but I remember him like yesterday, big, bluff, red-bearded Lanny, who was the toughest city editor in history. There was a suspicion of his native Texas in the way he talked; when he was excited he drawled. He was a slave-driver with a whip who could have given good advice to Simon Legree, but the best man in the world when you were in trouble.

'Hi, Larry.' He wrinkled his brilliant blue eyes at me. 'That female cop came on the line and bullied me into handing you a raise and a regular job.'

'I'm sorry, Lanny. I didn't ask her to do it.'

'No?' He leaned back, lighting up a Caporal, a habit he carried over from his days on the Paris edition of the New York *Standard*. 'No, maybe she played that one off on her own. Do you rate it?'

'I've got a story.'

'Sherbina? The *Noon Mercury* carried it, fudged.'

'The inside eye-witness story, Lanny. Hot as a gasoline fire.'

'Right. I'll confirm my promise. Laidler's sick. You can take over.'

'Laidler? But he's the crime man——'

'He's sick, kid. Dysentry. You'll stand in for him.' Lanny smiled at my expression. 'You're all right, Larry. I've taught you the tricks. From now on you're on your own. Oh, yes. You can have a by-line.'

' *Gosh!* '

' Forget it. What's the story? '

I gave it to him, straight. The blue pencil in his right hand made little motions now and again, as if he were subbing the lines he didn't fancy.

' That's how I hoped to write it, Lanny.'

' Fine. Get down to it. I'll give you a page one spot, and a streamer. I'll have pictures find me cuts of Nadia and Pym.'

' She wants the one we took of her in her office.'

' The greedy cop! Okay, I'll see to it.'

I handed over the telephone message.

' This was waiting for me downstairs.'

' God's truth! Is this genuine? Of course it must be. I'll check with the board. Larry, wait a minute.' Coager fingered his beard. ' Yep, we'll reorganize that story.' He scribbled on a piece of copy-paper—the *News* was not big enough to employ a headline-sub—and pushed it over. ' This bite you? '

It did, marked up for crisis-size type: NEWS REPORTER THREATENED! *Sequel to Dancer's Murder.* CONFIRMS MRS. PYM'S FEARS.

I walked back to the newsroom, with a million dollars in my pocket. Previously I had existed on borrowed machines, but now I went over, grabbed up Laidler's battered Limmington, and heaved it to my old desk back of the copy-boys' corner.

There were only four men in the room, but I had to take a ribbing from them, and fight off suggestions of drinks when I told them about my promotion. Every little thing is a reason for most Far Eastern newspapermen to drink; when there's no excuse, they just go and have a drink to celebrate it.

The story wrote itself from the lead I had been mentally chewing all day. It was sweet as a butter-nut and smooth as old brandy. I was proud of it when I took the wad of copy-paper into Lanny Coager.

He ripped through it, subbing not more than a third,

which was better than I expected. He suddenly stabbed the story with his pencil point.

'Larry, I like that name. The Cyanide Man. Is it yours?'

'You bet.'

'I can use it.' His glance was sly. 'You didn't figure that on one murder, did you?'

'Maybe not.' I told him about Leslie Chow. 'But Mrs. Pym won't release it.'

'Then we'll play ball. It's got promise, and with the Chow story in mind we'll build this Cyanide Man. Wait.' He picked up the external telephone receiver and asked for Dr. Fedor. When he came on the line Lanny switched on the charm. 'Dr. Fedor? Ah. Glad to catch you. This is Coager, of the *News*. Yes, sir, we certainly are! I want to build you up. Advertising? Why, Doctor, a truthful news report isn't advertising.' The hurt reproach in his voice was a masterpiece. 'Tell me, have you opened her yet? I see. Yes, thank you. Surely, any time.' He dropped the receiver into its hook, looking at me. 'Post mortem's just finished. He won't give me much, but he confirms hydrocyanic acid. It was a capsule right enough.'

'Then it was quick, poor devil.'

'Quick? Oh, sure. Larry, we've got to build Nadia. I don't want her fading out before the murder's solved. This stuff you've done is good. You've got the right slant, and I like your adjectives; "bright blonde lovely" is good Metropolitan stuff. Wait a minute.'

I sat on the only chair, loaded with old newspapers, while Lanny worked on a piece of copy-paper. Finally he pushed it over to me.

There is an atmosphere of foreboding over the Settlement to-night. Nadia Sherbina's murder is on every tongue, and there is a feeling that worse is to come. In the cheaper bars, where reputations don't count for much and nothing is sacred, they are already singing a jingle. Nobody knows how it started, but it is spreading, wildfire fashion:

> Sing a song of cyanide,
>   A pocket full of death.
> No one knows why Nadia died—
>   They called it loss of breath.
> When the corpse was opened,
>   Cyanide was there.
> Who will be the next to fall?
>   Death is in the air.

'But, *Lanny*!'

'Sure, sure, I know.' He winked at me. 'We know about Chow, so we're anticipating intelligently. There's no harm in giving 'em a crude jingle. If we don't supply it someone will think of one—they always do. It's an angle.'

'Could be. You think it's a big story?'

'The biggest yet. My bones tell me. And it's better stuff than Mutt and Jeff. People are damn well sick of them.'

It made me laugh, that office name for Wu Pei-fu, and Chang Tso-lin. They were our latest *tuchuns*, or warlords, fighting out their interminable squabbles around the Settlement. Wu Pei-fu was just one of the endless mob of bandits, blown to general-of-an-army proportions; Chang Tso-lin was different, a coolie who had climbed high, lording it in Mukden with quite an army. He was trying to be what Chiang Kai-shek could have been had the poor old generalissimo had one per cent of what makes Winston Churchill tick; it never worked that way, which explains why Mao Tse-tung and his bunch of doctrinaires are running the one country in the world to-day that is so like England in outlook and philosophy that I get mad thinking about it.

'But, Lanny, what about this Hop-Ley Dancers' stuff?'

'I haven't figured it yet. What do you think?'

'There's the item Mrs. Pym found in Nadia's place.'

'You think it stacks up?'

'Well, she nearly blew her lid when Laystall remembered them in connection with the Jovial Hearts.'

'Some secret society stuff, wasn't it?' Lanny dug into his beard again. 'Larry, there's the makings in this. Thing is, shall we play the Cyanide Man or the Hop-Ley Dancers? You can't do both. The readers will get confused. It's an old newspaperman's routine, kid: never play two slogans when they're both good.'

'I say the Cyanide Man.'

'Sure. It gets home. It's one man on, maybe, a murder campaign. That means you, me or John Doe is in danger. Nobody gives a cinder in hell for a Chinese *tong*, or whatever it might be.' He lit another Caporal. 'Sit on the Hop-Ley Dancers. If they break into something I'll run the story. Maybe it's just a red herring to fool you.'

'I hope so.' It suddenly struck me I lived in a fairly lonely section of the French Concession. If there was any queer business going around, I was a natural on my way home.

'Right. We'll spike this Hop-Ley thing. I'll run this story as it stands. Larry, you'd better get out into the city and see what you can find. Got a gun?'

It made me jump.

'A gun? Hell, no!'

'Can you handle one?'

That annoyed me. I was locally regarded as quite a light in the Clay Pigeon Shooting Club. What was more to the point, I was sharpshooter in my bunch in the American Company of the Shanghai Volunteer Corps—in China that didn't mean Sunday afternoon soldiers, but near enough the real thing.

'And you at the city desk, Lanny?'

'Sorry I hurt your pride.' He grinned at me, hauling a gun from his desk. 'Take this. It's an Ortgies thirty-two self-loader. It's no great shakes for target work, but at short range she's a beauty. Here's a pack of shells.'

'You mean I should carry it?'

'Why not? If the police kick, you've been threatened. I'll watch that end of it. Here, let me show you.' He made a demonstration for me. A Coager who loved guns and understood them was something new to me. ' I carried that baby in Paris, and, off the record, when Pershing and not the *News* was my boss. It got me out of a lot of trouble one time and another. But watch her; she's got a kick to the left. If you should ever have to empty the clip, remember that, or you'll hit the next block.'

I hefted the Ortgies. It handled nicely, then I put it in my pocket with the cartridges. I thought, at the time, Lanny Coager had been reading detective thrillers.

It's queer how a few hours can make a twenty-one-year-old grow up. That morning I had been a cub, mooning about my overdraft; after lunch, with plenty under my belt, something had changed in me. I felt grown up, capable and somehow wary. However Lanny Coager and Mrs. Pym thought about it, I didn't want any part of the Hop-Ley Dancers. I didn't know why; the name gave me feathers under my diaphragm every time I thought of it.

I had orders to look around. It took me, for a starter, through the afternoon sunshine, into Dinty Moore's. It stood on the corner of an alley off Szechuen Road, a low-slung bar that tried to be a reasonable imitation of a New York saloon, right down to shining brass cuspidors. Dinty Moore—whose real name was Schumansky—did all the work himself, a big, black-haired, broken-nosed character as like an Irishman as Joe Smith. But newspapermen favoured him, and Dinty's was a second office for most of us.

He gave me a yell as I walked in.

' Hi, Mister Baker. Gonna drink, huh ? '

' Sure. John Collins.'

' John Collins, he says? That ain't no drink. Here, this is *real* Scotch, I guarantee you.'

' John Collins, Dinty. I'm not poisoning my stomach with Highland Cream from Tokio.' He giggled; it was a sour old joke around there. I elbowed the bar and looked round. There was only one other man in the place, little Toby Garnett, of the *Free Press*, a mild little man who was usually half drunk. He'd been in Shanghai for years, married a Japanese wife, and lived somewhere in West Hongkew.

He greeted me, ambling across in that uncertain trot of his, small, stout, and grinning. Some time or other he'd had smallpox; it had left his brown face a legacy of faint pock-marks.

'Hullo, Larry. Grown since I saw you last?'

'Somewhat. What are you having, Toby?'

'Stengah—Dinty knows the recipe. Promoted, they tell me?'

I looked into the bleary blue eyes. Toby had his ear closer to the grape-vine than any man I knew.

'After a fashion.' I pushed his drink across and clinked glasses. 'What's new?'

'Oh, we got the Sherbina story, but you palling along with this female detective, I dare say you've got a story?'

'It'll pass. I'm standing in for Laidler.'

'Well, *well*! This would call for a drink if I had any money. However, good luck, boy.' He pulled me away from the bar to a space between the cheap metal tables. 'Larry, this is for you.' He suddenly nudged my pocket. 'Heeled?'

'Why, yes.' I think I blushed.

'Take that silly expression off your face, there's a wise boy. I remember, you can shoot. Larry, take your Uncle Toby's advice. Hire a boat and get out into the middle of Tahu Lakes for a week.'

'Look, Toby, what goes on? That's the second warning——'

He chuckled when I stopped, finishing his drink.

'Had one, have you? Here's another: you're running up against the wrong crowd, my boy. Pym's different. She's official. If she's killed, there're plenty more in Central Station. But you're an outsider, looking in. Get it?'

'But what the devil's at the back of this?'

'Trouble. I know them: Nadia; Laffin; yes, and one or two more. Stay out, there's a sensible fellow. I like you. You're fresh and keen; you'll make a good man

at the desk one of these days. But you'll never get there if
you don't keep your nose outside.'

I bought him another drink and tried to make him talk.
Either he was bluffing or it was genuine ; he began to get
maudlin. I couldn't get any more sense out of him.

I went into the sunshine, sauntering to the corner of
Nanking Road. It was barely tea-time and, like all cities,
Shanghai would have nothing much to offer me until after
the businessmen began going home.

I mooned along, staring into the shops, conscious that
I felt a big let-down after the excitements of the day, with
the inevitable hiatus. When I got to Wing On's I spent a
long time at the windows, went into the store and out of
the side door. The Chinese theatre was showing *The Four
Brothers*, and somehow I stuck out an hour of it.

My knowledge of Chinese was near enough to nil, but,
parrot-wise, I had mastered a certain number of phrases,
not that you needed much in the theatre if you had any
imagination at all.

But I had struck a bad patch. The hero, in full war kit,
was mounted on a step-ladder bouncing up and down,
declaiming in a high, artificial voice. I guessed he was
riding over some mountain, maybe going to war, because
he was armoured and one pike-man, on the boards, stamped
solemnly to show he was the great army.

It was something philosophical right enough. The hero
kept pointing to his head and to the floor, which carried its
own message. Somehow I wasn't gripped.

I raised an arm for a hot towel, which the watchful
attendant interpreted, slinging me the towel across the
heads of the audience. I wiped my face and hands and
felt better for it.

Then, as the scene-shifters were marching on with tables
and chairs, which they were arranging round the busy
hero, I realized a new scene was about to begin, so I got
back into the sunshine, glad to get away from the smell of
native tobacco, garlic and sweat.

The next move had me beaten. It was all very well

going out into the city to find news. You can't get news without contacts, and, until the Ritz-Carlton opened, I had none.

I was so bored I hailed a rickshaw and told the coolie to take me back to my home, such as it was.

The Route des Sœurs looked pleasant. The young trees along the kerb were showing their spring leafage, and there was a fresh smell in the air.

The rickshaw dropped me at the house where I was staying. It was opposite the Cercle Français—the French Club to us all—and as I went in the gate I could hear the voices of the tennis players on the far side of the long club building. If I closed my eyes for a moment it could have been an afternoon in Regina.

Sung, the No. 1 boy, opened the door to my ring. Mrs. McNaughton, my landlady, wasn't in, he told me; there were no letters for me and no callers.

I went up to my small room on the second floor. It all looked homelike and pleasant, with the pictures of my folks on the walls, my radio in one corner—a cat's-whisker job it was in those days—and my pennant, from Regina High, above it.

There was a small balcony, part of the fire-escape system, outside the window. I went on it for a minute to see who was in the garden, but as there were only a couple of the older roomers chatting in deck-chairs, I came back and took off my jacket and shoes.

When I was comfortable on the bed I reached out for my book—it was Russell's *Where the Pavement Ends*—but I got through no more than half a story before I was asleep.

It was dark when I woke. I nearly shot through the roof when I saw there was somebody in the room, sitting in my old cane chair, not two feet from my head.

What I saw was enough to scare anybody. It was not so much a frightening scene as a well-staged one.

There was a gun which looked like a heavy calibre revolver levelled at me. By means of a tiny electric torch, held in his other hand, the visitor had spotlighted the revolver so that I couldn't make any mistake about it.

The beam of light was so minute that I couldn't see much else, except that the unknown wore a black Chinese gown reaching to feet I assumed were there. On the third finger of the hand holding the gun, and being clenched it was just a hand, there was a gold ring holding a piece of mounted jade, a buffalo. It looked old somehow, and jade was something I had studied rather well—I was prepared to bet it was the genuine *fei-ts'ui*, ' kingfisher stone,' or else my studies had been wasted time.

The unseen eyes must have been watching me wake. When I had got on one elbow a soft, odd little laugh broke the tight stillness of the room.

CHAPTER V

THE MAN IN THE RITZ-CARLTON

' GOOD evening, Mr. Baker. You will, I hope, forgive these dramatics ? '

The voice was so deep and strange, after that laugh, and so artificial, that it shook me.

' Well . . .' I paused to clear my throat. I admit being scared, and wishing I had the Ortgies by me instead of in my coat pocket on the wall hook. ' It *is* a bit of an awakening.'

' Undoubtedly. First let me explain that this revolver is loaded, and that I used the fire escape, as I shall do again. You and I should have a talk.'

' Yes, of course.' The voice had me beat. It was perfect English, yet it was so contrived that I failed to understand it. Then I got it. That very afternoon I had seen the things in Wing On's toy section, little pieces of shaped rubber called ' Voicographs,' intended, the sales card said, for insertion between the tongue and palate. I remember the selling tag : ' Change your voice to a deep grown-up bass. Surprise your parents ! Make your friends laugh ! ' It was also a very ingenious disguise.

' You will be wondering how I know about you ? Do I have to tell you how easy that is in Shanghai ? '

' Oh, no, I suppose not. I've had your warning.'

' Warning ? ' For the first time the unseen was startled into showing emotion. ' What warning ? '

' About the Hop-Ley Dancers.'

' About . . . ? Ah, yes, I see.' There was a pause. Then that bubbling laughter, so soft I could barely hear it. ' Yes, indeed. Mr. Baker, I have a mission.'

' Yes ? '

' Yes. Certain people who must not live have died. You

have seen two of them. There will be others. I shall tell you about my mission in due course. Rest assured you are not one of them, unless you are foolish enough to move now.'

'Thank you.' I thrust fingers through my hair automatically. It was almost funny.

'There will be a letter for you. It will advise you of a death.'

'Another ! Look, Mr. Cyanide Man——'

'What was that ? '

'Gosh ! It's a name I'd figured up for you——'.

'Cyanide Man ? ' Then the laughter again. ' Now, that is very clever indeed ! Yes, I like it.' There was a rustling sound and something plopped on the bed beside me. ' I always reward clever people. Mr. Baker, I think you have quite enough to keep you busy for a while. Tell your readers all about me ; tell them that sinners shall die ! '

I nearly got heart failure when something moved and my head was tangled in thick cloth. Maybe I was scared. I know I hit out, yelled, and jerked the thing from me. The room was dark. I knocked over a couple of books, finding the bedside light. When it was on the room was empty.

Naturally the fire escape was clear and I came back into my room. The Cyanide Man, or whoever the nut was, had thrown my woollen comforter, that had been on the back of the cane chair, over my head to cover his getaway. When I was breathing normally I had a look at the roll he had thrown at me, a thousand dollars in old banknotes, mostly tens and twentys.

I was dressed for the street and into the warm spring night within ten minutes flat, checking to see no mail had arrived for me. When I got to his office twenty minutes later I found Lanny Coager brooding over the make-up blank for to-morrow's issue.

Lanny stared at me.

'Larry ! You look scared, kid. Trouble ? '

'Not exactly.' I sat on the visitor's chair, happy at being in the familiar smell and noise of the *News* building. 'I've been entertaining a goof.'

'Now, Larry . . .'

'I'm not kidding.' I threw the money on the littered desk and gave him the story, just as it happened.

'A thousand bucks? It's a lot of money.' Lanny pulled his beard thoughtfully. 'He likes the name, does he? You never got a glimpse of him?'

'He was much too cute. It was something out of a moving picture—Fu Manchu, except that I was scared.'

'Yeah? And he said sinners shall die?'

'That's about it, Lanny.'

'You know, I like it. I mean as news. We've never had a crazy man dressed up like something out of a dime novel doing things around Shanghai.' Coager gave one of his deep laughs. 'If he's going after sinners here in the Settlement, the guy'll be busy till for ever!'

'He had me mentally scanning my record.'

'Poor old Larry. You wanted to be a reporter, and now, by heck, you're there in a big way. And a letter coming about death, and the guy has a mission? *Boy!*' Lanny was radiant. 'I'll run to-night's episode, just as it happened. I'll state the thousand dollars is held here at the disposal of Central Police Station. What about this letter?'

'If it comes by post we get our mail at eight in the morning.'

'No, it rates an extra. There hasn't been one on the *News* since the Armistice of nineteen-eighteen. I still think it might be worth it. Question is, do we hold the letter and run an extra, or hand it over to Pym first?'

'She's played ball with us.'

'So she has. Grab the 'phone and tell her now.'

When I was through to Central Station, I was told Mrs. Pym had not been back since four o'clock. Nobody knew where she was. I talked to Laystall instead.

'Good evening, Superintendent. Baker here.' I gave him the story. 'We're naturally anxious to have your views before we do anything, sir.'

'Thank you, Baker.' The gentle old voice did not sound

in the slightest surprised. ' I'll talk to Mrs. Pym about it, but I see no reason why you shouldn't run the story since it happened to you. You've no notion as to the man's identity ? '

' He covered up too well, sir. He sounded crazy to me.'

' What he said certainly suggests it. Hold the money for the time being—you say it's used stuff ? '

' Yes, sir. Mostly Bank of China issue, and filthy. You'd get fingerprints all right, hundreds of them.'

' We could try. This letter is another matter.'

' Yes, sir ? '

' It might be important, Baker. Where will you be to-night ? '

' I'm going to dinner now, Böök's, I think, then to the Ritz-Carlton.'

' I'll get in touch with you. I'll see the General Post Office myself, and have all your letters put aside. The last collection is late, so after that I shall probably ask you to come to the Post Office. If the letter is what you think it is, you can have a copy for your paper. I shall probably want the original.'

' Yes, sir. Just a minute, please.' I covered the mouthpiece and told Lanny.

' Fine. I'll keep Benchley and his camera standing by and you can contact me for him to go along. Ask Laystall.'

' Superintendent ? I've spoken to my editor. Can I bring a photographer to make a copy of the letter ? '

' Certainly, and thank you, Baker. If you go anywhere else this evening let the office know where you are.'

Lanny Coager was rubbing his hands when I replaced the receiver.

' Nice going. It's a case of having too darn much news. Still, since you're going to the Post Office for a special scrutiny, I can hold back till midnight. Leave the visit to me. I'll scare-head it alongside the other story and leave enough space for a cut of the letter.'

' Perhaps we won't get it ? '

'I think we will. This is our lucky break, and I'm riding it. And, Larry...'

'Yes?'

'You might be a sharpshooter, but you don't know the angles. A wise man keeps his iron handy at all times. Get me?'

'Sorry.' I laughed. 'I hadn't thought about it.'

'If somebody's after you, you don't stop thinking. Now go eat, and I'll keep Benchley standing by.'

The Swedish restaurant was busy, but I got a table near the door and found my companion was old Charlie Voucher, editor and proprietor of *Voucher's Weekly*, a combination of magazine and shipping gazette. It had quite a vogue in the city, and it was not unlike my native *Maclean's Magazine*, which it cheerfully imitated.

Charlie was usually half drunk, but, like Toby Garnett, he knew a great deal about China. During intervals of listening to Charlie's stories I dug gently at possible lines in case there was anything he knew from which I could raise a lead.

He told me a few anecdotes about Laffin, nothing of importance. Nadia Sherbina didn't interest him, but the jade ring did. He knew the subject rather well.

'You don't know as much about it as you think, Larry, my boy,' he explained over his coffee. 'Jade's a fool-word, anyway. It's used to cover two different minerals that look alike. Nephrite, a calcium-magnesium silicate, and jadeite, a silicate of sodium and aluminium. In theory they're both white when they're pure, but you get the range of colours through impurities. I'll tell you this: polished nephrite is oily rather than vitreous and jadeite's the reverse. The ring you saw was apple-green, which means it's probably jadeite.'

'I thought it was old, Charlie.' I didn't much like my knowledge thrown in my face.

'*Fei-ts'ui?* The name used to apply to some very fine green nephrites in the year ten hundred and something. It dropped out until jadeite came here from Burma in the eighteenth century, when they dubbed it *fei-ts'ui*. I've seen the buffalo motif in lots of current work, and even in spinach-green nephrite, but that wasn't more than a hundred years old. Your ring's not unusual, and it's recent; if it was Sung dynasty, or anything like that, I doubt if you'd see it outside a museum.'

' Maybe the owner's rich ? ' I was thinking of the thousand dollars.

' Don't fool yourself. No Chinese would wander about with Sung nephrite on his finger. You met him, you said ? I mean, outside his home ? ' I nodded. ' Then it's modern stuff. He'd keep anything like that for some high ceremony, just like you'd treasure your great-grandfather's watch. Worn casually for no reason ? Not on your life, Larry.'

By the time I'd finished with Charlie Voucher it was near enough to nine-thirty. I said good-bye and went into the night, heading towards the Ritz-Carlton.

When I'd checked my hat with Daisy Ting, I had a few words with her. She was wearing her ordinary black gown. When the cash customers began to roll in, she always changed into a European gown with one of the first lightning fasteners I'd seen at the throat, with, soldered to the tag, a medal with an inscription, ' You can pull me for a dollar.' As Daisy wore good high underclothes beneath, the regulars never tried it and the tourists just felt silly.

She told me the place was busier than usual. The word of Nadia's death had got round apart from the reports in the evenings, and quite a few people had rolled up out of morbid curiosity.

The Ritz-Carlton is worth a description. The cinema and the main restaurant were round at the side. In the front was the money-making section. When you'd passed Daisy Ting's hat-check alcove you went down a passage into the bar, a cosy, airy room with plenty of seats and a strictly American style of decoration. It was mainly red leather and chromium. The whole end of the bar was a glass wall through which you could see the floor ; to get there you went down a short flight of curving steps, which also led from another passage, good wide steps which gave women a chance to show their gowns.

The floor itself was the best in Shanghai, surrounded by a low dais dotted with tables. The cabaret came in at the door far back on the right, the rear wall being a high platform on which Highlo' Harry and his men gave out the music. The setting of the big room was smooth—dark green leather, deep plum walls and soft lighting. Barbadoro knew how to put class into his place; the Ritz-Carlton had it. Not only that, it cost five dollars to go in, and there was a five-dollar table charge. Without my *Daily News* card I should never have gone near the place.

There was quite a crowd in the bar, with Leslie and Wesley Ho—known over the whole Far East as the Brothers Ho—serving drinks as fast as they could mix them. They both gave me welcoming grins. To the stranger they were dark-faced Chinese in white gowns, identical twins, but Wes always showed one eye-tooth when he smiled, and Les didn't; if they weren't smiling you just hoped for the best when you addressed one of them.

I saw nobody particularly interesting. There were one or two of the Country Club Americans, dressed correctly and behaving correctly. Two Britishers were there, one of them a severe, white-haired old fellow who was high up in the Chinese Maritime Customs Service. Other than one or two foreigners I didn't even know, the crowd was as usual.

The floor looked more interesting. I headed down the stairs, pausing to wave at Highlo' Harry, who was taking the boys through a fast, jazzy number. He waved back, a big, brown-haired, brown-faced man who could almost make a clarinet talk.

Barbadoro, waiting in the red-roped receiving area, gave me an ironical little bow.

'A table, Mr. Baker?'

'I'm roaming, but maybe I'd best sit somewhere.'

'If you please. You will not alarm the customers?'

I winked. 'Thank you.' He gestured to his aide. 'Rico, a table for Mr. Baker and a bottle with the compliments of the management.'

Rico Santonelli found me a good table, half-way round the curve of the dais. He settled me, whipped up a bottle of good Scotch and bowed.

'Plenty people, Mr. Baker. They com' because of poor Nadia. So sad. You call me if you want me? Thank you, sare.'

The death of the star did not seem to make the atmosphere any the less cheerful. About half the tables were full, with the flashy, happy crowd typical of the place.

I saw Mrs. Rotgers with her usual party, a tall, dark, graceful woman with a craze for mauve, the recognized leader of the Country Club Set. Lorrie Bala was there, his clever, somehow typically Armenian face absorbed in a discussion with a grey-haired man who looked like, and probably was, an American oil man. Benjamin Cudworth, who never had a penny, but whose ancestry was impeccable, was squiring a pretty redhead. Mrs. Erp was at the next table, and that really was her name, Mrs. Lester MacMahoney Erp. Where she came from nobody bothered to inquire: if she hadn't got millions, she seemed to spend them, and that was good enough. This huge, ugly, overdressed woman with a raw Arkansas drawl fought Mrs. Rotgers all over the city, socially, I mean.

My immediate neighbours were the most interesting. Paul Chang was a Chinese who looked like a Western artist's idea of a good-looking native. His father was old Lord Chang, who had been Ambassador to the Court of St. James years back, and had died with almost every honour under the sun in his possession, a fine old gentleman. Jennie Chang was there as well, a brown-eyed, pert little girl with a lovely smile. They were entertaining a man I had never seen before. He was so largely and broadly built that I figured him out for a northerner immediately, probably from Jehol, where they grow them big. His face was fairer than Paul's, a sculptured face with bone structure that would have enchanted an artist. His eyes were dark and impassive and his chin firm as his nose was hooked, a conqueror's head if there ever was one. Like his companions, he wore European dress, exact to the last item.

Paul and I were acquaintances, and he gave me a polite greeting when I had been settled in my chair for a few minutes.

'Good evening, Mr. Baker. Will you join us for a drink?'

'I should like that. Thank you.' I went over to the proffered chair, bowing to Jennie. Paul introduced their guest.

'Dr. Wu Hsiung, please permit me to present Mr. Laurence Baker, from the *Daily News*.'

I bowed, shaking hands.

'A great pleasure, Mr. Baker.' His voice was even more melodiously perfect than Paul's, and Paul had gone both to Harvard and Oxford. The name surprised me a bit. I didn't know a great deal about China, yet Wu Hsiung was not only odd, but it just didn't fit a northerner, unless I was up against one of those little puzzles of Chinese names which were always ready to trip you.

Still, Paul was talking to the man with great deference and treating him like a superior which decided me the doctor was a pretty important man, for Paul was about as far up the social tree as he could get, and he wasn't using college-boy politeness either.

'A fascinating place,' Wu Hsiung said when we were all smoking. 'You are often here, Mr. Baker?'

'Most nights, sir,' I took my cue from Paul. It seemed to please him. As a newspaper man I was anxious to know who the visitor was, but to broach the subject would have been a solecism of the worst order in that company.

'Mr. Chang tells me of a sad tragedy which has occurred. One of the dancers, I believe? You, as a journalist, will perhaps know?'

I told them about Nadia Sherbina, that is as much as we were printing. Paul and Jennie were interested because they knew her well ; the doctor just nodded, his eyes half-closed, as if he was hearing about a case.

'You mean there's a murderer going about?' Jennie gave a small shudder. Paul laughed and covered one of her hands.

'It's been assumed. Mrs. Pym is running the case.'

The name seemed to bring Wu Hsiung to life. He sat up, unstarched himself, and leaned on the table.

'A remarkable woman !' His eyes swept over the three of us. 'I remember hearing of her in Peking. She has a genius for detective work, great resource and a most complete lack of fear. A phenomenal woman.'

'I admire her myself, sir.' It seemed a bit flat as a remark, but I was feeling my way.

'Yes?' The doctor's sudden smile warmed his whole personality. 'As a man of conservative tastes, I should not care to see her example imitated by my people.' He nodded when Jennie giggled behind a polite palm. 'Precisely, young lady. But we have a proverb, Mr. Baker : *shang hsing hsia hsiao*, which means, to be completely literal, above does, below imitates, implying that those above set the example and those below follow them. Which, you will understand, is why I prefer Mrs. Pym to be of your race in her example.'

'I see, sir.' I had a good enough ear to realize his Mandarin was the perfect, slightly pedantic delivery of the profound scholar. 'I don't think there's another like her. My editor, Lanny Coager, thinks she will be a pretty big person one of these days.'

'I hope so, I sincerely hope so, to which I must add, if I am not being boring, *mou shih tsai jên, ch'êng shih tsai t'ien*, a Chinese variation of your own contention that man disposes . . . but let us hope great things for her.'

'Thank you, sir.' The conversation was getting me down. Either Wu Hsiung was a prosy old savant or else he was talking just to keep me away from any impertinent barbarian questions. Just then Highlo' Harry ordered a roll on the drums and got silence ; I blessed him for it.

The place had filled up since I came, and Highlo' had a full audience when he announced: 'Ladies and gentlemen, I need not tell you how sad we are all that our brightest star will not be present to-night, but she would be with us when we say, " The show must go on." Therefore we give you,' he paused and the orchestra came in on his wave as he began that famous locally composed song hit, ' Ritz-Carlton girl, you are the one I really do adore . . .'

Promptly, with the refrain, the lights went out and the spots picked up the curtained doorway. It opened and the twelve girls came on, in U.S. Navy summer uniforms, a trimly drilled chorus in clothes made whiter by the brilliant spots.

Nadia was not leading them this time. They went through the routine, to a vigorous background of *Anchors Aweigh*, as if she were there. It was well done, the dancing was as precise as gunfire and the excitement they got out of that fast-played tune was amazing.

The crowd rose to them, even Dr. Wu Hsiung clapped with the heartiness of a man unused to such a thing. After that Leda and Barney Procrusko gave us a murderous little scene of two overdressed socialites meeting one another at a party—a blatant and undignified tilt at Mrs. Rotgers and Mrs. Erp—then came the usual conjuror, who, being Chinese, made the European article look silly. Sally Loder, an early version of the modern crooner, sang some dull thing about a heartbreak to which I scarcely listened, then the chorus was back again, this time in the uniforms of the of the United States Marines. If their pepped-up version of Foster's *Oh ! Susanna* had nothing to do with the uniforms, the sheer vitality of the performance was enough to keep the audience applauding and shouting after the house lights were on again. The Roaring Twenties might seem archaic and dreary to moderns, but they packed enough energy and blazing vigour in everything that was undertaken to make the moderns, even when it comes to jive and bebop, seem slow and cumbersome.

Barbadoro had been waiting until then, apparently. He

came up to the table, bowing low to the others, asking me if I could spare a moment.

I thanked my host and said good night, following Barbadoro into the passage alongside the bar. A familiar, tweed-suited figure was waiting by Daisy Ting's counter. Mrs. Pym, in those exotic surroundings, was looking chipper as a sunny morning and tough as a liner's cable.

She waved.

'Hi, son.' She gestured to Daisy. 'Don't tell me you ever spent a dollar on that.'

I glanced at Daisy's inviting tag, grinning at the smiling Barbadoro.

'Tell her who gave you the idea, Daisy.'

'Yiss, Mr. Baker. Mr. Baker b'long talkee my do it.'

'Well!' Her grey-blue eyes had a new respect in them. 'Larry, I didn't think you were so smart. I'll take him along with me, Barbadoro.' She dropped a silver dollar on Daisy's counter. 'Pull it yourself, honey, and get a surprise on me.'

I was somewhat awed. Mrs. Pym is a nice-minded woman, and I did not think such a childish gag would have pleased her or appealed to her sense of propriety until it struck me that maybe she guessed it was for the tourist trade; she always possessed a profound contempt for suckers.

The Bugatti was at the kerb, placed neatly in the centre of a whitewashed oblong that insisted on no parking. Several of the Chinese chauffeurs from the expensive-looking saloons lined up across the road were grouped together, staring pointedly at the little red car. Her eyes raked them and they moved back at her sharp: '*Chi phau tien khe s le,*' a perfectly silly colloquialism which advised them to go and cook some hot water, a mild phrase considering the violent lengths one could go to in the vernacular, but, just then, it was something of a rude crack.

The chauffeurs moved back, smiling at her because they saw the joke. She climbed in the Bugatti and I got in the other seat. We stormed into the crowded brilliance of Nanking Road.

'You've been having quite a day, son.' She jerked her wild hat at me. 'Mysterious strangers and what not?'

'You've heard all about it, ma'am?'

'Plenty. We've got a letter for you, and nearly had to bring in the Court of Consuls to get it held back.'

'I wonder if it's the one that's expected?'

'We'll hope so. Tell me, Laystall thinks you regard this Cyanide Man as a nut?'

'He's got a mission, ma'am. I've got views about missions of that sort.'

'When it comes to wiping out sinners, so have I. Think this mysterious Joe Doaks is anything to do with the Hop-Ley Dancers?'

'I got the impression he was a bit surprised when I mentioned the warning.'

'Um? We'll consider it later. I've been stabbing at this dead Chow business. If he's ever done anything wrong in his whole life, I'll eat my funny hat.'

'You mean he doesn't tie up?'

'Chow? A born innocent. Studies—at least studied bird life in his spare time. When you hang around the feathered kind you've no time for the others. He didn't smoke, drink, or use bad language. He had a craze for eating lichees and pumelo. Far as I can see, he never did anything else. And if gluttony for fruit is a sin, you can write me off as a half-witted Pootung amah.'

'How about Nadia?'

'The usual sins, according to the Commandments, but I think she was reasonably half-hearted about them. I don't suppose she could've slung anything but very small pebbles in a glass-house—though, come to that, who can? No, Nadia was on the make in a mild way. If she's what the Cyanide Man is after, he'll get round to wiping out two-thirds of all the females in the Settlement.' The Bugatti sped up the slight incline of the Garden Bridge over Soochow Creek, tore along the embankment road, halting in front of the General Post Office. 'Out you get, son.'

We went in at the back, through the sorting-office door, where a very tall, very dignified Chinese was waiting for us, a living proof that the Civil Servant of any race is quite unmistakable.

'Good evening, Detective Inspector. Good evening, sir.' His bow was as reserved as a buff form of application. 'If you will please to follow me.'

We entered a whitewashed office containing three men standing round a plain table on which rested a solitary letter. They comprised the Postmaster, the Assistant-Postmaster and the Sorting Office Inspector—I never found out who the tall Chinese was. I had my eyes on Mrs. Pym, when she saw the solemn group round that poor little letter. There was a sardonic quirk in the nearest corner of her grim mouth—the pompous stuffiness of authority rampant usually brings out the worst in her.

'Detective Inspector Mrs. Pym? Good evening.' The Postmaster bowed, and so did the rest of them. 'This gentleman is Mr. Laurence Baker of the *Daily News*?'

Her sniff was surprisingly mild.

'You ask him. He can talk.'

'Mr. Laurence Baker, sir?'

'Sure. That my letter?' I reached out. I thought the four of them would throw a simultaneous fit.

'*Just* a moment, sir.' The Postmaster moved in front of the table, an undersized, moustached father defending his helpless young. 'You have proof of your identity, of course?'

'Why, yes.' I hauled out my press card, a couple of letters addressed to me, my Shanghai driving licence and a rude postcard from a cousin in Calgary, Alberta.

The four of them scrutinized every item carefully; I thought they would ask me for my passport and my fingerprints before long, but hoped to heaven they would hurry. Mrs. Pym's expression was getting to be choleric. In another minute I think she would have hauled out that Luger she always carried in her big handbag and started shooting.

The Four Bureaucratic Horsemen seemed to think I was me, and not some cunning ringer out to short-change the Post Office. I was given my letter and my belongings. We all bowed again, except Mrs. Pym, and she got to the Bugatti before she let off some words in dialect so tough that they had hairs on their chests.

I said, 'Yes, ma'am,' and handed over the letter.

'I don't want to open your damned letter. You do it. After all that high-handed hoo-hah, I hope it's a misdirection for the wrong party.'

It wasn't. It bore my name and the *Daily News* address, typed on a machine with a bad ribbon, and mailed in East Shanghai for six o'clock.

Inside was a half-sheet of thin paper, neatly typed : *Why doesn't Jacob Laffin take in his milk any more?* It shook me so much I stood and gaped.

Mrs. Pym's snort was violent.

'Hell ! I believe that freak's really got a sinner at last ! '

CHAPTER VI

STILL MORE CYANIDE

WE made the Central Police Station at fire-engine speed. The Bugatti was parked at the Foochow Road entrance, and we went into the Charge Room, the desk sergeant saying nothing when he saw me with Mrs. Pym, through the rear door into the long passage.

The second door bore Superintendent Laystall's name. He was inside at his desk, checking over something with Kelly.

'Ah, I see you've got the letter, Mrs. Pym?'

'Yes.' She pushed me forward. 'Show it, boy.'

Laystall's eyebrows nearly climbed into his white hair.

'*Not* Laffin!'

'That looks the way of it.'

'Incredible! I stayed on duty because I expected trouble; this is worse than I thought. Sergeant, take this and have the Fingerprint Department process it immediately, please.'

The letter was back almost instantly in charge of little Arthur Kee, a good product of the country where fingerprints were understood when the white man regarded furs and woad as smart winter wear.

'Quite clean, sir,' he told Laystall. 'There's a single accidental, which is all. May I have Mr. Baker's impressions, please?'

I was willing, and let Kee print my digits. He peered at the card on which he rolled my fingers after the inking.

'Yes, the left index finger, sir.'

'So the Cyanide Man wore gloves.' Mrs. Pym's voice was extremely tart. 'Now do we get along to Laffin?'

'Of course.' Laystall reached for his peaked cap, a bit put out at her tone. 'Sergeant Kelly, you will accompany us. Mrs. Pym and, I suppose, Baker, you will come in my car?'

'Thank you.' She spoke with sudden kindness. I think she liked Laystall a whole lot, but being kept waiting always made her mad. 'I'll take Larry in my car. Nanyang Road, isn't it?'

Though Kelly drove Laystall's car himself, and that big Irishman could handle a car like an inspired angel, the little Bugatti streaked way ahead of him, though, just beyond the Recreation Ground on Bubbling Well Road, we near enough bust ourselves to pieces.

The Bugatti was ripping along the luckily clear roadway at fifty when a stout old Chinese in a tatty blue gown waited till we were nearly level with him, and shot in front of us like a projectile, the off-wing just brushing his gown tail as he got clear. Mrs. Pym didn't bat an eyelid, but my blood pressure climbed right out of the top of my head.

She gave me a look of scorifying cynicism.

'Never seen that before, son? Well, you're learning now. The old mutt imagined he had a devil on his heels, so he waited for the first fast car and did what he did. He got by, but the devil didn't. Simple Chinese logic. It happens all the time; maybe you don't drive fast?'

'Not more than twenty when I'm in a car.'

'That's walking, son.'

'What happens if he doesn't jump hard enough?'

'You asking me? We turn here. The house is just about opposite the public garden.'

Nanyang Road was quiet and dim under the young moon. I could see people strolling in the gardens across the street, and somewhere a player was performing on a one-stringed fiddle and singing. If it sounded to me like a pup that had been trodden on, no doubt it was beautiful to Chinese ears.

Laystall's car arrived just then, halting behind the Bugatti. The superintendent joined us, the bulk of Sergeant Kelly at his heels.

Mrs. Pym did not say anything, but moved along the

wall, using a small electric torch she had brought from her bag. It spotlighted a gateway, showing the unseen house to be named Narkunda.

'Hindustani,' Kelly told us helpfully, 'though I don't know what it means.'

She glared at him and led the way towards the house. We somehow arranged ourselves in a row, staring, as the torch showed us a great deal of the frontage.

Narkunda had probably been quite a house in its day. Now it was just a massive derelict, a hodge-podge of unpainted frames, broken shutters and an air of completely ungraceful decay, as if the house had been allowed to fall to pieces without anybody giving a damn. Some houses die slowly and splendidly; others just fall apart like a slattern with a passion for gin. Narkunda was the second —ugly, unloved, and sordid in its neglect.

'And him with all the money in the world? Glory be to God!' Mike Kelly's mourning voice seemed a suitable epitaph. It did not suit Mrs. Pym. She jerked down the front of her tweed jacket, stamping up the creaking steps to the porch.

'He could've sold this in its prime for a lot of money, and bought something cheaper to decay in. But he wouldn't do that—oh, no, he had to waste a perfectly good house and let it go to spectacular pieces. These mammons!' She flashed the torch over half-a-dozen bottles of milk. 'I suppose we'll find him shot full of cyanide since he doesn't answer?' She studied the ancient double front door calculatingly, raised a neatly-brogued foot, with a leg that would have delighted a beautiful woman, and rammed the sole against the wood, just below the lock. The door burst open at the same time as Laystall cried out in protest:

'You shouldn't do it that way, ma'am!'

'Eh? He doesn't answer, so he must be dead; if he's dead he can't answer—oh, you mean I should do it legally?' Her glance was sardonic. '*Me*, Superintendent?'

Laystall shrugged helplessly. We followed her into a

dusty hall, almost bumping into her when she stopped unexpectedly, sniffing loudly.

'Dear land!' It was Kelly who spoke. 'He's dead, sir.'

'I'm afraid so.' Laystall peered uneasily into the gloom. 'It's going to be nasty. Mrs. Pym, perhaps——'

She did not even wait, marching into the darkness behind her little torch, following her nose. In all the time I have known her she has never shirked a job or used her sex to get out of something unpleasant.

She called us from somewhere in the gloom. We went forward, beckoned by the torch beam, just as she found the electric light switch.

The dusty, shadeless bulb revealed a dreary little room, a sort of cubby-hole stuffed with tasteless Victorian furnishings. There was an old roll-top desk against one wall. Seated on the chair before it, crumpled on the desk surface, was a man. He was dead, very dead indeed. Laystall shuddered visibly and Kelly looked unhappy. I'd seen death before, but not like this. I admit it. I went into the black hall and stood there, fighting down my queasiness by sheer power of will. If you don't know China, then you don't know we have a line in insects and scads of queer little flying pests, even in early spring. And Chinese rats are like any other sort of rats, but tougher and nastier because nobody bothers them very much. Six milk bottles on the step meant six days had gone by. A dead man in an empty house could have quite a lot happen to him in that time.

They came out eventually, Mrs. Pym shutting the door behind her. Laystall, Kelly and I lit cigarettes with a sort of unanimous reflex.

'That's Laffin.' Mrs. Pym was quite unperturbed; in fact she sounded thoughtful and interested. 'You know, he doesn't look like Sherbina or Chow to me.'

'I'll say he doesn't——' Kelly began, and had it bitten off.

'Let's not be funny about it, Sergeant. He's dead. You can see them dead early or you can see them dead late: it makes no difference in the final result. Thing is, I'd bet one of his millions there's nothing cyanotic about that face.'

'You mean he was shot or something?' Laystall asked.

'Could be. But he looked very peaceful, wouldn't you say? Sergeant, there's a 'phone around here somewhere. Locate it and call Fedor. It's his pidgin. We can have a look meanwhile.'

She led the way through the rooms, the dreariest chore I've ever endured. There must have been about twenty rooms in all—over-furnished, dusty, refuse-littered, and decaying. Even the stack of clothes held by an old wardrobe in Laffin's bedroom must have been bought when I was in diapers. The dress suit, which Laffin probably wore when he went to the Ritz-Carlton, was green with age. There was a great hole in the seat of the pants, cobbled with coarse black darning wool.

It shook me, but not as much as a letter Mrs. Pym disinterred from behind the foxed mirror over the mantelpiece. It was from the China Mission to Foundlings, a Methodist organization that did a great deal of good, dated for the previous December:

My Dear Mr. Laffin,

My fellow-workers and I have no words with which to thank you. In asking you for toys to help make happy the Christmas festivities of our little charges, we never, in our wildest dreams, expected to receive so huge a quantity.

Indeed, there are far too many even for our seventy children, and I trust I may express my hope that you will permit the surplus to be sent . . .

It went over the page, and that was not all. Tucked in with it was a money order counterfoil for five hundred dollars, the payee, in crabbed old clerkly writing, being the Rickshawmen's Mission. It was for the day after the China Missions letter was dated.

Mrs. Pym sighed.

'I don't get it. The crazy old coot builds a reputation

for being a miser and holding his millions tighter than a
native cherishes his ancestors, yet here's proof that he
turns handsprings at Christmas.' She gestured at the
bedroom. 'And he lived in this crummy flea-nest!'

We were still probing when little Dr. Fedor came in,
blowing his nose loudly, Kelly at his heels.

'Most distressing.' He greeted us with a small wave.
'There are times . . . however, you have your own views
about the death, I hear, Mrs. Pym?'

She turned, hands on her hips.

'I have, Doctor. Would I be right if I said natural
causes?'

'Well, well.' Fedor carefully avoided committing himself. 'I won't say yes and I won't say no. But it's highly
possible. I can see no sign of a destructive act. You mean,
of course, that the position suggests a natural collapse?'

'Precisely.'

'I must say I am inclined to agree. The autopsy may
have something to say; I still believe it may turn out as
you think.'

It shook me. I had been expecting something dramatic
and terrible. But when you came to consider it in a
reasonable light, Schyler had said Laffin was eighty—I can't
say I really checked the body to see if he looked it. Just the
same, eighty was a big stretch for any man, and he could
have quietly laid down and died as been pushed into
Eternity. It was just that I was all keyed up for some sort
of wildness.

'That letter,' I said. 'It doesn't make sense.'

'Not good sense. Unless somebody wanted him found.'
Mrs. Pym went and thrust up a squeaking window irri-
tably. 'The place st—smells! Doctor, I'd be grateful if
you can get down to work at once. Superintendent, can
you make the coroner get a wiggle on and have him cut up
to-night?'

'To-night?' Fedor was dismayed. 'I was going to
bed early.'

'I'll stay up with you.' Mrs. Pym's voice was as soothing

as a buzz-saw. ' So will we all. You can think of it while you're doing the job.'

Fedor rubbed his bald head unhappily and trailed out with Kelly to telephone the coroner.

She looked round the room, considering it.

' A notable day,' Laystall said. ' Sherbina, Chow, and now this. I could count the murders I've investigated on one hand.'

' Laffin isn't murdered yet,' Mrs. Pym told him. ' I wonder who his estate goes to ? '

I remembered Schyler's opinion that there must be about two hundred million in it. The amount was so huge that it was silly. I also remembered the story of Laffin's distant relative in Yangtzepoo and wondered if it were the only one : if the wills of other wealthy old misers meant anything, Laffin had probably left all his millions to a dogs' home.

Just then I remembered I was working on a newspaper.

' Can I have a release on this ? ' I asked Mrs. Pym.

She glanced at Laystall, who shrugged.

' I don't see anything against it, ma'am, though perhaps it should stand until after the post mortem ? '

She nodded.

' Fair enough. You heard, Larry. Sit on it for the moment. Darn it, I'm sick of this rag-shop ! Superintendent, what about leaving a man here and I'll come and look round in the morning ? '

It was so decided, and we went to the front door, where Kelly was waiting with Fedor.

' The coroner is issuing the order,' he told Laystall, glancing at the gloomy little doctor. ' And Dr. Fedor himself will be doing the work.' Kelly shuddered. ' He's waiting for the cart this minute, so he is.'

The party broke up after that. I nearly fell through the ground when Laystall asked Mrs. Pym where she would be so that she could be informed about the post-mortem result.

' I'll go along to the Ritz-Carlton with Larry.' She twiddled her outrageous hat and gave me a small leer. ' Think I'd pass as a dance-mad matron, Larry ? '

We all had too much sense to smile. That stolid, tweed-suited, formidably English figure was the last thing in the world I could imagine moving around to Highlo' Harry's music.

'It'd be swell if you'd like it,' I said in the most diplomatic voice I could manage.

'The younger generation.' She sounded completely affable. 'I'm asking him to play Valentino to me as a red-hot momma, and he's as lukewarm as an hotel bath ! C'm on, son, you're for it now. If nothing else, you'll go down in Shanghai history as the man who took Pym to a night spot.'

I thought Barbadoro was going to fall flat on his face when I trailed down the stairs behind Mrs. Pym. The floor was packed, the air thick with noise and busy music.

She stood in the roped-off space, where incomers paused to have their gowns admired, looking as if she wished she had a machine-gun and was using it.

'*Signora?*' Barbadoro bowed low. 'An honour. A table for the *Signora*? *All'istante!*'

She did not move a muscle of her stern face on the journey to the magically conjured table : I saw Mrs. Rotger's eyes go round, in the arms of her dancing partner ; Mrs. Erp put down her glass and frankly stared. Highlo' Harry nearly dropped his clarinet, and I don't think there was a soul in the room who wasn't watching us. Some of the people at the far side, wondering what the changed hum of conversation was about, stood up to see. I felt like something the dog had been chewing.

It was better when we were sitting down. My bottle, presented by the management, appeared. Barbadoro was startled when Mrs. Pym demanded still lemonade, but she got it.

She dropped her bag on the table—I heard the solid thud of the Luger—crossed her arms and leaned back in her chair. I suppose her slow glance over the scene was an interested inventory, but some of the guests ducked their heads as if a naked sword blade had come too near. Mrs.

Pym's eyes usually gave strangers the feeling of a wind blowing straight from Siberia. I was used to them, but I dare say they made uneasy consciences hop like a jabbed nerve.

She nodded when she was looking at me again.

' I suppose they wouldn't come here if they didn't enjoy it. You're a child. I can see your point. But what about things like that ? ' She gestured openly to the over-dressed figure of Mrs. Lester MacMahoney Erp. ' She'll never see sixty again, but that flowered organdie she's wearing'd look silly on a schoolgirl. Does she dance ? '

' Crazy about it, ma'am.' I was beginning to have fun.

' It must be a strong floor.' Mrs. Pym said something in Mandarin, which she spoke even better than Shanghai dialect. It sounded terse and rude, and I think it was. ' This go on every night ? '

' I believe so.'

' It beats me. I wonder where the wives go ? '

' You mean ... ? ' I hesitated. There *were* a lot of oldish men with young girls. ' Maybe they're on business ? '

Her look was so outrageously cynical that I chuckled.

' Son, it's called monkey business in simple circles like mine.' Her nod was suddenly pleased. ' The Cyanide Man would have the time of his life if he's after sinners. Look at 'em ! Half of them gaping openly at me on my innocent pleasures.'

' And the other half ? '

' Looking the other way, hoping if I don't see 'em I won't haul them off with me. Why don't you drink your liquor ? It cost you enough.'

' With the management's compliments, ma'am. It doesn't taste so good when it's free.'

There was a very small twinkle in her eyes.

' If I had that sort of mind I'd give you a philosophical lecture on the implications of your remark. However ... who's the big, handsome Chinese two tables down ? Looks like a twin brother to Genghis Khan.'

' Oh, I met him earlier. That's Doctor Wu Hsiung. I

don't know what he's a doctor of. He thinks a lot of you.'

'Im'phm?' She scrutinized the doctor, then turned to me. 'Wu Hsiung? That's a phoney, son, like you calling yourself McGonigle Baker. Where's he from?'

'I wasn't told. He's with Paul and Jennie Chang. I figured he might come from Jehol.'

'Respectable company, anyhow. Jehol? That's not bad guessing. I've a notion I've seen him in Peking.'

'He mentioned hearing of you there.'

'Did he, dammit! Ver-ee interesting. I'll keep him in mind. He's been staring at me in a polite way ever since we came in.' She took one of her famous flyers. 'I wouldn't trust him farther than I can throw the band.'

'Eh? But, ma'am!'

'Don't yammer. If you dropped him down a chimney he'd still fall zigzag fashion out of choice. He's as crooked as a Chinese-fashion bridge.'

'But you haven't——'

'I haven't met him?' She looked at me blandly. 'Son, women's intuition is always supposed to be a big laugh. I'm using it just the same. It's the thing a woman sizes up a man with, when she uses her head and not her heart—and I, as rumour will tell you, have a lump of concrete where other females keep what is dubbed the seat of their affections.'

Just then Highlo' Harry announced the cabaret, and the lights went down. The Ritz-Carlton Girls came on in their white uniforms. I've no doubt Nadia Sherbina's successor had been absorbing her routines when the earlier show was presented; this time she was at the head of the troupe, Lydia Tschenko.

I remembered her as one of the Astor House dancers. I dare say Barbadoro had brought her in quick and groomed her. It was a swell job. If she was almost a dead ringer for Nadia Sherbina in looks and colouring, she was more lithe, more youthful, and there was something that smacked of ballet in the way she handled her

feet. She was deft as a feather, her voice really good.
She got such a reception that they had to go through
Anchors Aweigh all over again.

While Leda and Barney Procrusko were doing their
sketch Mrs. Pym said :

' That's high life, eh ? I'm learning ! Is that blonde
item Nadia's successor ? '

' I think so, though Highlo'—though the orchestra leader
didn't say so. Maybe he's trying her on us first ? '

' If the tongues hanging out mean a thing, she's a
success. It couldn't be . . . no.'

' What was that ? '

' Just wondering.' Her glance was gently satiric. ' A
far-fetched thought that perhaps she put the skids under
Nadia to get her place ? '

' A pretty little blonde like that ! '

' Hooey ! One day you'll learn that seven female killers
out of ten are blondes—I mean natural blondes, not the
peroxide and ammonia mob. It's a loose thought, anyway.
Unless she was an understudy or something, it doesn't stand.'

' I think she was at the Astor till a few days ago—at
least I saw her there last week.'

' Put it down to Pym, thinking wild.' After the Marine
dance and the return to normal lighting, she glanced at me.
' Going to haul me round the floor, Vernon Castle Baker ? '

I was saved from that one by Barbadoro suddenly appearing. I wondered if he'd come through a demon trap in the
floor.

' Your pardon, *Signora*. The telephone. In my office,
if you wish ? '

She decided to take it in one of the outside booths, and
followed Barbadoro to the entrance. At her gesture I
stayed where I was, watching the dancers.

Association with Mrs. Pym seemed to have achieved
something for me. People appeared to be noticing me ;
some of them smiled in a friendly way as they passed.
Others looked at me with a sort of interested pity, in much
the same manner as they would study a man whose nearest

relative had just been hanged. As a simile I've heard better : it still conveys what I mean.

Paul Chang came over to me, raising one hand when I went to stand up.

' No, please. I was wondering if you could use your influence ? Dr. Wu Hsiung is so anxious to meet Mrs. Pym that my sister and I hoped, if we gave a small reception, she would come ? Do you think you could broach the subject ? I could, of course, arrange the party to suit her.'

' That's nice of you. I'll ask her, anyway. Shall I call you ? '

' At the house, if you will. You will find it in the book.'

He smiled and thanked me, returning to his table.

If I knew anything about it, she was no party-goer, but the meeting promised to be interesting. I decided to see if my charm would work on her.

When she returned her expression was grim. She came marching between the tables, looking neither to left nor right. I had an idea it wasn't going to be the best time to bring up the question of parties.

I said nothing, standing while she sat down, making a business of lighting a cigarette until she was settled.

' You're a tactful cuss, Larry. Waiting for the female fire-eater to simmer down ? '

' You looked a bit mad, ma'am.'

' It'll keep for the moment. What's on your mind ? '

' Me ? Gosh, do I look it ? '

' Come along, son. You don't hide things well.'

Curiously enough, it made me feel easier. I brought up the question of the party.

' Paul Chang would be very honoured, ma'am.'

' I wonder why he's toting this Wu Hsiung about ? ' She looked at their table without pretence. Luckily, again, the trio were watching the floor. ' I'll think about it. I wonder why the fellow wants to meet me ? '

' He seemed pretty impressed with your reputation, ma'am.'

'Bilge ! He might be impressed, but not all that much. I'm a noisy dabbler in a small pond at the moment. One day it'll be different, but right now I don't get it. Unless,' there was a look of interest in her eyes, ' he's up to something and wants to size me up to find out if I'm as tough as they say. Yes, maybe that's the answer. Okay, Larry, you fix it. I may be able to nail him on that phoney name.'

' Yes, ma'am. What day shall I say ? '

' I'll tell you about that. Now, Laffin. You can have a release on the news.' She glanced at her wristwatch. ' You'll make your edition with time to spare.'

No doubt I was wrong ; I just couldn't help feeling disappointed.

' It's according to Hoyle, then ? '

' The death ? Sure. Heart. He just went out like a light, which shouldn't've worried him at eighty. Might've happened at any time. The cadaver was all it should have been.' Her little bomb knocked me clean sideways. ' The only thing Fedor couldn't figure was who fed him cyanide after his death.'

' *Cyanide !* '

' S'sh, boy ; you'll have the neighbours staring. Yes, somebody pushed a cyanide capsule down his throat—maybe with a pencil or something—right after his death. The thing had just about melted, not that it had gone far.' Her look was oblique and pregnant. ' Your Cyanide Man must be a nut if he thought that was going to fool the doctors.'

' Gosh ! It's a big story. Can I use that as well ? '

' Why not ? ' She waved a hand in the warm, smoky air. ' The Country Club ought to get a big kick out of it.'

I thought so, too, and plenty of other folks besides the Country Club set.

CHAPTER VII

HOME OF THE DANCERS

AT its breakfast-tables in the morning the city of Shanghai must have just about taken off like a rocket. Not since the Foreign Settlement was laid down in 1846 had the morning papers carried quite so many sensations.

The *Daily News* had a front page that was a record for civic murder—indeed, not a single item of news was printed concerning anything else. Nadia Sherbina; Leslie Chow; Jacob Laffin—they were all there, including the threat against me, and all the rest of the day's events. The Cyanide Man had celebrity coverage, but even the Hop-Ley Dancers got a look in. Lanny Coager had done a job he could boast about.

And, dominating the whole thing in a classic build-up, was Mrs. Palmyra Evangeline Pym. Coager was playing a hunch, and, when he'd finished, our lady cop was something between Sherlock Holmes, Woodrow Wilson, and William Jennings Bryan. If anybody had been uncertain about her in the past, there was no doubt of it now. 'The Settlement,' Lanny wrote, ' is in the grip of a terror-wave of crime, unprecedented in its history. Luckily the hour always brought the man—or, let us amend, the woman. Detective Inspector Mrs. Pym is big enough to fight this mass murderer and squash him.'

The rest of the papers carried their stories, though the coverage was comparatively routine. The *News* couldn't have thrown bigger headlines or better stories, not if it had got an inside flash that to-day was the end of the world.

Mrs. MacNaughton, my landlady, tackled me on my way out of the dining-room after breakfast.

'Mr. Baker, *surely* that isn't all true in your paper?'

'Sure, every word of it.' I smiled at the plump little woman who was the model for all good landladies.

'You mean men with guns in *my* house?'

'I'm afraid so. Don't let it worry you.'

'Worry me? I'm scared to death. The idea, breaking into respectable homes! I shall go to the French police this very morning.'

'But why? I doubt if he'll come again.'

'Maybe not. I won't have it. I'm an old widow woman and I won't be murdered in my bed. Why, you might have been killed!'

I left her talking to Sung about bolting and barring the doors at night, and insisting he should get a policeman to occupy the empty first floor front, for safety's sake.

It wasn't Lanny Coager's habit to get to the desk till noon. He was there when I rolled up out of the warm sunshine just before ten. He had every daily in front of him, his beard cocked at a derisive angle over them.

'Seen the bunch?' He greeted me. 'Man, we've cleaned the lot! Like our layout?'

'Hottest yet, Lanny.'

'That's what I thought. Larry, keep this up and you'll get your job permanently.' I accepted the Caporal he threw across the desk, and we both lighted up. 'You rate a bonus on this page alone.'

'I've had a raise——'

'The hell with it! You get a bonus. See the compradore and draw twenty-five. It's not much, but you can use it.'

'Lanny, that's——'

'Phooey! Now, how do we rate for to-day? After this front page, anything else will be an anti-climax.'

'That's how it strikes me. There's Laffin's will.'

'I've already called Schyler's office. He's not in yet. I've been promised a call the moment he can see me.'

'Fine. Could we get the inside on it?'

'It's unlikely. Lawyers don't talk under such circumstances.'

'You try. You can get it out of him if anyone can.'

'Why, thanks——'

'I'm not flattering you, Larry. Got any ideas?'

'A side issue, for a beginner.' I told him all about my evening at the Ritz-Carlton. 'This Wu Hsiung bird. Mrs. Pym thinks he's a fake; the name sounds queer to me. Could somebody do some leg-work and check him back?'

'Leave that to me.'

'I'm sorry I didn't call you for the photographer about that letter. You ran it, anyway.'

'That's Pym service. She must've left orders to have a print sent to me. I got it in plenty of time for process to work at it.'

'She's a swell girl, Lanny. Think she can stack up to your promises?'

'I'm using your enthusiasm as a guide. I like the old faggot. She's God's gift to newspapers.'

The house telephone rang and Lanny scooped up the receiver.

'Yeah?' He added 'Okay' and handed the line to me. 'Charlie Lee on the door; for you, Larry.'

'Thanks. Yes, Charlie? This is Mr. Baker.'

'Missy have got, masta. Wanchee talkee you. Can do?'

'What name missy have got, Charlie?'

'No savee. She talkee me wanchee you chop-chop. My tella she you come?'

'Right. Waiting room-side, Charlie?'

'Have got. My pay she. An hyih we.'

'Zia-zia, Charlie.' I put down the receiver, grinning; when he thought of it, Charlie could be as formal as a red-button mandarin. 'Some woman,' I told Coager. 'She's downstairs. It'll be one of those things, I dare say; saw an odd stranger hanging round her house last night.'

'You get along, Larry. Maybe you'd best go round to Central Station? You might get a lead.'

'Right. I'll see the woman and go straight there.'

The *News* waiting-room was pint-size, and it smelled old.

HOME OF THE DANCERS

There were a few ancient magazines on the table, and the place itself was opposite Charlie's box by the main door—I always believed Charlie slept there, nights.

The woman knocked me for a loop the moment I saw her. This was no worthy housewife with some scatter-brained story, but a redhead who could have pinch-hit for a Leonardo da Vinci angel.

She was as tall as me, dressed in a slick bird's-eye suit. She wore a Chinchilla wrap—I did not know it then, but it was one of the rare Rex mutations from France—trim shoes and a cocky little hat. She wore no jewellery; with that face she didn't need any.

'Mr. Larry Baker?'

'Sure. You wanted me?'

'Yes. My name is Irina Roberti. You won't know me.'

One of the Russians, but her English was better than mine. This was no cabaret girl, but real class. The fine, miniature-like features told me she had the best White Russian blood. I was no push-over for women in those days; I was too busy making a career for myself, but if anybody was going to push me, she could. One touch from those little hands and I would have taken off like a modern jet—I can be as poetical as Herrick when I feel like it. I did then.

'Mr. Baker, is there somewhere we can talk?'

'Anywhere would suit me, but there's Dinty Moore's along the block. If you don't mind a saloon?'

'I should like that. Will you show me the way?'

Charlie Lee's eyebrows were up as we passed him, the nearest the Chinese can get to a wolf-whistle. He was so shaken that he tore out and opened the door for us, which was pretty big of him. In China they regard red hair as the unluckiest thing in the world—I noticed the old chap had his first and last fingers crossed, the ward-off-devils sign.

Dinty Schumansky Moore practically climbed over the bar when we entered the empty saloon. He brushed down one of his tin tables, arranged two chairs and leered over his broken nose, appraising the cape. I never knew a

Pole from Ireland, which he was, who didn't know everything about anything worth money.

I said I'd have a stengah; she settled for a Hong Kong Pink Gin Swizzle, but we didn't start talking till the drinks arrived and Dinty was back behind the bar, trying to listen.

'Mr. Baker, do you think you can help me?'

'I dare say.' I looked into her grey eyes and figured this was no swooning maiden, but a tough-minded woman who knew what comes after ABC.

'I read your story this morning in the *News*. Mr. Baker, I believe I know where you can find the Hop-Ley Dancers.'

'Eh? But——'

'You're going to ask me why I should come to you?' She gave me a dazzling smile. 'I have certain reasons of my own. In case you wonder who I am, I was born here, in Shanghai. My father was a Social Democrat, but just before I was born, in nineteen hundred and three, the party split into the Bolsheviks and the Mensheviks; my father hated Lenin from the very first moment, and, when the split occurred, he left Russia and we came to Shanghai, that is, my father, my mother, and my two brothers. I was born soon after that. When my parents died they had left me a little fortune. I've been here ever since because, since I grew up, I have no country.'

'Are you in politics?'

'Russians are always in politics, Mr. Baker. Do you think you could take me on trust and come to see what I can show you?'

It seemed good enough to me. Many of the lines a reporter picks up come in from public sources, from busybodies, from public-spirited citizens or, more usually, from people with a grouch against other people. I decided she was more or less in the last category.

'I'll take a chance. Where do we go?'

'It's down by the Riverside Power Station, just off Yangtzepoo Road. We could get a taxi?'

'Okay.' I got up and went over to Dinty. 'Stop eating the lady and get me a cab, will you?' I rubbed his black hair.

'Going places, huh? Want a little help, maybe?'

'Khwa-khwa, you big lunk, or do I have to sock you?'

'Przepraszam? You and who's else?'

'Just me.' I coiled a fist and waggled it at him. 'See that? We Canucks are mild, but rouse us and a Kwangtung Blue Tiger's a gentle kitten in comparison.'

He gave me a huge, lopsided grin and went to the 'phone, calling the Willys Knight garage for a cab.

It arrived within ten minutes, speed for China, and I walked to the door with the girl. She gave the native driver a direction in dialect so expert I couldn't keep up with it. I didn't realize it at the time, but she said *zaung* instead of *kyi*, meaning godown, or warehouse. And *zaung* is used when it refers to the godown belonging to the speaker. It came back to me later, like things do that you hear without hearing at the time.

It was a long run through the bright morning, across the Garden Bridge to Broadway and then to the straight length of Yangtzepoo Road. She leaned slightly against me all the way, talked on the city like an expert. If I'd been more susceptible I should have fallen for her, but if she knew men it wasn't my sort of man. She used *L'Origan* perfume, like so many of the Russians; it happened to be one scent I hated. And, further, I was on a story. The Cyanide Man assignment was my first personal baby. Ten thousand redheads as pretty as an angelic choir wouldn't have diverted me from my job.

We stopped on the corner of Tinghai Road, almost at the end of the International Settlement. It was fairly quiet just there. When I got out at her gesture I could smell the mud from the nearby river, mixed with the sharp odours from the Gasoline Landing Station.

She gave the driver his money, and a nice tip which had him grinning all over his face.

'Hadn't he best wait?' I asked her.

'We might be some time.' She took my arm companionably. 'There's a hire garage next to the Power Station when we come back.'

'Tuk Dzo's? I'd forgotten that. Okay, Miss Roberti. You show me the way.'

'Irina, if I can call you Larry?'

'It's a deal. Now, where do we go?'

'Over there.' She pointed to a long, low warehouse standing back from the main road, behind a hoarding boosting somebody's fertilizer. I could just see the name on the frontage: Hello Storage Concern. That made it Chinese, for Enormous Universal Company is as common a name in Shanghai as Smith and Company is in Regina: Hello Storage fell into the same category.

She led the way along a path, ignoring the closed front entrance, pausing when we reached a little pass door.

'This is it, Larry. I can't tell you how I know about this, but I've checked it myself. If I'm wrong in saying this is the home of the Hop-Ley Dancers, you can demand any forfeit you like from me.' It was a game that didn't interest me just then, but I saw what she meant.

'You're coming with me?'

'Why not? It should be exciting. Have you got a gun?'

'Eh? Why, do you think I'll need it?'

'I think you should be very careful.'

I pulled out the Ortgies and checked that the safety catch was off; I felt silly, there in the bright sunlight, holding a gun, with the cheerful sounds coming from the Gasoline Landing Station where a tanker was at work.

I tried the door and pushed it open. There was nothing inside, only darkness. She was at my heels as we crept in. Beyond the patch of sunlight, oblong to the shape of the doorway, there was nothing until we had gone about five more yards.

Then the place split with noise. A mass—as it seemed—of Chinese descended on me, whipped away the Ortgies and held me tight; Irina Roberti let out a small scream as she was caught, too.

We were hauled furiously into the darkness of the godown.

CHAPTER VIII

THE PATHWAYS OF MIDNIGHT

IN a wide, empty room, the walls of which bore bins full of boxes labelled as ping-pong balls and golf balls, we came into some light. The mob broke into component parts and turned out to be seven Chinese, coolies by the look of them.

Four of them were holding me, two had a grip on Irina and the remaining one, who wore a cap, seemed to be in charge.

I said, ' *Auh-tshauh siau koong !* ' to him. He went puce, while the others snickered. It was not so much that he minded being called a dirty street coolie—it also meant that he was a man who collected certain kinds of manure. If I'd dug up his ancestors and thrown them in the river, I couldn't have insulted him worse.

Irina turned an anguished face to me, then rattled at the man in her expert vernacular. It was some sort of apology for my ignorance as a *Me-kok nyung*, or American (the whole continent is American to the Chinese). It made me pretty mad, though there was nothing I could do about it.

I was wondering about Irina. She'd been handled roughly, right enough. Her expensive wrap was torn ; there was a small cut on her, and her grey eyes were frightened. I still wasn't convinced.

' How fashion what thing you pay me this ? ' I asked the head coolie.

' *Maskee, maskee.*' He shrugged on that universal negative, which meant about anything you wanted. ' You catchee this side. Bimeby masta come.'

Just then I remembered the difference between *zaung* and *kyi*. I glared at the girl.

' Irina, you told the chauffeur to bring us to *your* godown. You own the damned place ! '

'I know, Larry, I know. Truly, you must believe me—it's not my fault.'

'In a pig's eye! There's a trick in this somewhere.'

'Please believe me . . .' The words trailed away. The door had opened and a Chinese stood there. He was about the biggest man in the whole world, so fat that I felt you needed a hand-lens to find his eyes. He wore a blue European suit, his hair cut *en brosse*, and there were rings on his hands. I looked for the jade buffalo, not that there was one.

Irina Roberti was scared sick. I was so angry I could have kicked him to death without worrying.

He waddled into the room, followed by a couple of natives in black suits, hatchet men if I ever saw them. The head coolie did a low bow and brought out a chair in a hurry, which the fat man took without a word.

He considered us for a long time before he spoke.

'Good morning. You have had a little trouble?'

It shook me, hearing perfect Oxford English from a man who looked like a country farmer gone to fat.

'"Trouble"? Are you the head man around here, you bladder?'

'*Mis*-ter *Baker!* Is that a sample of Canadian education of which one has heard so much?' He was smiling at me, showing a mouth loaded with bullion.

'That's how we talk when a bunch of dirty-necked coolies act this way. Just what's the score, anyway, and is this girl in it, too?'

'Miss Roberti?' He glanced at her and she nearly went through the floor with fright. 'A means to hand, you might say. You were asked very nicely to forget all about the Hop-Ley Dancers.' A sort of quiver went round the group. I'll swear none of them, except the head coolie, had any English. They didn't seem to need it when they heard that name.

'Dancers or Cyanide Man, it's all the same to me, fatso. The *News* prints the truth and nothing you can say or do is going to stop it. Just try, brother, just try.' Fine words and bold ones, I thought. At twenty-one a man will chin-up to a berserk female grizzly and dare her to come on, which is just as well. When the spirit goes out of the twenty-one-year-olds you can wash up this world as finished.

'Notable, my dear Mr. Baker. But, you see, I am not in the habit of making jokes.' He shifted his bulk to greater comfort. 'Let us be sensible men. Suppose I offer you five thousand American dollars and this woman here? I will also see that you have every comfort on a one-way journey to whatever port outside China you choose.' He raised his hand as I opened my mouth. 'Just *one* moment! Irina Roberti is a nice girl, and five thousand dollars is more money than you will make in years. Just for one little thing.'

'What do I do, cut my throat?'

'Oh, *please* stop being childish! You will go to your editor and to Mrs. Pym. You will tell them the Hop-Ley Dancers is a figment of your versatile imagination.'

'That's all? And how do I explain away the fact the words were written '—I caught Irina's eyes, wide, pleading, and anguished—' in . . . in my story to-day?' I don't exactly know why I made that switch. I was going to mention the paper in Nadia Sherbina's flat, and I think Irina knew it.

'Smooth, extremely smooth.' The fat man chuckled. 'You were thinking of a little note in Russian in the possession of Nadia Sherbina?' His glance of malignant dislike at the redhead must have made her toes curl. 'You are a gallant man, Mr. Baker. By the way, I forget my manners completely. My name is Fong, Albert Fong.'

'It's nice knowing you. Tell me, how come you can hand out dishes like Irina and all that money? I'm only an ordinary reporter, you know.'

'I know *all* about you. Irina does as she is told, whatever she may think about it. The thing is that *you* have concentrated attention on the Dancers; you can take that attention away.'

'It's like that? Not me. I'm going to uncover this

story, Al, my lad. Far as you're concerned, you can *tsun ah* . . .' I let him have the rest of it, and I thought he'd react to it, a coarse phrase which makes any normal Chinese go clean mad.

His face reddened. The coolies hid their snickers this time; the hatchet men stepped forward together, halted by a sharp word. Fong made an excellent recovery.

'You must forgive me if I am sensitive. You have the American knack for finding raw spots. I had hoped we might settle this like gentlemen.' He made a small sigh, and I'm darned if the fellow wasn't sorry. 'Mr. Baker, will you accept my offer?'

'Not for a boatload of taels. I want to know who the Hop-Ley Dancers are, and when I know they'll be able to give a public performance.'

'How foolish.' Fong said something and the coolies took Irina out of the room. She looked scared, but never said a word.

'Where's she gone?'

'Why, does it worry you?'

'Me?' I chuckled. 'If you think you'll get me to keep off by stripping pieces off her hide, you're wrong, mister. Anyway, I couldn't change my mind and take her and the dough if she's all mussed up, could I?'

'Oh?' Fong was worried by that. He'd made his offer and, whatever he was, he had the Chinese desire to keep face by honouring his word. 'You may change your mind?'

'Give me your word the girl doesn't get hurt now or at any other time, and I'll think about it.'

'Very well, you have my word.' He gave a direction to the head coolie, who went out and then came back, nodding. 'Well, we do business?'

'I've thought about it. No deal, chum.'

'Ah? Then the girl——'

'You gave your word. Remember?'

If looks could have done it, Fong had me on a hot griddle. But I'll say this for him: he wanted to keep his word. My own showing was pretty poor. Just the same, I was playing the cards as they fell.

'Let us put an end to this, Mr. Baker. Yes or no?'

'No.'

'That is most unfortunate. She's a nice girl, and it is a great deal of money.'

'Surely. How do you know you could trust me?'

'Isn't this becoming rather elementary? You appear to trust me more than I can trust you. The girl and the money would be waiting for you in the ship off Woosung when you have carried out your part of the bargain.'

'Just what have you got on Irina?'

'That would be telling, don't you think?' Fong creaked to his feet. '*Now*, Mr. Baker, is it still no?'

'Yep. I'm staying on the story till I break it.'

'Indeed. May I point out that I am not the slit-eyed Oriental of your Western romances, but, I must say, those romances have given us Chinese quite a few ideas that had never previously occurred to us. You won't change your mind?'

It would seem, from the perspective of people living in big cities, that Fong was taking a lot of trouble over a junior reporter. But, rich as it was, Shanghai was not a big place. Its European population was not large, and personal journalism was no small thing in those days. Because of it I mattered quite a lot more than would have been the case in a western city. Fong wanted the heat taken off: if I retracted and backed it up by running away, the Hop-Ley Dancers and whatever they meant could go on without any further attention. More than that, no local editor would have touched the subject in a hurry if any further news broke.

I said I wasn't changing my mind.

'That is your sorrow.' Fong seemed quite contrite. 'I don't like violence, particularly crude violence, but it seems indicated.' He turned back the lapel of his jacket and pulled out half-a-dozen ordinary pins which he gave to the taller of the hatchet men. ' I read about this in an American romance of the San Francisco Chinese section. The most ingenious author mentioned the age-old torture used by us of pushing these pins under the nails of the subject's fingers and toes for promoting accordance with the—let us say—torturer's demands.

' As a student of Chinese history, I must say the idea is quite new to me. We are, perhaps, more refined when we use persuasion. But never let it be said a slit-eyed Celestial disdained to learn from the enlightened West.' He gave me a most unexpected smile, then said something to the hatchet man which, from its classifier, I recognized as Wuhu dialect.

My restraining coolies gripped me when I started to struggle, dumping me unceremoniously on my back. My right leg was lifted, the sock and shoe being ripped off.

I was no hero. I admit it. Canadians are tough as they come ; they're also human. I let out a yell before the darn pin even touched me. You read of men undergoing tortures with a stiff upper lip. That's novelists' stuff. When a man's being hurt he usually lets rip a howl and even if he shuts his mouth when the pain stops, he always yells when it starts again. If I disgraced myself before I was hurt, I guess the feeling of that pin going under a toe-nail scared me before it began to happen.

At least it would have happened, but the yell brought a shout in response. Even from where I was, the men in the room looked startled at a sound of running feet. Both the hatchet men hauled out Colts, which they probably trusted more than their little axes. The door slammed back and the U.S. Marines came striding in, wearing a funny hat, a tweed suit and answering to the name of Pym.

Her scorifying ' What the blazing hell ? ' was unladylike and effective. The next minute one of the hatchet men had fired and that blessed Luger barked back like the big German cannon that it was.

The hatchet man folded ; the second one dropped his gun either because he was scared or he just dropped it.

Mrs. Pym jerked off the electric light switch, grabbed me by the collar and hauled me on my back into the outer darkness and round the corner.

There was an outbreak of chattering, a sound of men running, and silence. I tried to get off my back, but she thrust me down again.

I got the idea when she took something from her pocket and threw it outwards and away from her. Four guns from four different points went off as one, all aiming, I guessed, for that same spot.

I found I was alone and stayed down, nearly jerking out of my skin when the Luger went off again, a little to the right. From the howl that resulted, it went home.

It was nervy business, flattened out in the darkness. At any minute I would be a dead duck, and wished the Ortgies was where I could get at it.

Something rustled somewhere, and the four guns banged again. This time the Luger's uproar went on till the clip was empty. I heard someone moaning when the din was over, and faintly the sound of a new clip going in with its characteristic little *snick* as it was slapped home.

How Mrs. Pym managed it I don't know. She must have put her electric torch on something, pressed the switch and jumped out of reach. In one breathless second the thin beam picked out Fong, dead centre, then the guns chattered, but, a shaved second before the torch was doused, the Luger banged once. I heard a heavy thud and guessed it was Fong: the nicest piece of snapshooting in years.

She had her targets marked now, since the gunmen hadn't the sense to move, for the second lot of shots came from the same points. Methodically, cold-bloodedly, the Luger began firing, paused as a third clip was used, and began again. The godown reeked of gunpowder, echoed with noise, and you could smell that queer, aromatic scent of spilled blood.

With an impact that nearly shot me on my feet the pass door smacked back. After that darkness the oblong of sunlight lit up the whole place and Mrs. Pym, standing there like an idiot, feet apart, Luger levelled, and apparently rooted to the ground as solidly as an oak tree.

The Luger's mouth quested from side to side. My flesh crawled to think, at any minute, she was going to get it. But her ears were sharper than mine. She had checked the target of every bullet, and what had seemed a woman acting like crazy to me was nothing but a little shrewd playing to the awed press. There wasn't a soul standing up to her.

Ignoring me altogether, though I tagged behind shaken to near paralysis, she checked the results. There was the head coolie and the second hatchet man, both dead, one of the coolies who had held on to me with a bullet in his chest, and Albert Fong with a slug in the middle of his nice suit, the biggest and deadest man I had ever seen.

I think the others must have got out by a ladder against the wall. It reached to a sort of storeroom, and, beyond this, a second storeroom with double doors for working a fixed hoist.

'Mrs. Pym, I just don't know how——'

'Can it, son. I told you nobody's going to fool with me.'

'How the heck did you find out?'

The grey-blue eyes were satiric.

'Want to make something of that? Use your loaf, or I'll begin to think you're a moron as well.' In an impatient voice she added: 'I called at your offices about twenty minutes after you left. The doorkeeper said you'd gone to Dinty's; Dinty told me you'd gone haring off with some redhead angel in a Willys Knight hire car. It was just a question of getting hold of the driver to find out. Does that put me in Baker Street class?'

'You bet it does! That dead bird, the fat one, was named Albert Fong. He was going to jam pins under my nails when you came in.'

'Unfriendly soul. What about the redhead?'

'Isn't she here?'

'Can you see her?'

It had me beat, so I told the whole story from the moment Charlie Lee called me.

'H'm. You're a bigger sucker than I thought you were. Still, men always zoom when they get tangled with pretty redheads. Irina Roberti? I'll find her, and all about her. So Fong's a Hop-Ley Dancer? Bet it shook the floor when he tried—and don't giggle at that, son, it's a lousy joke. You say he knew about that bit of paper in Sherbina's room?'

'He said so.'

'Huh? Then tried to buy you off with five thousand American dollars and the redhead as a bonus?'

'That's what he said.' I mentioned my thoughts about the importance of getting me to retract and out of the case.

'Could be, Larry.' She tried to turn Fong over with one foot and failed. 'This thing has stepped into big time.' She scratched her strong chin with the Luger muzzle. 'It's got me floored for the moment—sorry, Larry, I never asked if you're hurt.'

'Just plain scared, ma'am, but I've got over it.'

'Good. Help me search these birds, then I'll do some heavy thinking. Gun business always makes me feel brighter. Maybe I'll get an idea.'

I was glad if she was going to get some ideas. I was dazed and my mind would not stop brooding over those pins if they had gone home. The part of my mind that could attend to business was busy writing the story of that indomitable woman slamming into a dark godown alone, handling a proposition that could have had a squad of men acting warily.

It was just her way. Mrs. Pym kept herself fit with ju-jitsu lessons from Oko Tamawake, whose judo gymnasium was somewhere around the North Station, where he was our great expert in Dr. Kano's system. I think she knew as much as he knew, and, apart from that, was perfectly capable of wading into trouble with only her fists and using them well. If I had to nominate the woman I would most like to have by my side if I landed in a hostile mob, she would have been my pick. Come to that, in such a situation, I think I should have sat on the sidelines and watched : I should only have been in her hair.

'Larry,' she came from the search, 'there's nothing on them. I'm going to lock up this place—no, I'll find a uniform man and leave him in charge until Central gets here.'

'What shall I do, ma'am?'

'You can come with me. I'm going to have a word with Yüan Chou. Maybe he knows the answer to this. Don't look so vacant, son; the old boy's got his ear very close to the ground, and he should know. It's in Tuen Kee Road, in the Chinese city, where we're going in a hurry.'

A native constable was providentially standing by the side of Mrs. Pym's Bugatti, parked at the kerb in the main street. He was sent to guard the godown while she found a telephone and called Central Station, to return in five minutes with the news that Sergeant Chum-Kwat was on his way down.

She climbed into the driving seat, waving me in.

'Hold your hat, son; we're going to move.'

We did. Yangtzepoo Road and Broadway are busy at that time of the day, but we went along those streets as if all the devils in China were at our tails. I thought we should ease off on the Bund; I thought wrong. We slipped past streetcars and rickshaws in a manner that had me crossing my fingers, then we right-angled to Avenue Edward VII, left-angled and snapped across the Boulevard des Deux Républiques, slowing down in the Chinese city because we had to. Shanghai in general was bad enough; the purely native section was a snarl of traffic and people that would have driven a Regina cop stark crazy.

Using the hooter, or Mrs. Pym's violent vernacular when needed, we more or less fought, bit and gouged our way into Tuen Kee Road and stopped before a native house with me rubbing one finger along the door top, wondering if I was still alive.

She gave me a brief, sidelong look before getting out.

Concession did Mrs. Pym say anything; when she did so her eyes were metallic.

'If Yüan Chou's so scared, this is big, Larry. The Cyanide Man and the Hop-Ley Dancers have me beat if he's too scared to talk. He wanted to.'

'What did the boy tell you, then?' I was so puzzled that I said it for my own comfort.

'Said his master was deeply sorry, that all Chinese are very frightened just now, and that you and I were on the pathways of midnight.'

'Eh?'

'Got you?' Her glance was grim. 'Just a high-flown literary allusion for imminent death. In other words, son, our necks are stuck right out.'

'It's like that, is it?'

She suddenly smacked her hand on the hooter button when a dawdling coolie got in the way.

'Damned fool! Yes, Larry, it's like that. Want to quit?'

'Do you, ma'am?'

'*Me?*' Her expression was malevolent. 'If they don't get me, I'll get them first, and I don't play for tin pennies!'

'Okay, ma'am, I'm at your heels—so long as I get the story.'

She didn't say anything, but her grey-blue eyes made me want to throw out my chest and crow.

I knew when she brought out that one about '*chung jên shih shêng jên*' we would be getting down to things. It usually marks a period in conversation, the intimation that 'all people are sage,' the Chinese version of our own *vox populi vox Dei.*

My guess was right. She went smoothly into English and told him, with nothing left out, the story of her case.

Yüan Chou had been kindly, interested and just an amiable old gentleman up to that, but even his placid face and gentle nods, as prescribed for a host, began to change. Curiously enough, he did not show any interest at the description of the jade ring worn by the man who held me up in my bedroom : it was the Hop-Ley Dancers that got him. He was polite about the Cyanide Man, sorry about the murders, and absorbed in everything, yet I saw little beads of sweat on his nose the moment the Hop-Ley thing was out.

He was deeply worried, how worried I did not realize at the time, for he did not even look when I crossed one leg over the other to make myself comfortable, which, Mrs. Pym told me later, was the height of disrespect on my part.

Once he tried to speak and could not. His old eyes were anxious and pleading ; he wanted to speak, but dared not do it. Mrs. Pym must have taken pity on the old chap. She waved to the servant, standing by the door. He brought the teacups and she took one, me following, raising it and looking towards Yüan Chou. This time we drank it, and, apparently, it was our leave-taking. He stood up, negotiating so that we were both on his left side, and went with us to the door.

There was a great deal of bowing, and an invitation to return at a propitious time, but, to put it succinctly, we were out on our necks.

But not quite. As we were about to go into the street the houseboy bowed, and said something so softly I wasn't dead sure he spoke at all.

Not until we were crossing the tongue of the French

Gradually we got to chairs and there was so much bowing and exchanging of courtesies that I thought we would never get down to them. But we did. The boy appeared with a little red lacquered tray on which were three cups without handles, thin, fragile ware I assessed as valuable.

Mrs. Pym nudged my foot when we were all holding these things, filled with something golden that I thought was tea. I followed her exactly, so we never got down to drinking the stuff. The host put it to his lips, then his eyes and finally his forehead, replacing the cup on the tray; we did the same. I guessed it was the highly precise business of ceremonial greeting tea which the guests insist they are unworthy to drink. The host, not to be outdone, would not dream of touching it if his guests did not.

It might have gone on for a week, but it worked out. The boy took back the cups, bringing us a tray of sweetmeats and little oaten biscuits, each stamped with a red Chinese character: these we did nibble politely.

You have to be patient in China. Mrs. Pym lapsed into Mandarin which both she and Yüan Chou chose to speak. I heard her say, '*Tso-t'ien nuan-huo*,' which indicated that yesterday was warm; the old boy came back with a fast one that it was cool the day before yesterday, '*ch'ien-t'ien liang-k'uai*.' Then she pointed out there had been a heavy dew in the morning. It went down well, then they got on to affairs. Yüan Chou told us that '*luan ch'i pa tsao*.' I knew it meant everything was in confusion, or, to be literal things were 'at sevens and eights'—the Chinese prefer this to 'sixes and sevens,' but I never found out why.

It went on for another six minutes. From what I could get of it, they touched on the state of China, the railways, the new schools, the strike at the cotton mill in Hongkew, and the low habits of the younger generation. It shook me that Mrs. Pym, who hates wasted time, had so much patience. But she was bland, courteous and polite—I noticed in her dealings with the better class of Chinese h attitude was always impeccable.

'You don't talk when there's no need ; you'll do, son.'

I didn't spoil it by saying I was too dead scared to speak, following her across the pavement, where a small knot of idlers had gathered to watch. Foreigners in the Chinese City, other than those who went to gape at the big temple or the Willow Pattern Tea House, were rarities.

The building was small, one-storied, with the usual brick screen hiding the front door, something like the blast walls erected in front of doors in London during the air raids of World War Two. The roof of the place bore the usual curled metal ornaments—both brick wall and ornaments having simple reasons. Devils could not enter the house because devils cannot turn corners ; the ornaments were the same, since devils cannot sit on anything but a smooth surface. This might sound silly, but the Chinese have done well on such notions.

A houseboy in a dark blue gown received us in the hall. Mrs. Pym addressed him in vernacular, and we were led into a low, native-style room. It was a beautiful place, with scrolls on the walls—the real thing, not tourist junk—and redwood furniture that must have been worth a great deal of money.

When the boy returned he stood aside for an old, old gentleman to come in.

He was quite a picture, with a seamed, kindly face, and faded eyes behind tortoiseshell spectacles. He wore a mauve gown and his round cap was that of a scholar of degree—in China a scholar, or savant as we have it, ranks, or did rank, at the highest level of all with, very sensibly, at the bottom of the social scale, soldiers and refuse collectors.

The old boy tucked his hands in his sleeves and bowed low ; Mrs. Pym bowed back and I did, too, feeling slightly silly.

It was all very impressive. He told us, in perfect English, that he was ashamed of his house and his dress ; Mrs. Pym told him we were disgusting creatures to soil his floors by walking on them.

CHAPTER IX

WILD PURSUIT

MRS. PYM, with me behind her, walked into Superintendent Laystall's office without knocking. Her chin was out and the set of her shoulders suggested she was in a belligerent mood. It was just as well. She walked smack into big trouble in the form of a tall, thin, austere-faced man beside Laystall's desk. He looked like a backwoods minister with a knack for rabble-rousing.

I knew him immediately, Edward Carter Bowne, chairman of the Shanghai Municipal Council and, around the Settlement, bad trouble for almost everybody.

Laystall was looking worried; Bowne, trim as a new automobile, had his dragon-killing expression on. His pale eyes brightened as he saw us; he ignored me and took a sort of spiritual dive at Mrs. Pym.

'Ah, you are with us, madam?' His small sniff indicated that he wasn't impressed. 'I have been talking to the Superintendent.'

'That's nice for you.' I saw her hands go on her hips and sort of effaced myself into a corner of the office, trying to look like a chair. It was going to be a battle.

'I understand you are in charge of this holocaust?'

'If you mean the Cyanide Man, I am.'

'That, I believe, is the cant newspaper name in use.' It was no good; I tried to smile when he glared at me. 'Is that the creature who wrote all that nonsense?'

'Larry Baker, Mr. Bowne. A good friend of mine.' If I'd been at the receiving end of the rasp in her voice, I should have dived neatly from the window.

'A journalist!' Bowne tore me into little shreds and threw the pieces away. 'It is immaterial. May I ask precisely by what section of the Municipal Police Code you have bludgeoned your way into taking charge of this sorry matter?'

'As a police officer, duly accredited by the Council, at the head of the duty rota——'

'Ah! Superintendent Laystall, I am under the impression that *female* officers——'

'And where does the Code say female?' Mrs. Pym's demand was icy. It infuriated Bowne, who had a lawyer's pride in knowing his facts.

'*Mrs.* Pym, as a councillor, I opposed your appointment. Belper, who was chairman at the time, was with me, but we were overruled. As present chairman I am calling a meeting to-day to have your appointment nullified, *on* the grounds of incompetence, inciting unnecessary alarm, and the admission of reporters to police routine——' He paused and glared at poor Laystall, who tried a diplomatic intervention. '*Thank* you, Superintendent, I am capable of handling this situation. Mrs. Pym, I shall expect you in the board-room at three, when we shall deal with you direct, and put the matter to vote, a vote, I need hardly add, destined to a foregone conclusion. Why,' he suddenly became human, ' the town is in a panic, an absolute panic.'

'Indeed? And am I responsible for that?'

'Indirectly.'

'Nonsense! I am handling this investigation in my own way and I shall go on doing so.'

'I beg your pardon?'

'Bowne, you heard what I said. Police officers in the past have been hamstrung by fiddling little S.M.C. actions. This is one investigation that goes through to the end, with me in charge.' Her tone of voice was colder than the deep-freeze chamber of a refrigerator. Bowne's face went white, then it went red. He stamped to the door.

'There will be *other* criticisms after this interview, madam, and,' he added in a waspish voice, 'we shall be well rid of you.'

'Fine.' She turned, looking after him. I wonder the

back of his nice suit didn't smoulder. 'We'll go together, as I shall be bringing along a few bald details regarding a Miss—well, let's be charitable, and use the initials, A. H. S hyphen M.'

Bowne stopped dead in the doorway. He neither turned nor spoke. When he did, his eyes were on the window.

'Superintendent Laystall, I shall—er—consider the matter for the moment.' He went out, slamming the door.

Laystall's kind old face was worried to death.

'Mrs. Pym, I don't know, I can't think——'

She was brisk and cheerful.

'Bowne? Don't give it a thought. He's feeling his oats and now he'll run away and try to digest them. Now, this murder business.'

'But, Mrs. Pym. Those initials——'

She beamed at her chief.

'I said don't give it a thought. It's woman business, and unless I'm attacked I don't hit back—Voltaire said it better than that ; you know what I mean.'

I sat down quietly. My legs felt uneasy and I had quite forgotten, until then, that Mrs. Pym had the iceberg's quality of keeping most of her really dangerous potentialities under water. I should have guessed that she always carried ammunition for her gun, literal or figurative, and, come to that, I *had* heard something about Bowne and a woman, but it had never been proved.

'It was somewhat disconcerting.' Laystall sat down. 'He gave me a very uncomfortable ten minutes before you appeared.'

'Maybe he's scared I'm too good, or somebody's been prodding him ? Forget it, Super. I'm here and I'm staying. Pitfalls like Bowne I take in my stride. We'll forget it, shall we ? '

'If you say so.' He seemed relieved if anything, looking at her with a sort of dependence that surprised me. She had that knack, a sort of omnibus power of taking over everything in sight as a matter of course. Her personality was so strong that I don't think Laystall thought it in the slightest odd that she was running things as if she had the higher rank.

'Now, this godown business.'

'Yes.' He seemed pleased to get back to routine. 'Kelly is down there now. He was on the telephone to me when . . . my visitor came in. Chum-Kwat is with him. He does not know any of the Chinese, which makes him think they're either from the Chinese City or up-country. We're cross-checking with the Chinese magistrates.'

'How about the godown?'

'Hello Storage Concern? Founded by Igor Roberti some years ago and now the property of his daughter, Irina.'

'Larry, tell the Superintendent your story.'

I did as I was told. When it was over, Laystall fingered his white hair.

'I find it quite extraordinary. It sounds to me like a conspiracy, but a conspiracy about what? You say Yüan Chou would not tell you anything, Mrs. Pym?'

'Scared to death. All I got out of him was that Larry, here, and I are chalked on the tablets for early death.'

Laystall remained unimpressed. In China, if you were involved in anything touching crookedness or native rascality, death threats were a matter of course. Just the same, he didn't like it.

'I am being obvious when I say this is bigger than we imagined. I still don't like it, but that doesn't help us. Have you got any ideas, Mrs. Pym?'

'They're rudimentary.' She was sitting at right angles to the desk, staring at her square, strong hands. 'Nadia Sherbina touched it off; that we know. The piece of paper with the name of the Hop-Ley Dancers seems to me an oversight on the part of the murderer. When Larry broadcast it in his newspaper, it lifted the lid off something. Against that, we have Leslie Chow and Laffin. Chow could've been mixed up in it, though nothing will make me think Laffin was.'

WILD PURSUIT 91

'No. Perhaps it was a grudge-crime and a crude attempt made to copy the others?'

'It hadn't got round then, sir,' I interrupted. 'I mean, if it was a grudge-crime, where did the murderer get the details to copy the Sherbina and Chow murders, apart from the time element, and how did he cotton on to me?'

Mrs. Pym nodded approvingly.

'Good boy! Mind you, nothing stays secret in Shanghai for long. Just the same, your visitor mentioned that letter about Laffin?'

'Yes, ma'am.'

'There you are, Superintendent. Larry, was that visitor your friend, Fong?'

'No, ma'am.' On that point I was sure. 'He was big, what I could see of it, but not as big as Fong. I mean, he was big, not fat, and Fong's enormous.'

'Yes. Then where do we go from here?'

The telephone rang and supplied an answer. It was the West Hongkew Police Station. Laystall's face was a picture as he listened—interest, surprise, then downright dismay. He said Mrs. Pym would be on her way within a few minutes, then dropped the receiver on its hook.

'Another.' He stared at us, including me in his worry, which made me feel good. 'The Cyan——' he stopped and sniffed. 'That poisoner.'

Mrs. Pym stared back.

'You mean, he's killed again?'

'I do.' He wrote on a scratch pad. 'This is the address. Back of the Elgin Market. A Chinese house.'

'When——' She bit off her own question and stood up. 'I'll get down there first. Larry, come along.'

'You're taking him, after . . .' Laystall shrugged, smiling at me. 'I've no objections, Mr. Baker.'

Mrs. Pym's nod was brisk.

'That's nice of you, Super. Larry goes with me. I can keep an eye on what he writes if he's handy. Besides,' her compressed lips might have held a threat, 'he may want to write a book about me one day. I never heard of a Boswell who didn't hang around all the time.' Her wink was friendly and off we went.

Our destination was a native boarding-house again, this time a clean, extremely westernized place run by a Chinese owner who probably charged rates in keeping with the glamour; it included wash-hand basins in the bedrooms, which was something in those days.

I was astonished when we got into the elaborate sitting-room, as the door sign indicated it, and found a mob of Chinese present, including one who was familiar and a native uniformed sergeant.

Mrs. Pym sailed in with an amiable ' *tsau-'a.*' Everybody rose and gave her a good morning in return. The native policeman came to attention like a German soldier.

' *Ih-pak ling lok; ngoo sing Chwang.*'

' We'll speak English, Sergeant Chwang. You sent for help ? '

' Please, Detective Inspector. This gentleman Mr. Wesley Ho, please.'

I had already caught the glimpse of the eye-tooth in Ho's quick smile.

' One of the Brothers Ho, ma'am; bar-tenders in the Ritz-Carlton.'

' Ah ? I know you. What's the trouble, Sergeant ? '

' Poor Mr. Leslie Ho, please, ma'am.'

Wesley didn't take any notice of the interested onlookers, bowing politely to her.

' I go shopping, ma'am. My brother, Leslie, he very tired so stay bed. Last night work very late. When I come back poor Leslie quite dead.' He beamed as if he was happy, not that it fooled me. The Chinese never do what you expect and, with most of them, a display of inner emotion is a distinct loss of face.

' I see. Did somebody call to see him ? '

A stout little man, in a brown house-gown, bowed.

' My name b'long Tuk. This b'long my house. All time I sit desk-side by door. Nobody come Mr. Ho till Mr. Ho catchee house-side after go shop. Mr. Ho b'long shout he look-see bedroom and Mr. Ho no have got. Have go Heaven-side.'

She managed to sort this out, as I did after thinking.

'These people, Mr. Tuk. How come, what thing?'

'B'long people live this side, please. Also my friend and family. All b'long very proper. My talkee you who they b'long?'

'No, thank you. You tell me, Sergeant Chwang.'

'All very proper, ma'am. I know every person. Nobody go Mr. Ho bedroom. Maybe you like look-see?'

'Yes, please,' She waved back a sudden surge. 'You please catchee this side. My talkee you.'

Sergeant Chwang led the way up the stairs to the second floor. The bedroom belonging to the Brothers Ho was a big and very well furnished place. It was dominated by a huge gramophone against one wall with, alongside, a partitioned cabinet that must have contained hundreds of records. At the time radio was small cheese, an interesting toy that didn't excite a lot of people. Gramophones —or, to me, phonographs—were the craze. By the look of it, the Brothers Ho were fans.

Leslie Ho lay on the European-style bed, in bright mauve high-necked pyjamas. There was no mistaking the cyanotic pallor this time.

Mrs. Pym stood over him, scrutinizing the clenched hands and the tight grin of the mouth; her eyes moved slowly until she found a box that had rolled under the bed.

Holding it delicately by the edges, she looked at the box. Neatly reposing, in separate cardboard compartments, were a number of capsules made of gelatine. The label on the top said: 'Anglo-China Pharmacy Co. One to be taken on retiring and before breakfast if needed. 85576.'

'Larry, got a pocket-knife?' She turned to me. I had, giving it her with one blade opened.

She found a newspaper and carefully prised one of the capsules from its nest, sliced it with the knife and smelled it cautiously. Frowning, she touched the oily mess running over the newspaper and put the finger to her mouth, making a grimace of distaste.

"What is it, ma'am? Not cyanide?"

'Don't be dumb, boy. Would I be doing this? It's just ordinary medicinal paraffin. Somebody, the Cyanide Man I daresay, rang the changes on one of the capsules. It has Leslie Ho's name on the label, which means he probably took the stuff regularly. Damn! That means it was planted any time.'

'But Leslie!' I was angry. 'Why pick on him? I've known them both ever since I came here, my first friends, in fact. You couldn't meet a nicer pair.'

'I don't get it, I don't get it at all.' Her voice was almost mild. 'Larry, think he's a nut who's spreading the stuff wholesale?'

It beat me. I couldn't for the life of me figure an angle. It was just wanton, crazy murder without a vestige of sense behind it. When I considered the list of dead, it looked the maddest thing ever. I thought of Lanny Coager's last line to the Cyanide Song,' 'Death is in the air.' It was blind prophecy that hit the nail clean square on the head. For so much to have happened in that brief space of time, I began to wonder if we really were in for an epidemic. If I knew Shanghai at all, this latest murder would just about start a panic.

I watched Mrs. Pym making a search of the room. She didn't miss a thing, even to digging through the record albums. She shrugged when the job was finished.

'Not a thing, not even a line on the Dancers. Sergeant Chwang, do you know of the Hop-Ley Dancers?'

Chwang was so surprised, he said, 'No savee' before he realized his English was good, and changed it quickly to 'Please, I do not know the name, ma'am.'

'I see.' She looked at him, satisfied that he was telling the truth. 'There's nothing I can do here. I'll leave it to the doctor and your station. We'll go down. I want to talk to Wesley Ho.'

But Wesley had nothing to tell us at all. He was utterly

baffled by the crime because, as he said, he and his brother lived quiet and self-contained lives. They spent most of their time with their gramophone, occasionally went to the movies or the Chinese theatre. Neither of them were engaged nor married, and they didn't so much as belong to any sort of political faction, which was something of a rarity. Wes had certainly never heard of the Dancers nor, even, the Cyanide Man—I don't think, at the time, the vernacular newspapers had got around to taking any notice of the *Daily News* stories.

I went back to the Central Police Station in the Bugatti. Laystall was out and Sergeant Kelly had not returned from the godown. Mrs. Pym was in a gloomy mood. The case had her up a tree but she wasn't going to admit it.

She turned over the reports in her desk correspondence tray.

' Routine stuff, Larry. The Settlement's upside down over Laffin. Everybody's waiting to see how he's left his money—dammit, I don't know. Look, son, suppose you get back to the *Daily News* and leave me to worry at this thing ? '

' Yes, ma'am. Can I have the story ? '

' Anything you like.' Her grey-blue eyes were sardonic. ' Print what you wish, but leave out Bowne. I don't suppose we'll have any more trouble with him.'

' I hope not. Can I come around later ? '

' I'll call you. Now beat it, I want to think. Somebody is trying to ride me ragged and I'm getting mad, so flaming mad that I'm liable to bust out sideways. Dancers ! Cyanide Men ! The place is crazy and I'm going to know why. Out, Larry, before I throw you.'

I smiled and went ; I knew her well enough by then to realize she never started getting ideas until she began to spit. The *News* was the best place to be, and I went there.

The shortest way was to turn left into Foochow Road and, when I reached the corner, left again to Szechuen Road. I went that way, thinking of the case, and then somebody shot at me.

It was so startling that I didn't think of jerking out the Ortgies, which Mrs. Pym had found and returned to me ; I stood dumbly and stared. A small car was moving away towards the Bund, the only thing from which that wild shot could have been fired.

Then I think the adrenalin must have started pumping through me. I was good and mad, and got out the Ortgies right at that moment. Simultaneously, with one of those lucky breaks, a broker's cart came level with me, containing Randy McCallum, a broker and a member of the American Company of the Shanghai Volunteer Corps.

If you don't know what a broker's cart looked like, it is worth a description. They were low-slung vehicles, almost on the ground, made for getting on and off while moving. The hoods were raised in wet weather, which left the mafoo, or driver, high on his seat above the pony—Mongolian ponies, as slick and surefooted as polo ponies—and those little carriages could do anything a London taxi can do, and more.

Randy was beaming at me, standing up.

'Larry ! Wow ! The beggar shot at you, in that little Standard—oh, you saw it.' He nodded at my gun.

'Sure.' I jumped for the carriage. 'Can we chase him ? '

'Can we ? Yip*ee* ! ' Randy McCallum, who came from Wyoming, was one of the best drivers in town. He ordered the mafoo off, told him to wait at his office, and swarmed into the seat, snatching up the ribbons.

The fast-gathering crowd on the pavement stared openmouthed at the sight. Randy flicked the pony and it went off as if it had been stung.

We sighted the Standard when we tore round to the Bund. The pony, enchanted at the possibility of doing some real work, got down to it. I hung on, standing in the back by the grab rail, the Ortgies ready. Randy was whooping like a crazy man, his fair hair blowing in the wind, back again in his fence-riding days, which was how he started work.

We angled in and out of traffic, the pony happy as the bright day. It was no more than accelerated work to him : in his daily job he spent his time nipping in and round the tangle of narrow Shanghai streets, taking Randy on his daily business. This was exactly the same thing, with pep in it. Randy hardly had to drive at all.

There is something that gets into men in a hunt, a kind of ecstatic madness. It gives you a kick like nothing else on earth and I don't mean a lot of pink-coated funnies after a fox but a real hunt, a manhunt.

You could hear Randy's ' Hi-yi-yi*pee* ! ' a mile away, I am sure of it. My own howl was a reasonable copy of an *habitant* pal of mine in Quebec with whom I used to stay. He had a Sioux Indian body-servant who could imitate a coyote but on a higher note, and my pal improved on it. I think my noise and Randy's must have stopped half the traffic on the Bund.

The little cart tore along, the Standard well in view. We rattled up the incline of the Garden Bridge, past the frontage of the Astor House Hotel—where heads popped out of windows by the dozen—and somehow, Fate alone knows how, made it through the chaotic mix-up of Broadway on a busy day.

The pony was going like a champion. He was sweating and lathered, but his reins were slack on his neck and he was happy. How he dodged I'll never know : he just did, tearing the cart through gaps I don't think Randy would have risked in his normal senses.

The Standard was one of those square, boat-like things popular in those days. The top was up so that we couldn't see who was in it, but the driver knew his business. His rear mirror must have shown him the crazy set-up on his tail. He kept ahead all the way, but he couldn't get clear. I was being shaken around so much I dared not even risk a shot.

We hared into East Seward Road, where the going was better and less crowded. They must have heard us coming, for a gang of startled native constables were on the steps of

Wayside Police Station when we passed it. Randy changed his yell to a screaming ' *Banzai !* ' which got them shouting back before they realized what they were doing. We hurtled into Ward Road with nothing but a straight run between us and Ying Hsiang Kong village.

Somehow or other the pony picked up its heels. The carriage rattled, bumped and swayed. Randy was standing now, ululating with demented excitement. I thought he was going overboard at any moment. It didn't worry me ; I was on the bouncing seat, gripping the frame of the hood, yelling anything I thought of, the pair of us infecting the pony with such excitement that it began to gain on the Standard.

How we missed a crash I shall never know. People ran into the road, shouting and waving ; vehicles stopped in the craziest fashion, their drivers whooping us on our way. I figured Wayside Police Station must have come to life. A long black Buick began to gain on us, rattling a tinny bell for us to stop, and a uniformed policeman beside the driver was making futile motions at us.

' Randy,' my voice was a hoarse croak, ' cops on our tail.'

He turned, waving to the Buick.

' *Zowie !* ' He used the whip lightly. ' Attaboy, Lightning ! Cops on your tail ; *up* the Marines ! '

And the pony did it, blazing along like a champion. It couldn't last. Nothing could, at that pace, but one single moment came for me, a sort of hiatus in time, space, and motion. The Standard seemed poised and so did we. I remembered how Randy had told me about turkey shooting in Kentucky, when you had to drill the thing clean through the eye or you stank. I took one shot as if I was target-shooting, and saw a round hole appear in the Standard's hood. For what seemed hours nothing happened at all, then Randy whooped his head off. The Standard turned leisurely to the left, over the sidewalk, and into the gates of the cotton mill at the end of Ward Road with a report we could hear, above the thunder of our carriage wheels.

Randy McCallum took up the reins from the hook, eased them gently and we stopped twenty yards farther on, the little pony shivering and trembling. We both ran, with shaking knees, to him. I patted futilely at the sodden neck, Randy rubbed the hero's nose and found a slab of chocolate in one pocket which, in between panting, nearly choked the pony.

We walked towards the wrecked car, feeling singularly silly as every person in the gathering crowd turned to stare at us, chattering with excitement, and a big native sergeant in uniform marched sternly towards us.

Randy McCallum had the gift of tongues. He knew a dozen native dialects and his Shanghai vernacular was impeccable. He rattled out the story for the sergeant. It cleared his face when he learned about it; the crowd, in the partisan way of all Chinese crowds, slapped our backs as we eased through, shouting encouraging things and offering to chase the policemen away if they worried us.

The Standard was a wreck all right. It had piled up against the steel gates, bending them inwards. The radiator was flat as a wall and the front wheels were folded in half.

The man inside was the deadest thing in this world. Apart from the bullet-hole in the back of his balding head, the steering-wheel had transfixed him like a spear, the spokes bent forward and the steel column fair and square through his chest.

Randy McCallum and I recognized the corpse even as we saw it, but my 'Jerusalem! It's *Guido Barbadoro*!' made the Chinese sergeant jump back with fright.

CHAPTER X

THE FIRE-BUG

The Bugatti was at Wayside Police Station within twenty minutes. Mrs. Pym came storming through the mob outside into the gloomy Charge Room, her eyes chill as a winter morning. She considered us all, then waved to the native sergeant to tell the story.

'Hm'fh! So that's what you do the minute you get out of my sight, Larry?'

Randy McCallum, who could charm anything that ever wore a skirt, even Mrs. Pym, put on the smile the whole American Company called 'the Mickey Finn, female special.'

'Now, Mrs. Inspector, the boy was shot at. Gosh all sakes, you wouldn't want him dead, surely?'

'No–o–o,' but she didn't sound too certain, then took her hands off her hips. 'Well, maybe you couldn't help it. Damn it, man, did you have to go through the Settlement like a bunch of Red Indians on the warpath?'

'Aw, ma'am! My maternal grandmother was a Senecan Iroquois. She was on that buggy seat, spurring me on, wasn't she, Larry?'

'Oh, sure. I expected the whole of the Six Nations to come haring out of Ying Hsiang Kong village, mounted on rickshaws. *Boy!*' I looked at Randy and we giggled together.

Mrs. Pym's granite mouth showed a slight easing; we took it for a smile. Randy beamed at her.

'You know how it is, ma'am. The guy took a crack at Larry; I hoisted into my cart and we went after him. Glory be to God, it took me clean back to Green River Basin where my old pop died cleaning up a bunch of greasers who tried to burn us out. Now, if you'd been there you'd've gunned that car right away, but Larry? Hell, he's good but he's not Mrs. Pym.'

The outrageous flattery and that smile did it. Almost girlishly she adjusted the revolting hat, gave her face a brisk rub with a pocket handkerchief—equivalent to another woman hauling out a compact—and nodded.

'Well, if that's how it was . . . where's the body?'

We all trooped into the station yard. The Standard had been man-handled to get it behind the screening gates and there it was, the most wrecked-looking car in the world.

Mrs. Pym bent over that shocking corpse and went through its pockets. She found nothing except a Smith and Wesson revolver, with one empty chamber.

'Barbadoro?' She wasn't at all surprised. 'How the blazes does he come into this? You mean, he shot at you, Larry?'

'A yard wide of my knees. I'd say he's just a passable shot and didn't know those revolvers should be squeezed, not jerked. That means he'd've pulled his muzzle down when he fired.'

'You surprise me.' Her face was blank: underlining the obvious never pleased her. 'What I mean is, Barbadoro isn't the type of man to go gunning for anybody. Just . . . um.' She considered the body thoughtfully. I wondered if she had thought of the same thing as I had; if he were mixed up in this, it might explain something of the Nadia Sherbina business. Whatever it was, she wasn't saying.

'He's got a big house on Avenue Petain, near the Community Church,' Randy told her. 'I've been there Sundays, now and then. Quite a joint.'

'We'll try it. It's getting crazier and crazier. *Wait* a minute! Young Ho worked at the Ritz-Carlton, and Nadia . . . well, well, well.'

'And Laffin went there,' I added helpfully. 'Maybe Leslie Chow has a connection, too?'

She glared at me.

'Don't show off, Larry. You leave this to me and get

along to the *News*. Do me a favour, will you? Try and get there this time without another riot. Mr. McCallum, will you restrain yourself in future? I don't say you haven't done a job of work, but the rest of the brokers might start getting ideas, and running chariot races in their carriages.' She shuddered at the thought.

Randy and I found the hero of the day, the Mongolian pony, outside the police station in charge of a constable. A stout Chinese was giving the animal pieces of bamboo shoot to chew and we had to wait until it was finished, for public opinion was against us. The native outlook was always ready to give honour where it was due. The pony, far as I could gather, was a re-incarnation of Kublai Khan's grey charger gifted with an equine sense of harmony at one with Yang and Yin. I thought Randy and I rated a sugar-stick each, but all we got was a jovial '*man man chi*' from the onlookers. As it meant good-bye, but, literally, go slowly, it was probably one of those subtle Chinese *doubles ententes* that always had me guessing.

We returned at a sedate pace, both sitting on the driving seat—it caused a certain amount of comment from passers-by—and having the time of our lives.

'You know, Larry, if this is the sort of thing you have on your plate, I'll quit money-chasing to be a reporter. Got a spot for me?'

'It's the first time it ever happened to me. I nearly got tortured this morning, though.'

Randy McCallum's mouth opened. I thought he was going to fall off the box.

'No kidding? You did? Gosh, tell your old pal.'

I gave him an edited version of the Fong story. It lasted till we reached the Bund Club and there I was led inside to drink at the longest bar on earth. When I got back to the *News* building, I felt my prestige had risen a great deal. If I'd drunk all the liquor I had been offered I could have floated out to sea in it.

Lanny Coager gave me a welcome that warmed my heart.

'Hi, Larry. Seems you've got a story?'

'You've heard?'

'Just a few rumours. Snatched by a flaming redhead, I'm told; running races down Ward Road in a carriage, shooting up cars.' He scratched his beard. 'If this goes on, I'll have to move Laidler someplace else and give you his desk.'

'Golly!' I looked at him to see if he meant it, and he did. 'You want to hear it, or shall I write it first?'

'Give it me in sequence. I want to build my front page for to-morrow.'

'Right.' I didn't argue because Lanny liked to plot his layout from a verbal story, picking the headlights on a sheet of copy-paper in front of him. It probably explained why the *Daily News* always had the best front page make-up in the Far East.

When it was all told, Lanny whistled long and low.

'Man, oh, *man*! You know, Larry, you've got the best of all reporting gifts, the knack of being there when the news breaks. One of these days it's going to land you in big-time back in New York.' He sighed briefly: that had always been his ambition, but he never made it. 'This Irina Roberti. Know anything about her?'

'Other than she's the girl I'd most like to come home to, after a hard day here—no.'

'You mean, you've fallen for her?'

'Hell, no! She probably sold me up the river; just the same, once you've looked at her you never want to stop.'

'I wonder where she went? Wait, I'll check with Matsy Stein.' He went to work on the inter-office telephone while I sat there. Matsy Stein—she apparently had no other first name—was our lady reporter. If Mrs. Pym was hewn from granite, Matsy was cast steel. She had no heart; she would have sold her old grandmother's liver for offal if it had made a good story, and the sure way to get Matsy to tell the world was to give her your confidences on her oath of honour that she would never say a word. I think her mother was a lady dog, and her father a moronic mass murderer, but there wasn't a bit of social dirt in the whole world she didn't know.

Lanny was puzzled when he replaced the receiver.

'Never heard the name, which is something. She's going to work on it; that means your Irina's for it. Matsy'll find the unfortunate girl, if she's hiding at the bottom of the Mindanao Trench.' He glanced at his copy-paper. 'Larry, we'll highlight the Leslie Ho murder, play over to Barbadoro and give the Fong business a passing touch.'

'Spike my big scene in the godown?'

'No, I'll run it, but played down. It's Hop-Ley Dancers' stuff. I don't want the spot taken off the Cyanide Man. He's our big special and I don't want him lost.'

'But, Barbadoro?'

'He's anybody's baby—we don't know, yet. Nadia Sherbina is the pivot and we can't lose sight of her. The godown stuff is colourful, but the Cyanide Man's getting into his stride, and how! What about Yüan Chou; can we use him?'

'Better leave the old boy out. He's only a source of information, and publicity might get him hurt.'

'Yeah, there's that.' Lanny leaned back, rubbing his pink-shirted chest. 'It's a lulu, whichever way you slice it. Oh, by the way, I've fixed an appointment for you. Nathan Schyler at his house to-night for eight o'clock. He'll give you some inside dope on Laffin and his money.'

'Sounds useful. What's been happening there?'

'Oh, there'll be an inquest, along with the others. But the will stands until the coroner's had his say. Schyler's ready to give you the angles, though. The place is called Bronze Gates: it's a big house at the end of Tracey Terrace.'

'Few minutes' walk from my home. Okay, I'll be there.' We went into a purely technical huddle to get the best angles from my story, then, fully briefed, I went into the main room to get it written, sitting at my desk back of the copy-boys' corner with a slight feeling of surprise that I was there again.

The material wrote itself. All I had to do was bang the typewriter keys. I took the copy back to Lanny, waiting while he worked through it. His blue eyes were pleased at the end of it.

'You're coming along nicely, Larry. This is terse and clear; you're losing that habit of using superlatives, and letting your story tell itself. Your English is better.'

'I should hope so; I majored in English——'

'The hell with it! I'm trying to cure you of college English. There's no place for it on a newspaper, but you're letting your sense of style get rid of your education. Keep it up and you'll pass.'

'Thank you.' I stopped being clever, remembering Lanny was the best newspaperman in the East. 'What's the next one?'

'Stand by for the moment. There won't be anything else from here, though something may turn up—at the rate things are breaking, you never know. See what you get out of Schyler. Maybe we can use it.' He fingered his beard. 'You realize why you ought to stay around?'

'In case a story——'

'No, my boy, because you shot Barbadoro to death.'

'Golly!' I gaped at him. 'Do you know I never stopped to figure that one out? Think there'll be trouble?'

'Not with Pym siding for you, and she will. It was justifiable. It's probable you'll get a lamming from the coroner for having a gun and using it; why don't you tell Schyler about it? He's an able guy and he'll probably handle the legal end for you.'

'I'll do just that.' I went back to my desk in an uneasy condition. Until Lanny had said it, it hadn't come home to me that I was a killer. With World War Two under their belts, folks don't think about killing in the way they should; to me it was something that made my stomach queasy. I was a little scared, as well.

I hadn't anything to do. Ten minutes staring at my old typewriter—that is, Laidler's typewriter—gave me an idea. All the detective stories I had ever read stopped somewhere around the middle and chalked up the score, recapitulating to clarify, as the authors liked to put it, the detective's mind. I had always regarded it as nothing but a stunt to fill a few pages. It dawned on me it was one way of giving the reader all the angles in case he had forgotten some of them.

Rolling a sheet of paper into the machine, I tried it, itemizing the case since the moment I had come into it. The game was so absorbing that an hour passed by the time it was finished. I was just reading what I had written when it came, a relayed telephone call to get round to Mrs. Pym's office pronto, a word she never used unless she wanted action.

With my synopsis in my pocket I left word with Lanny's secretary; it seemed he had gone out. I was at Central Station in the shortest time ever.

Mrs. Pym was in her office, alone.

'Hi, Larry.' She waved to a chair. 'I've just had word from Bowne's office. Apparently he doesn't want to tangle with me; he's going after you, instead.' My stomach felt as if it had turned over. 'He wants you charged with driving to the public danger, disturbing the peace, carrying firearms, and with manslaughter. McCallum's to go along with you as an accessary—it's spelled with two a's, if you're interested.'

'You mean . . .?' My face must have been dead white.

She shook her head, nearly bringing down the pile of untidy brown hair.

'And I meant that as a little joke to ease it off! Larry, you poor, boneless fish, are you scared?'

'I'm not in the mood for singing, ma'am.'

'Because of Bowne?' She was honestly baffled. 'You mean, that bag of vitiated air worries you?'

'Nobody's ever wanted to charge me with anything like that before.'

She smiled, for the first time since I'd known her—that is, the corners of her mouth creased so that I thought it was hurting her, but the grey-blue eyes were twinkling, probably an epoch-making moment if I had been in the position to enjoy it.

'Well, for biting off buttons!' She was genuinely staggered. 'You'd let a yard of Whangpoo mud like Bowne worry you?'

'He's the head of the S.M.C., and, besides, nobody likes having the book thrown at them.'

'Larry, if I didn't think you were useful, I'd pan your rear end for you and throw you to the wolves. Besides, I've already told Bowne you were under my orders and if he didn't like that he could jump in the creek. Don't let it faze you, son; can't you see the wings of the great god Pym protecting you?'

I had to chuckle. It was my fault, forgetting the one I'd decided I'd sooner have with me than anyone else when trouble was coming up.

'I'm sorry, ma'am.'

'It's just that you're not conditioned, and I forgot things loom big at your age. Forget it. The coroner will say a few things, primed by Bowne. I'm handling this so it's Bowne-d to come out just the way you want it.'

I laughed then, remembering the English peel off puns the way a hash-house waitress deals plates off the arm.

'If you can laugh at a stinker like that, you'll do. Larry, I'm nowhere, but I'm going somewhere fast. Now that I've frightened the pants off you, want to come along to Barbadoro's house in Avenue Petain? I'm going to have a look round.'

'I'd like that.' Relaxing, I felt the copy-paper in my pocket and pulled it out. 'I made a synopsis of the case, ma'am. There's a carbon attached, if it interests you.'

It did. She stayed right there and read it through, making corrections as she went along.

'Nice work, son.' She handed back the top copy. 'I've put in my end of it. Type it again for me, will you?'

'Glad to, ma'am.'

'Fine. We'll get along and see what we can find—oh,

hold it.' She sat down again, hooking up the ringing telephone. 'Yes? Yes, Pym here. Who? Yes, let me have it.' She listened, her lips compressed. 'Thanks. Petrol, eh? Nobody there, and nobody seen? Fine, there's nothing I can do about it. No, leave it at that.' She replaced the receiver, leaning back to gaze at me. 'Son, somebody's got a fast-thinking mind. That was Bartozzi, the French fire chief, relayed from downstairs. We won't be going.'

'To Barbadoro's?'

'Exactly. The house was empty, except for the servants who, naturally, couldn't see whether it was Sunday or half-past nine. Some slick fellow emptied a can of petrol over Barbadoro's sitting-room floor and threw in a match. If we're interested, the ruins are worth seeing. Everything we might have looked at has gone, including any evidence as to Barbadoro's game. Fast work?'

There wasn't a thing I could think of worth saying.

CHAPTER XI

BACKGROUND TO FONG

'OF course,' Mrs. Pym went on after a pause, 'there's his office at the Ritz-Carlton. Does he own it?'

'Barbadoro? No, ma'am. A private company. He was everything from *maître d'hôtel* to general manager. It was in the red when he went there; the dollar shares were worth a dime. Now you couldn't buy them for two-fifty each.'

'Like that, eh? You're a queer kid. Sometimes you act plain dumb, at others you come out with facts.'

'I'll take that as a compliment. You know, I've just thought of it. What about this reception to meet Dr. Wu Hsiung?'

'Let it ride for the moment. I've got other things on my mind. Yes?' The question was in answer to a knock on the door. Sergeant Kelly came in, his grey eyes bright. Little Chum-Kwat was behind him, smiling as usual.

Kelly settled his bulk in a chair, the sergeant at his side. Mrs. Pym's face was affable; she had a warm spot for the Irishman.

'Well, full of news?'

'Yes, and no, ma'am. First, the godown isn't important. It belongs to Irina Roberti, but has been rented out for years to a Chinese company. The Hello Storage Concern will probably close down since you shot the owner through the tummy.'

'One of the mob, was he?'

'Yes, ma'am. But they're all, with this exception, you will be remembering, from up-country. Sergeant, you tell the inspector what you know.'

Little Chum-Kwat came to attention, showing the radiant smile in which his eyes did not join.

'Albert Fong I have been able to find out something about. He is not a good man. He comes from Peking. He studied at Nankai University in Tientsin; very clever man, I have heard. Also, he was student at Whampoa Military Academy.'

'Ah? We seem to be getting somewhere.'

'I hope so, ma'am. He is a rich man from his father. In nineteen hundred and nineteen he was arrested as a revolutionary with a certain Mr. Chou En-Lai* for leading a demonstration which the government did not approve.'

'Oh, Lord! Chinese politics?'

'I fear so, ma'am.' He smiled even more brightly. 'This Mr. Fong, he is said to be a good friend of a Mr. 'Veh.' This wasn't very helpful; 'Veh was vernacular for ' not ' and was about the same as our omnibus for an unknown, Mr. Smith. Mrs. Pym grimaced at it. 'I cannot find out who Mr. 'Veh is; perhaps he might be the Cyanide Man?' Chum-Kwat gave me an oblique glance.

'Anything's possible.' She moved uneasily. 'Any more?'

'A little. Mr. Albert Fong, he is foolish, with many ideals. I think he give money to them. His father make all his money in America, in San Francisco, where he once have a very fine restaurant called '—Chum-Kwat made a mouth of distaste—' the Hop-Ley Food Shop.'

'*What!*' Mrs. Pym stared at him, then at Kelly, who nodded. 'So that's it!'

'I have found out more,' Chum-Kwat went on. 'Certain people who are frightened to talk tell me because they are afraid of me more. It is said that old Father Fong was once a member of the Jovial Hearts,' Chum-Kwat made a dry spitting motion on the floor to show his good contempt of such societies, 'and steal much in Peking during the Great Trouble. He goes to San Francisco and there opens his restaurant with his capital. He returns, and, when he is dead, his money goes to his son, who becomes associ-

---

* Present Premier and Foreign Minister of China, involved in 1919 as leader of a demonstration part-Communist and part-Kuomintang.

ated with many queer people. He founds a society called the Hop-Ley Dancers, so called,' he anticipated the inevitable query, ' because they dance, a metaphor if you please, ma'am, to the tune called by Mr. 'Veh. In Chinese this would be like a pun for puppets who permit somebody else to arrange the strings.'

Mrs. Pym's face was a study in consternation.

' It's getting worse every minute. This revolutionary, Chou En-Lai, is he in this, too ? '

' Oh, no, ma'am, he has been abroad, where he went just after his arrest.'*

' Um. So we're still nowhere. Can we find Mr. 'Veh ? '

' I will try, ma'am. He is very discreet.'

' All the more reason we should dig him out. What happens now that Fong is dead ? '

' There'll be somebody after taking his place,' Kelly said comfortably. ' There always is, ma'am.'

' Thank you. You're a lot of help, I must say. Chum-Kwat, can you bear down on this ? I want to get at the Hop-Ley Dancers and somehow we're going to do just that. Leave it with me while I chew on it. Larry, you keep this Hop-Ley stuff to yourself, and play the subject down a bit, will you ? '

' Yes, ma'am.' I was ready to agree with that. The Cyanide Man was the person *News*' readers liked ; if we brought in the Hop-Ley bunch and intimated there were Chinese politics at the back of it, interest would die within one minute. Shanghailanders didn't give a hoot for them.

The discussion broke up and I went back to Szechuen Road. Lanny Coager was at his desk, beaming cheerily, when I came in. I gave him the complete details of all that had happened, which made him scratch his red beard.

' Barbadoro, eh ? Was he mixed up with this Hop-Ley stunt, do you suppose ?'

' It looks like it. I suggest we either ignore his death or play it down, Lanny.'

---

* Chou En-Lai went to France and Germany from 1920 to 1924, not returning to China until after this narrative ended.

'Yes.' He nodded slowly. 'Seems the best way. I'll run it and the house burning as separate news from your stories. We don't want any part of Chinese politics, so we'll keep to Mrs. Pym's wishes as a matter of policy. You say they considered Mr. 'Veh and the Cyanide Man as the same person?'

'Chum-Kwat suggested it and Mrs. Pym thought it might be possible.' I sighed heavily. 'Look, if that's the case, does it make the murders any the more sensible?'

'Lord alone knows, I don't. It smells to the sky.' Lanny pounded the desk. 'You know, it's a lovely story, but, as I've been saying, you've got to keep them apart. The Cyanide Man's hot; the rest of it stinks. What are you going to do now?'

'If I'm not wanted, I'm going to bang out a synopsis of what's happened. I did one for a time-filler and showed it to Mrs. Pym. She liked it, did some corrections, and asked me to make a new copy for her.'

'Nice work, Larry. Do one for me as well. You'll be at the desk?' I nodded. 'Right, be seeing you.'

At my desk I brooded over it before I did any work, baffled by the whole thing. China, in those days, was in a mess. There was a so-called Republic of China, but who it was and what it did nobody quite knew. The country was full of fighting bandits, called *tuchuns* or warlords, of whom only two mattered: Wu Pei-fu, who was just then entrenched outside Shanghai and trying to get hold of the port—later, if my memory serves me, he cleared out to Japan with a fortune—and Chang Tso-lin, whose headquarters were in the north, and who was trying to be a unifying force to create a real China. Neither of them ever amounted to a thing; the only other one was Chiang Kai-shek, down in Canton, organizing and running the Kuomintang (or Nationalist Party). Being hundreds of miles away, he never bothered us at all.

Most of these warlords pretended to be patriots, but none of them, with the exception of Chiang Kai-shek, were worth a plugged nickel. They were bandits, pure and simple, running wars because they hated one another and grabbing all they could as a sideline. Somehow I couldn't see the Hop-Ley Dancers or the Cyanide Man mixed up with them. I threw the subject out of my mind and turned to the machine, and the undisputed facts.

I had never made a synopsis before, nor, for that matter, had I been involved in quite such an elaborate investigation. It had puzzled me for a time how the matter should be dealt with; obviously the first duty of a synopsis was to give the pertinent facts. The job of re-typing the original synopsis, as Mrs. Pym had amended it, got under way.

CASE OF THE CYANIDE MAN

Went with Mrs. Pym to a block of apartments, where we found apartment owner, Nadia Sherbina, dead in bed. Aged 22, born Kiev. Character believed sound enough; drank; no known enemies.

Cyanide murder being decided by fact she had gone to bed without make-up, and had an appointment for a permanent later in the week. Advice of murder given by man who 'phoned Central Police Station, which, on my questions, did not seem to be the doorman.

Sherbina had about $6,000 in bank; a year's contract with the Ritz-Carlton. Apartment contained many friendly and even intimate letters from men; none of these can be regarded as significant.

Found was a telephone slip bearing some Russian characters meaning 'the Hop-Ley Dancers'. This was apparently something to do with an old secret society, the Jovial Hearts, according to Superintendent Laystall's memory of the 1900's.

Fingerprint men and photographer on job. Poison thought (later confirmed) to be contained in a capsule. Death took place roughly between 5 and 7 a.m. that same morning.

On journey with Mrs. Pym we were halted outside the Ritz-Carlton by a policeman with a request to visit a house in Kulun Road, where we went to find the body of Leslie Chow, an apparent cyanide victim. Came in at 11 o'clock the previous night. Character seems blameless; born Ningpo; for seven years a ledger clerk in Cathay Oil. No known reason for his death.

Visited Guido Barbadoro *re* Sherbina. He knew little about her and his information was of no service. Contract he signed last January was handled for Sherbina by Nathan Schyler who had met Sherbina at Jacob Laffin's table, having had drinks with her. Took care of her contract at Laffin's request. He told us Laffin worth about (according to hearsay, but not to his knowledge) $200,000,000. Told us Sherbina had tried, unsuccessfully, to dig Laffin for money, but had no entanglements to his knowledge, that she wanted to go to the U.S.A.; he thought that if she'd found a way of making money, she would have done it.

When I returned to *News* an anonymous telephone message warned me to keep away from the Hop-Ley Dancers. Curiously enough Toby Garnett, of the *Free Press*, more or less advised me the same thing. What does he know? Mrs. Pym intends to find out.

Went home after a brief spell at the Chinese Theatre, and slept, woken by somebody with a gun whom I could not see in the poor light. Had a revolver; wore a black native gown; on third finger of gun hand a gold ring with a mounted jade buffalo. Warning about Hop-Ley Dancers does not seem to have been sent by him, but this may be wrong. Told me a letter was coming for me. Talked a lot of drip about 'sinners must die', which Mrs. Pym is inclined to regard as a notable red herring. Threw me $1,000 in old bills and cleared out. Told all this to Lanny Coager and advised Laystall. Talked to Charlie Voucher, of *Voucher's Weekly*, about the jade buffalo, he telling me that he did not think it was as valuable as I imagined it was. Laystall took steps with Post Office *re* the letter coming to me.

Went Ritz-Carlton where I met Paul and Jennie Chang, entertaining a queer bird named Dr. Wu Hsiung, who wanted to meet Mrs. Pym. She collected me and told me investigation had showed nothing wrong with Leslie Chow. Collected my letter which said: 'Why doesn't Jacob Laffin take in his milk any more?' At Central Police Station this was processed, unsuccessfully, for fingerprints. With Mrs. Pym to Laffin's house, Narkunda, where he lived alone. Six bottles of milk on doorstep. Found him, a heavy old man, dead over his desk where he must have been for all those six days. In spite of his reputation for being a miser, he seemed to be pretty generous to charities. Dr. Fedor thought the death was from natural causes.

Went to Ritz-Carlton with Mrs. Pym. While she was on the telephone, Paul Chang asked if she would come to a small reception he had planned so that she could meet Dr. Wu Hsiung. She decided she would think about it, telling me that Laffin's death *was* natural causes, but somebody had thrust a capsule containing cyanide down his throat.

Called Schyler's office for any handouts regarding Laffin's will; *News* checking Wu Hsiung. Had a caller who gave the name of Irina Roberti who wanted me to take her on trust, and said that she knew where the Hop-Ley Dancers could be found. Like a half-wit I went along. She seemed a nice enough girl, born in Shanghai after her father left Russia, being a Social Democrat and, obviously, anti-Communist. Her vernacular was expert, but I caught her using a phrase which meant the place we were going to—the Hello Storage Concern's godown—was her property though I never got it till too late. Bit of a tight corner with a character named Albert Fong who seemed to scare Irina to death. Was going to mention to him the paper found in Sherbina's flat (about the Hop-Ley Dancers) but it scared Irina so much I changed it halfway, but, anyhow, Fong seemed to know all about it.

He propositioned me in excellent English. Wanted me to back out with a retraction and I could have $5,000, Irina, and free transportation for doing it. Got rough when I refused. Mrs. Pym sailed in, wiping out everybody in sight, including Fong. Irina had vanished and is now being looked for.

Went with Mrs. Pym to Yüan Chou in the Chinese City for angles, but he clammed up on us. Back at Central Police Station where Edward Carter Bowne, of the S.M.C., tried to be clever and was sent off with an open threat from Mrs. Pym. It was shown that the godown where I was in trouble originally belonged to Igor Roberti (the father?) and is now Irina's, but she has been pretty discreet and is unknown.

Newest victim was Leslie Ho, of the Brothers Ho, who got a shot of cyanide. Next I got in the way of a gun in Foochow Road, but not too much in the way. The car from which the bullet was fired was chased by Randy McCallum and me. I got in a lucky shot which killed him right enough—Guido Barbadoro, but nobody knows where the devil he fits into this. The car was Barbadoro's own, one he did not use very often, police checkings show.

Lanny Coager put Matsy Stein on to Irina to see what she could find out. An appointment fixed for me to-night to see Nathan Schyler at eight at his Tracey Terrace house, Bronze Gates, for, presumably, some sort of handout.

Barbadoro's house burned down by a fire-bug, which shows good fast teamwork and left no clues of any sort. From Kelly and Chum-Kwat certain news came in that Fong was a rich man with quite a history, largely political, and that his father had the Hop-Ley Food Shop in San Francisco where he made his pile before he returned to China. Albert Fong began a society with the title of the Hop-Ley Dancers, which, according to Chum-Kwat, had something to do with a Mr. 'Veh (or, as we have it, John Doe). There is the problem as to whether this Mr. 'Veh is the Cyanide Man.

Vetted by Mrs. Pym, this material contains all that I know and, as she has said, all that she knows.

Just what is behind this nobody can tell. The murders have no sense behind them. It might be argued there is a political end, in which case they become reasonable to a certain extent, though every instinct in me is against this—I can see all of them as political murders until we come to Laffin and that blows it sideways. Laffin never touched any sort of politics in his life, I am certain of that.

There is the problem as to whether Mr. 'Veh and the Cyanide Man are one and the same. It is possible, for I think the bird who held me up in my room was Chinese, the thing he had in his mouth to disguise his voice suggests that he might be somebody I know (as a very wild notion, can I bracket this with Dr. Wu Hsiung?).

The Cyanide Man, and/or Mr. 'Veh—what is behind this? Where do the Hop-Ley Dancers come in? I cannot see any political angle on which they might work. There are the warlords, of course, but they are too local to worry us here, and anything like a society of this nature working here in the Settlement is right against all the ideas of the warlords as I know of them. The list of dead simply does not make any sort of sense. Mrs. Pym and I are in danger; we knew that but Barbadoro proves it, though why a man of his success and standing should come into this is anyone's guess, unless, as a crazy thought, is *he* the Cyanide Man? There is the little tie-up between Barbadoro of the Ritz-Carlton, Sherbina and Leslie Ho, of the same place; still it does not make sense.

I read over what I had written. It didn't seem very bright to me, but it was the best I could do. It was a fascinating puzzle, screwy as a chipmunk in springtime.

Leaning back with the clipped typescript in my hand, I stared over the untidy newsroom, wondering what it was all about. By the pile of overseas news stories from A.P. I could see the Cyanide Man had got everybody excited. There was a feature from a Los Angeles newspaper bannerheaded CYANIDE POISONER STALKS CITY, which I read right through, and got a thrill to read of myself as ' youthful, courageous Larry Baker, local newshound, is singlehandedly stalking this dangerous killer.' I did not think Mrs. Pym would take to this, though there was no reason why she should ever hear about it. At least, the Cyanide Man was exciting the rest of the world as much as he was stirring Shanghai.

The day was getting along and there was no reason for staying any longer. Lanny Coager was busy with some caller when I looked in. I gave him the carbon of the synopsis, which he tucked in his drawer, and told him I was going home for a while.

The second carbon I put in an envelope and sent round to Mrs. Pym by boy, then went out and found a rickshaw to take me back to Route des Sœurs. Since I was due at Schyler's for eight o'clock, I felt I could manage a quick sleep before dinner.

I locked the balcony door before I settled down this time.

CHAPTER XII

WAR

It couldn't have been more than six o'clock when Sung, Mrs. MacNaughton's houseboy, woke me. I nearly jumped out of the bed because I thought it was my visitor back again.

'Masta, you wanchee telephone. Come now?'

It was in the hallway, a public coin-box. I pulled the door shut and picked up the receiver, hanging by its cord.

'Yes? Larry Baker here.'

'Larry?' The voice was faint and far away. 'Oh, Larry!'

'Who—for crying out loud, is that *Irina*?'

'Yes. Larry, listen, please. I'm in trouble. I can only stop a minute. Fong sent me to a house. I am there now. I've sneaked out of my room.'

'Where are you?'

'I don't know, oh, I don't know. The number on this 'phone is Rubicon double seven, seven. Can you do anything? I don't know what's going—*oh!*' I heard her gasp and the line went dead. For a moment I felt mad, then realized she sounded in real trouble. I had a grudge to work out with her, but, after all, I figured I had to do something.

At twenty-one you don't stop to reckon up the score. I checked with the numerical section at the back of the telephone directory. Rubicon 777 belonged to a Mr. Tee and was called Ih-da-zu—something to do with trees— and the address was Saung Tsing Thien village. I knew it, a place well outside the Settlement limits in Chinese territory.

For a space I thought it over. I was ready to be St. George Baker; the trouble was I hadn't a charger. Then I remembered Jimmy Markham, a fellow roomer in Mrs.

MacNaughton's. He was in hospital with dysentrey, but he had a two-seater Citröen in the garage. I knew it would be all right if I borrowed it.

I went back to my room for my jacket and the Ortgies, then down to the garage. The little car was there, so I took it after telling Sung, who didn't seem to worry since it wasn't his business.

It was getting dark outside. Somewhere out in the China Sea there must have been a monsoon at work, for the sky was heavy with racing clouds, the air was chill and the wind high.

One of the things I knew well was Shanghai and its surroundings. The route was in my head and I set off. At the end of the French Concession, where Avenue Joffre became Jordan Avenue, there was a road block with a bunch of French police and some of the Light Horse Company standing by. I recognized one of the sergeants, Arthur Finlay, holding his pony.

'Hullo, Arthur. What's the trouble?'

'Who's that? Oh, Larry Baker.' He came over to me. 'On a story?'

'Yeah.'

'You go out at your own risk, then.' He nodded. 'Hear that?' I could, a sporadic sound of distant firing. 'Wu Pei-fu's lot retreating again. The stand-to order came an hour ago.'

'Oh, lor', trouble again?' It annoyed me. Every time one of the warlords got driven back on Shanghai, the Volunteer Corps had to stand by to keep refugees and deserters out of the city limits. It wasn't that we were a mean lot; we just hadn't the space or food for a bunch of newcomers, quite apart from the fact many of them would carry arms and bring trouble. 'My company in it?'

'No, not yet. Just us and the Field Artillery Battery. I dare say the stand-to order's at your office.'

'Thanks, Arthur. I'll chance it.'

'Okay, it's your neck. Which way are you going, just in case?'

'Saung Tsing Thien village. I've got to be back before eight.'

Arthur waved me on, grinning.

'If you ever get back, you crazy Canuck! On your way.'

I didn't feel quite so heroic, pushing into the darkness. If I'd had any sense at all the thing should have been thrown in Mrs. Pym's lap, but I had to be the big brave man and do it myself.

The route was entirely deserted, with only the Citröen headlamps to show me the way. The paddyfields and vegetable patches were empty, the only sign of life an occasional native pushing a barrow or a sweating man hauling a produce-cart on which were his portable possessions, his wife and family—outrunners of the stream of frightened people that would turn up before midnight.

Away to the north, on my direct route, I could see flashes of gunfire and, a bit nearer, dots of lights signifying rifle fire. The wars of those days were, to a certain extent, a joke. The soldiers, in uniforms when they were lucky, carried paper umbrellas to a man, for they hated rain and every battle stopped dead when it poured. Now and again whole regiments changed sides without objection if the other side handed over enough *cumshaw*, or bribes. Casualties were low, chiefly because nobody could shoot very well, but they *did* happen. Give a few thousand natives rifles, ammunition to half of them, and the law of averages saw to it that people did get killed. If I landed in that lot, both sides would fire at me as a matter of course.

I got more and more worried when I was off the made road. The native roads were tracks, passable because there had been no heavy rain recently. When I got to Tso Ka Jau village, close by Soochow Creek, I scouted for a hiding-place. There were rifle shots and noise ahead; if I had to go through that, my feet were the most reliable to use.

The nearest thing to a hiding-place was a Chinese burial place, a vast earth mound, grass covered, twenty yards from the road. I bumped the Citröen over to it and parked on the far side, hauling brushwood and foliage to cover the little car.

In the darkness on my own, I felt insignificant, but at least the road lay dead ahead. I skipped off it quick when I heard a noise. A bunch of native soldiers came by, mounted on ponies. I could just about see them in the dimness from the thicket where I crouched, men in the usual thin grey uniforms with silly-looking military caps. They were hauling an old-fashioned Maxim machine-gun mounted on wheels, disappearing with a chatter of voices along the road I had come.

It was a question of Indian tactics after that. I didn't know where the battle-line was, or whose territory I was in. There was plenty of firing now, a yelp or two at times, and a great deal of shouted defiance. Bunches of refugees, hauling their worldly goods, crawled past now and again, and once I came across a couple of dead soldiers, efficiently stripped of everything except their underwear and caps, the usual custom.

On the edge of Saung Tsing Thien village I ran smack into trouble, a mortar section comprising an officer and four men. I came out of a bamboo thicket just as they fired the damned thing.

The belching flame of the mortar made the scene like daylight. The officer, Chinese fashion, was standing well away from his men, facing me, on the sensible basis of not being too near if the mortar blew itself up with the crew, a common happening since no soldier ever dreamed of cleaning his weapons. His ' *ts'ung na-li lai?* ' was in excellent Mandarin and though he was entitled to ask me where I came from, I knew enough to realize he was addressing me as a peasant. It made me mad.

' You go and fry.'

It brought the rest of the crew together and they loped towards me, hauling their knives. I didn't quite know what to do. If they caught me it might be weeks before I got home again, if I ever did, which depended on how they considered me.

I raised the Ortgies and shot the nearest soldier in the leg, then doubled back to the thicket and out the other side, as if they were all after me. They must have stopped there, but they had me baffled. If they were using Mandarin, that meant they were from the north, probably Chang Tso-lin's lot. If that were so, they faced the wrong way. It made me think a bit, and I went with a great deal of caution after it.

The house was not hard to find. Telephones, outside the International Settlement and the French Concession, were rare. All I had to do was find the poles of the wires. I tried two places which were wired, but neither of them were private houses, and, in any case, they were both deserted.

Another wire led off, skirting the village, and it meant slowing down. There was a hell of a battle going on ahead, about a mile away. Rifles were really being used, and I could hear a couple of machine-guns. There was even a big one, some sort of field gun, that went off every two or three minutes—rapid firing for a native gun-crew —and I didn't like the wild way the thing dropped shells all over the landscape. Then I found the house, a secluded villa, well back from the dirt-track of a road.

It had a line of trees behind it and Chinese characters on the gate. I recognized the first character, something like an extended hyphen, which meant ' one ' or ' a,' and presumed the house-name was guided by its trees, probably meaning a line or row of them.

There were four Chinese crouching by the far wall in the front garden. They were chattering like a bunch of magpies. It wasn't easy to make out their conversation, but, since it was in Shanghai vernacular, I managed to work out that they were debating whether to pay the soldiers *cumshaw* and chance it, or get back to Shanghai.

The problem was the front door. Some fool was using star-shells, backed by an occasional rocket. The door was wide open and the hallway sent out a splash of light from the electrics. The rising wind would hide my movements, though I didn't think I could get in without being seen:

it certainly wasn't a clever thing to ask the Chinese if Irina Roberti was inside.

I crept along the road side of the garden wall, found some rocks, and heaved them right over the house into the back garden. Two of the rocks made falling noises, the third went smack into glass. It sounded like the end of the world, but it did the trick. The quartet ran jabbering towards the back garden.

The house door lay ahead. I was inside as fast as I could make it, the Ortgies levelled and my heart nearly choking me. I did not even bother about the downstairs level. I've never known somebody held under restraint in a private house being anywhere but on the upper floor. I was right, and found Irina in the second bedroom from the stairhead.

There was a key in the lock. I turned it and sailed in. She looked as if she was going to faint.

'Larry! Oh, *voydite—speshite! Speshite!*'

It was plain enough in any language. I dodged in and shut the door. She was frightened to death, her red hair mussed and the cut on her face she had got in the godown angry and sore-looking. She hung on to me till I couldn't breathe.

'Take it easy, Irina. There's trouble outside.'

'The fighting? I know, I can hear it. I've been here since they took me from the godown. I tried and tried to get out, then sent one of the men to get me some water when he brought my tea. I just managed to get to the 'phone and call your house when he started coming back.'

'Yeah? How did you know where I lived?' I was suspicious, and had every reason to be.

'Lar-ee! I know a lot about you.' She smiled and then shivered. 'I'm so frightened of Fong.'

'Fong? Lord, don't you know? Mrs. Pym shot him to death when she got me out of the godown.'

'*Oh!*' Her grey eyes were wide. 'They told me you got away, but not that——' I thought for a moment she was going to keel over. 'Fong is dead?'

'Sure, and most of the bunch with him.'

'But that means——' she never got around to completing it. There was a burst of yelling outside, a trampling of feet and a rattle of small-arms fire. Somebody was yelling his head off in the back yard, something about they were coming. It was enough for me. I grabbed Irina's hand and would not even let her stop for her fur cape.

When we got into the front garden I couldn't see a soul, only hear the noise on the other side of the house. The lights went off a moment after a colossal crash in that direction. I figured that field gun had got the small power generator which most of those country villas owned; if the gun had the house range, it was just as well to get away.

I snatched her hand and we went out to the road, running like frightened kids in the general direction of my car.

During the run I remember thinking what a fool I had been not to bring Mrs. Pym. This was a tight corner and Chinese armies or no Chinese armies, she was the one to have around. Then yelling began behind us and I could hear the rattle of hoofs.

I hauled Irina almost bodily off the road into a paddy-field where we landed up to our knees in the yielding slime: the water was ice-cold and I thought my feet had gone forever.

A machine-gun began to rattle close by. I shivered at the cry of a wounded pony. Next minute a bunch of mounted men had shot past our crouched bodies, the machine-gun went on steadily and a mounted rider and his pony seemed to leap over our heads smack into the paddy-field, where they lay behind us.

The machine-gun stopped, giving way to a chorus of screams, intermittent rifle fire and that most extraordinary of sounds in modern warfare, the clash of swords.

The whole area began to erupt. Every sort of weapon was going off; the field gun was getting in its ten cents' worth almost every half-minute, and an orderly clatter along the road heralded a troop of mounted men riding well, picked troops obviously, wearing cloaks and carrying swords at the ready.

The leading man, weighed down with braid, said something and the troop broke into a trot just level with our heads, reached out their swords and suddenly went off, down the road. This time they really mixed it, coming up against opposition that seemed to be standing its ground, no doubt entrenched in Saung Tsing Thien village.

Irina was shaking with fright. I jerked her arm.

' This way. We'll try and get out of range.'

We oozed over the paddy-field, skirting the dead rider and his pony. There was a path beyond this which we followed, though I wasn't feeling hopeful. The fighting was on every side of us. The Ortgies felt horribly inadequate.

For perhaps ten minutes we kept going steadily in the right direction, neither of us speaking. The wind was ripping at our frozen legs, the cloud-rack now and again permitting a glimpse of moon to get through, which gave us no more than a few moments' light before it was gone again. When it was out I could see the flat countryside, groups of men moving all over the place and, in the darkness again, the steadily increasing sparking of rifles and machine-guns. Something big was happening. Somebody was standing up to somebody. My only solution was that the picked troops of both sides were in action, which meant they would fight because, in all probability, they were trained, had weapons, uniforms and their back pay. It wasn't a joke any longer.

We stopped just after that. From somewhere behind there was the most shocking clatter I'd ever heard; it sounded like fifty tractors coming along, backed by machine-guns and the intermittent roar of what seemed to me like six-pounders in action.

In the general row I couldn't figure where the sound was coming from, and, for safety, we stayed where we were, on a path between two paddy-fields.

We could hear frightened yells. A group of men without weapons went running past not ten yards away, two riderless ponies followed. The tractor sounds grew louder, then, lurching, crashing, its tracks slapping as it went, a tank loomed out of the darkness, firing furiously in every possible direction, a real, genuine, British Mark IV infantry tank. How it got to China was anybody's guess, but the crew inside knew how to handle it. They were rooting men out of their hiding-places like hounds flushing foxes. From inside, above the rattle of the armament, you could hear the crew, screaming with sheer excitement.

Irina was trembling with fright. She had never seen such a thing before, nor, for that matter, had I except in war books. I told her what it was and to stay down, then we saw something really brave, typical of the unexpectedness of the Chinese character.

The mounted troops in cloaks appeared from the darkness, bunched at the sight of the tank, squatting and spitting in the middle of a field. The officer shouted something and the ponies tensed, and the whole lot went at the tank, swords at the ready, howling their heads off. There must have been a good hundred of them.

They made it, too. The tank's guns were going at a wonderful rate, bringing down ponies and riders. The rest of them went straight on. It was so damned crazy and brave that I was on my feet, howling my head off with excitement. It was beyond me to keep quiet, for the way the troop went at that spitting tin can was stark loopy.

The officer went down and whole swathes of his men. The rest of them got there, a bewilderment of ponies, dismounting riders, guns, screams, and equine shrieks. They swarmed on the tank, some belabouring the sides with swords, others, with more sense, on the top, digging weapons into any place they could find. The tank revved up and tried to squelch from the field while one cavalryman, squealing his head off, stood under one of the tracks and tried to hold it. The tank nosed down on him.

The moon, that had given me light for the picture,

vanished again. It was silly, staying there. I turned to Irina, who had been crouched down, and told her we were getting on.

She never answered me. I thought she was petrified with fright, jerking at her arm to make her hurry. It gave in a peculiar boneless fashion as if she had let it go slack. Out came the moon again for the briefest of moments. It was like a photograph, or the momentary brightness of a flash-bulb. Irina sat there, slumped slightly forward, on her haunches. Her left hand was supporting her and her face was towards me. Some bullet I had not even heard had gone between her eyes.

I went on my own knees, sick and shaking. This was death in a personal sense, real death, of somebody I had known and now realized had mattered to me more than I had imagined. There I stayed, the clatter of war round me, with a sourness in my mouth and, I remember so well, one knee on her purse which, womanlike, she had brought with her.

The tank was moving slowly, firing from one gun, men all over it like leeches on a jungle animal. It struck me that my neck was out about as far as it would go. If I didn't move, I should join Irina.

The purse went into my pocket as I stood, orientating myself. The landscape was semi-luminous from moonlight behind a thin cloud. The wind was strong now, dead in my face, bringing with it a queer mixed tang of wood-smoke, cordite, wet soil and, oddly enough, garlic. I could see the tank still firing, shuddering slowly to the right as if an uncertain hand was on the controls. The firing in the village was growing and shrill yells from somewhere suggested an attack was in progress. I began to run.

It was a wild journey, over fields, sloshing through sunken paddy-fields, and, once, into a small, icy brook, and, beyond this, an earth road. I hared at it in the darkness, running into a small body of marching men.

It was a wild chaos of insane confusion for less than a minute, a tangle of groping hands, shouts, and rifle shots which went nowhere. I tore and bit at every hand, and was over the road into the emptiness beyond.

I thought I was being chased. What luck helped me I'll never know ; even to-day that journey has me beat. The fighting seemed to be on every side, disorganized, untidy, and almost like guerilla warfare. It was those mounted men with cloaks I feared ; they seemed to have the knack of being in the most unexpected places.

I was moving fast, going over a low grave, the faint moon guiding me towards Tso Ka Jau village. It was not too difficult when you remember that Canadians born in small towns learn a lot of woodcraft and tracking as kids, which meant I was capable of finding my way.

What I didn't expect was the machine-gun emplacement I went into on the other side of that low grave. The sentry was on his toes as well, letting rip a rifle shot as I landed on top of him. Why it didn't hit me I can't think ; what did happen was a bunch of men threw themselves on me as if they had been waiting.

I vanished under a tangle of arms and legs, choked with damp cloth, the smell of sweat and the paramount odour of garlic inseparable from the poorer Chinese.

Normally I would have quit there and then, but it didn't happen. I hit, bit, gouged and kicked like a madman, one hand hanging firmly on to the Ortgies. The moment I came up to the top of the struggling mass I fired that gun into it until the clip was empty.

Whether it was that or a sudden thunder of hooves as those ubiquitous ponies turned up, I don't know. Anyhow I broke clear, rolled over and over and went off full tilt into the blackness with, it seemed, ponies breathing over my shoulders. Elbows in sides and my stamina to help me, I lit out, running as fast as I could. When I stumbled I was up again at once : if the Chinese wanted to have their battle, they were going to have the damned thing without me in it. Self-preservation was so strong that even Irina's face, as I had last seen it, went out of my mind's eye when I had thought it could never be forgotten.

Panting, gasping and cheeks stung with my own tears from pain and the sharp wind, I went on. With that blessed second wind I really got down to it and though the battle seemed always with me without growing less, it was the following wind that carried the noise.

Fool's luck sent me into that huge grave with a jolt that made me nearly take a lump out of my tongue. By the time my eyes had stopped running I was tearing at the crude litter hiding the Citröen. Then came the worst part, driving into the darkness by guess and by God, without the lights I dared not use.

I hit a native road with the moon for company again, steering with arm pressure. By holding the Ortgies under the steering-wheel I could use both hands on it and be ready if I had to make a quick steering manœuvre, putting in a new clip of cartridges from my pocket. I had forgotten it until then and had I possessed more than one working suit, it would have been at home when I needed it most.

The road was becoming familiar now. The lights of Shanghai were coming nearer. My heart seemed to jump clean out of the car next moment. There was that familiar clatter of ponies again, and those darned cavalry were on my tail.

It was a question of quick timing. Far as I could make out, from a quick glance behind, there were about a dozen of them, moving fast. Obviously they heard the car, and either I could stand up to them with the little gun, or turn on the lights and run like hell for home.

Home sounded pretty sweet to me. I switched on the headlamps and the parking lights. The road lay ahead, flat and clear. The Citröen actually jumped when I rammed my foot down and brought my head low as I dare.

Thirty, forty, and then fifty, but I had to drop down again. The road was too uneven for the light body. Thirty was as fast as I could move, so I held on to it, yells at my tail and my neck flinching because, any minute, a sword might go in my back.

Where the refugees had got to I didn't know ; at least they weren't in my way. Once I held the Ortgies in my right hand, reversed it over my shoulder, and fired three shots, nearly bursting my right eardrum. It wasn't supposed to be anything but a warning that I had some sort of armament, not that it did much good. They were still on my tail, a good way behind, hanging on. If I got a blow-out or anything like that, I should have had it.

I'm damned if the car didn't begin to jib. It wasn't much, just a slight falling off in momentum. I trod hard on the accelerator, not that it made much difference except that the bunch behind realized it and were speeding up, yelling as if they were going to get me.

I came round a small thicket of bamboos and there, perhaps half a mile away, were the lights of the barrier on the French Concession limits. I had made my point and the car was failing under me, a choked jet or something like that, and failing it was. I did the only thing left, banged on the hooter like a maniac—three dots, three dashes, three dots. I pounded that S O S until the car began to slow to a running pace.

The hoofs were coming nearer, making up the gap at racing speed. The boys on the barrier were no fools. I saw their small searchlight go on, and fired one shot into the air. Swinging into the light of the questing beam, which was now in my direction, came five men on ponies, small figures growing larger every second with good, honest-to-God Anglo-Saxon yells to help me along.

I let the car crawl as it would and swung round. The cloaked cavalry were not more than two hundred yards behind, coming up fast. It had to be steady, and steady it was, two snapshots as if I was on the target range. I hit one man and he went off his pony, not that it stopped the rest.

With that crazy imagination of mine, I was working out just where the swords were going to spit me. But they began to slow down. It never struck me they were round the bamboo thicket and could see the barrier. I stood and

gaped like an idiot until hoofs rattled from behind me.
The five mounted men went by, trim in khaki and little
blue forage caps, led by the blessed figure of Arthur Finlay.
He let rip a ' You bloody fool ! ' as he passed me with his
men, who, faithful to the worthy principles of democracy,
law and order, were carrying nothing more lethal than *lahthis*.

The Light Horse Company was the aristocrat of the
Shanghai Volunteer Corps, a bunch of the *élite*, usually
called the ' Tight Horse ' and regarded strictly as Sunday
afternoon soldiers as distinct, for example, from the Field
Artillery Battery, a bunch of veritable, tough-living, hard-
drinking men who never gave a hoot for looking pretty.

But Arthur Finlay's crowd did their stuff beautifully,
keeping in a smooth, disciplined, parade-ground group.
They went after those cavalry and caught up with them,
using the *lahthis* like veteran schoolmasters, impervious to
the fact they were on forbidden territory, attacking armed
men who, had they stood their ground, might have preci-
pitated killing and an international incident that could
have blown us all sky-high.

The cloaked men ran. Probably they weren't scared ;
they just didn't want to tangle with white folk and the very
real threat of the watchful Allied warships of which there
were always a few patiently moored in the middle of the
Whangpoo.

Finlay and his men came riding back out of the darkness
ten minutes later, the lot of them grinning like kids.

Arthur sat easy on his pony, watching me while I delved
under the Citröen's bonnet, using the Billingsgate for which
he was famous, but so crazily jubilant he even forgot to
tell me what he thought of me.

The car started when I climbed in. We rode majes-
tically towards the welcoming searchlight, Arthur ahead
and a pair of men on either side of me.

I got away in the end, after a combination of criticism
that made my hair curl, praise from the demonstrative
French police, and a shot of whisky from Arthur's hip-
flask that about burned the skin off my throat.

It struck me as completely mad, riding sedately through the well-lit streets of the French Concession. My suit was solid with muck, I ached all over and, above all, my watch told me it was still short of nine o'clock. To this day I don't know how I crowded so much in less than three hours.

The Citröen, running as sweet as a nut now, was eased into its garage. I got into Mrs. MacNaughton's house and found the bathroom free. I showered and changed into another suit, then went out again, headed for Nathan Schyler's, a bit late but on my way.

There was no time even to brood over Irina. The thing had lost its impact for the moment. I was looking forward to a nice, non-committal statement from Laffin's lawyer, a bit of sanity and a return to the mundane after living half a lifetime in three hours.

Bronze Gates, Schyler's house, was a big place at the end of the cul-de-sac that was Tracey Terrace. It stood in its own grounds, reminding me of New England in its architecture.

I went up the garden path. By the noise at the back, I guessed the servants were having some sort of singsong. I would have gone to the front door but, to the left, a lighted room showed open french windows. I was enough of a reporter to have an initial look-see.

Nathan Schyler was at his desk, his white-haired head on the blotter. When I stepped in and ran to his side, I could smell cyanide this time. In that lovely room the scent was unmistakable and pungent.

After the crazy excitements of war all round me, I was back again with the more civilized world as personified by the Cyanide Man.

CHAPTER XIII

THE LITTLE TALL RABBITS

It was perhaps natural, as a reporter with a proper respect for facts, I had read up the cyanides to make sure my reports contained no bloomers. When I went to Schyler's side, I knew what to look for. The insensibility was there, right enough, the limbs were flaccid, the skin clammy and cold. I saw something else that startled me. Under his nose, so that he was lying on it, was a shining brass paper-knife. In the brilliant light of the room I could see it, a faint, intermittent clouding and clearing on the polished surface—he was still breathing.

I went out of the room like a rocket, discovering a telephone on the hall table. It was sheer luck that I got through to Lanny Coager immediately.

'Lanny, this is Larry. Jump to it, Schyler's here in his house, been given cyanide. Rush a doctor, for God's sake.'

'Got you, son.'

'And Lanny, Lanny! Tell him it's cyanide. If he doesn't know, bring a stomach pump, hydrogen peroxide, and sodium thiosulphate and a syringe. That's all I know. For pity's sake, *rush* !'

I banged down the receiver, not waiting to listen if he had got it, then tore into the room again. There was no time for anything but work and the hell with police rules.

Schyler was a weight, for he was a tall man, but I got him on the floor, ripped off my jacket and began artificial respiration, forcing myself to do it sensibly, according to the rules and not like a madman, which is what instinct dictated.

It must have gone on for hours, as it seemed to me, though it was really only twenty-five minutes before I heard cars outside. Somebody was banging at the front door; simultaneously Mrs. Pym came charging past the french windows, Dr. Fedor and Superintendent Laystall at her heels.

Little Fedor smacked his things on the floor and got to work with the stomach pump. None of us said anything, standing helplessly as he slid in the long rubber tube and began squeezing the bulb attached to the glass container.

I was sweating and hot, trembling with exertion, yet it was impossible not to concentrate on the drama of it. I barely noticed Sergeant Kelly come in through the house door.

Fedor's balding head looked hot when he went back on his heels, extracting the tube.

'I think there's a chance. I'll give him an intravenous glucose injection. Kelly, know artificial respiration?'

'Yes, sir.'

'Get down to it, quickly.'

After the needle went home, Kelly got astride the still figure and took up where I had left off. An hour later and with other injections, Schyler's slow, convulsive breathing had changed to something more normal; there was even a little colour in his face.

Fedor went to the windows, gesturing. Two native attendants in white came in, carrying a stretcher, which they unrolled.

'Load him up.' Fedor waved and began grabbing his things. 'We'll finish this at the hospital.'

'Think you can save him?' Mrs. Pym spoke for the first time.

'He's as good as saved now.' Fedor watched Schyler being carried out. 'This young feller here has a head on him.' He followed the attendants into the night, an engine started, and with it the deep clang of the ambulance bell.

Laystall patted me on the back of my damp shirt.

'Nice work, Baker. I'll see that Bowne hears of it for his soul's good.'

Mrs. Pym looked insufferably complacent, as if she was

saying, 'That's how *my* young men do their stuff!', not that she would have uttered the words for a million.

With the chief actor gone, the room seemed to become normal. I flopped in a chair and lit the cigarette Kelly gave me. Mrs. Pym characteristically checked over the place before she said anything.

'Now, Larry, tell me exactly what happened.'

'Yes, ma'am. I had an appointment for eight; I— well—got held up and didn't arrive till a good hour after that. The french windows were open and I peeked in before I tried the front door, saw Schyler sprawled on his desk. When I ran to him I smelled cyanide right away.'

'On his desk? I thought cyanide killed 'em dead.'

'That's what I thought. There was that brass paper-knife under his nose,' I indicated it, ' and he was still breathing enough to mist the surface. I tore out to 'phone Lanny, as I knew he'd be there, came back and dived into artificial respiration.'

'Did you, dammit! That was smooth observation, son. How come you knew what to do?'

'I've been reading up cyanide to learn what it was all about. I figured you wouldn't mind him being disturbed when I thought he had a chance.'

Laystall beamed at us.

'You've done a sensible thing, Baker. Mrs. Pym, if Schyler pulls round he may be able to tell us just what happened.'

'That had struck me.' Mrs. Pym looked a bit grim about it. 'Larry, what were you going to see Schyler about?'

'Coager hoped he might spill some material regarding Laffin's will. Schyler fixed the appointment with him. That's all I know about it.'

'Yes?' Her eyes were suddenly hard. 'Now, young Larry, what were you doing in Chinese territory? The French police contacted us. It seems you practically started a war right on the Settlement doorstep.'

'Yes, ma'am.' I was stuck for a moment. After all the

excitement the whole thing seemed to come back and knock me for a loop. It was only then I realized Irina Roberti really was dead; it made a sickish feeling in my throat.

I began the tale. Mrs. Pym, Laystall, and Kelly sat down, facing me. It made me uneasy until I got into the swing of it, and I let it go. Descriptive reporting had landed me the job with the *Daily News*. Even if I sound like a brash Canuck in saying it, my descriptive stuff *was* good. If I pulled a few fast ones as I talked, it was no more than a sort of literary licence; the way the audience watched me proved the narrative was going over well.

Mrs. Pym let out her breath when it was told. She gave me the second smile on record: it shook Laystall and Kelly enough to give her the floor.

' Larry, I take off my funny hat to you ! ' She tried it, but the pins wouldn't yield, so she just touched it with two fingers. ' Ver-ee nice indeed, son. So you went charging into the middle of a battle because you had a crush on this redhead——'

' I did *not* have any such thing ! '

' —because, as I said and damn well continue to say, you had a crush on this redhead, and don't glare at me. Your ears are pink, which means you're covering up.' She gave me a mild little wink. ' She got a stray bullet in her face. That's bad; I hope you weren't so gone that it's cut you up ? '

I glared at Kelly's grinning face, making a gesture.

' I suppose she was all right.'

' That's an admission ! Still, you're a kid and the world's lousy with redheads and every other colour as well. Hearts don't break at twenty-one, so cheer up. Irina's off the case, and that means we don't get to know what she knows.'

' I hadn't thought of that, ma'am.'

'Well, I had. What about this Chinese house she was at ? '

' If that fight hotted up any worse after I left it, I doubt if either the house or Saung Tsing Thien village are still on the map.'

'There's that. You say she was shaken to hear Fong was dead?'

'Shaken and, I think, pleased. She did get as far as saying "But that means——" when hell broke loose and there wasn't time for any more.'

'Pity it wasn't in a story-book. Thrillers always seem to wangle it so the girl spills the beans while the villains considerately take about an hour to load their guns in another room.' She sniffed loudly. 'However, it strikes me we're still nowhere. Irina's out of the picture and Schyler's been attacked.'

'It worries me,' I told her because it was on my mind, 'that I left her there. I should have brought her back.'

'What on earth for?' Mrs. Pym gaped at me. 'She was dead, wasn't she? Oh, I see, you didn't like leaving her body just where it was—sentiment and what not? Son, when you've been round this world for a bit you'll cotton on to the idea that a body's just a body; it's the impact on living people that counts, the unwritten things left behind.' She looked so malevolent that I had a most uncanny feeling she was thinking of the late Richard Pym. 'But that——'

'Gosh! The purse!'

'Eh?' She glared at me. 'What purse?'

'I never told you. Irina grabbed her purse and brought it with her. I put it in my pocket.'

'By purse do you mean handbag, you confounded young foreigner?'

It made me chuckle, and Kelly took it up.

'I'm sorry. Yes, I guess it was a small handbag. It's in my suit, back in my room.'

'Ah! Either she grabbed it because she was a woman, or because it held something useful. Kelly, you go along with Larry to collect the thing and bring it here. I don't want him hijacked on the way, and he's not to peek, understand?'

'Yes, ma'am.'

I put on my jacket and went into the night with Kelly. It was such a short journey that we walked, a perfect night. The wind had entirely gone and the sky was clear of clouds, bright with moonlight.

Kelly bulked beside me, nearly as big as a house. He was fascinated by my adventure on Chinese territory and wanted to hear it again.

' Did you ever know the like of that ? ' He beamed at me, banging my arm in a friendly way. ' A fight of that size and you didn't have a Kelly in it. But that's the way of it, and me who took in fighting with my mother's milk.' He held an enormous fist in front of my nose. ' Look at that now, will you ? Wouldn't it have been joy to your heart to have it beside you ? '

' Heck, Mike, I wanted to get out, not in ! ' I shuddered when I remembered the tank falling on that cavalryman.

' Shame on you, for a Canadian ! If you were an Englishman I would be after understanding it. The English, God save them, can fight, but they'd sooner not ; they're peaceable folk, just as likely to ask you to talk things over. But fight ? They can when they have to—you won't remember the Curragh mutiny ; I was there, and I saw British officers who were after refusing to fire on their own race . . .' Kelly stopped talking and said an added ' No-o-o ! ' as if he didn't believe it. I stared and couldn't help flinching, probably because my bones were still aching.

We were in the Route des Sœurs, nearly level with the Cercle Sportif Français, where, on our side of the road, was an open space, real estate still undeveloped beyond the partially completed foundations of two houses. As we paused several figures moved in the dimness, beyond the radius of the street lights.

The group was Chinese all right, ragged, unpleasant men marked with that uniform appearance which distinguishes the hoodlum of any nation in the world. They were heading towards us in an enveloping movement.

Kelly asked what they wanted, grimly. They came on

silently, one of them pointing to me. I saw some of the group were carrying sticks.

'Trouble!' Kelly sucked his teeth with excitement. 'The Blessed St. Patrick heard me and himself remembers me!' He did not even wait for my reasonable demand to find out what it was about, diving straight for them with the impetus of a runaway truck. I tried a bit of mental encouragement for my own aches, and dived after him.

That they wanted me there was no doubt at all. Four of the swine jumped straight at me, and once more the Ortgies wasn't handy. Still, I was six-foot tall and tough as they come. I forgot any pacific intentions when I got a whack in the middle of the back. Kelly and I tried to stay shoulder to shoulder.

What I disliked was the intense silence of the hoodlums. They grunted, raised the dust and muttered, though there was none of the yelling, the hysterical 'ki-yi-yi'-ing which distinguished a Chinese mob mixing it. Because Route des Sœurs at night is pretty deserted, we had that vacant lot to ourselves.

They weren't fighting for peanuts either. I had to use every bit of craft in me to keep on my feet, especially when some of the men brought out those filthy narrow-bladed Canton knives.

I kicked one man in the stomach and got his stick from him as he went down, a nice handy piece of mahogany, heavier at one end than the other. My back was stinging so with the stick to support me, I smacked into them, fighting mad after I got a kick on the shin. It was only from a Chinese slipper. Still, it had a leather sole.

Kelly was having the time of his life. His great hands were alternately fists or hooks. Whichever way they were and however he used them, they hurt. I think the group totalled at least a dozen, maybe a few more. I don't know. My memory of it is confused.

We fought, stamped, and whacked over that patch. Once I lurched flat on my stomach when my foot caught an unfinished foundation wall belonging to the nearer of the two houses. The man who had apparently been about to jump on my back fell on me as well, went head over heels and got my mahogany stick on his noggin as I came to my knees. It began to speed up, both Kelly and I using everything we had. My contribution was fair; if I hadn't gone through all that furious running earlier on it might have been better. Mike Kelly was the star of it, a pounding, cursing, chuckling mountain of sheer destruction. I wish to heaven I could have watched; it was something of an indication of what was to happen when dear old Mike went down to his death in Singapore when the Nips marched in.

He charged, punched, kicked, and threw men clean through the air. He moved like a dancer and smote like a Behemoth, a raging inferno filled with that mad Irish fighting spirit I had seen more than once on eastern waterfronts. The Irish can be rats, minor saints, or fighting fools, according to their outlooks—Kelly was king of the last group.

I never realized the way he was covering me up. Otherwise, I figured later, somebody could have cut me down easily. The mahogany stick was lightning in my hand and it did one hell of a lot of damage. Just the same, Mike Kelly, veteran of dozens of fights, had long ago checked up the odds and all the time his blazing destruction was centred on keeping my tail free of those knives.

Then they broke and ran. Three of them weren't moving at all, and another three were just sitting down, thinking things out. Kelly said something scorifying, glaring into the darkness; his inviting 'Come back and take it, you water-gutted bastards!' wasn't even answered.

He grinned at me, rubbing his hair.

'Thanks, Larry. Boy, did we slay the dirty killers!'

I stopped verifying my limbs to grin back.

'Did *you* slay 'em, you big baboon! Heck, I didn't do a thing and you know it.'

'Aw, you and your beguiling.' I could see he was pleased. 'Gangsters, would you be saying?'

'I would—are you all right, Mike?'

'Ready for a hundred more. Your chin's bleeding.'

'They had knives. Did you see?' I dabbed at my chin.

'And just when I was beginning to enjoy myself!' He forgot himself and roared out a violent demand for the bunch to return and stand up like men. Naturally nothing happened. It made me chuckle the way he went round, pulling the six remaining men about like so many loaded sacks until he had them rolled together at his feet. He studied them fondly. 'Look at them, will you? One, no, two, with broken necks!' He looked at his right fist and kissed it. 'Mike, you're a real Kelly,' then kissed the other one and added: 'Sure, Pat, and you were just as good, blood of my heart to you both.'

I hated being the voice of cold reason.

'What were they—Dancers?'

Kelly chuckled.

'Not bad, Larry, not bad at all.' He saw one of the men at his feet was stirring and slapped him awake. 'Who sent you? Damn it, *noong sing sa*, you dirty kitchen refuse.' The man cringed and babbled something in vernacular. Kelly nodded. 'The Little Tall Rabbits, is it? Well, well!' He raised his face to me. 'Gangsters, Larry. Chinese City rats, professional roustabouts. You hire them when you're after wanting somebody beaten up and his home smashed, or some John Chinaman has to be flattened out and killed, at so much a time.' He questioned the man vigorously, slapping his face when he didn't answer quick enough, and shrugged at his frightened answers. 'He doesn't know a thing. Hired, they were. Did what he was told, like the others. The leader got away, bad cess to him.'

Kelly calmly borrowed one of the cars parked outside the Cercle Français, loading the six in the back and sat on them, directing me to drive to the French Police Station in Avenue Joffre. It epitomized the Chinese knack for keeping out of real trouble that, during the whole of the fight and after it, never a single spectator turned up.

The moustached little French *sous-inspecteur* at the police station was enchanted with our story, shocked to hear of what went on in his own territory, and gratified to learn how we had come out of it. When he saw our credentials, especially Kelly's, he was our blood brother. The dead men he waved away as of no consequence, a veritable *bagatelle*, and begged us not to disturb ourselves. He did not even question the impropriety of Central Police Station officers from the International Settlement being in the French Concession, along with an accredited S.M.C. police surgeon, on official business. The French police believed strictly in the policy of *laisser-faire* between the various white officials on the very sound principle that there was enough work for everybody without splitting hairs when the Chinese had to be dealt with—the Republic's attitude towards China was far more realistic than our own. If all Shanghai had been a French concession, no warlord would have got within fifty miles of it.

He insisted on coming back with us in the car, to explain personally to its owner where it had gone. He went in the French Club to do so and when he hadn't returned after thirty minutes, Kelly and I decided he was probably having a high old time. We cleaned up a bit in my room, taped my chin with adhesive plaster, and headed back towards Tracey Terrace with the purse.

Kelly was in a mental heaven, sailing into Schyler's parlour and into Mrs. Pym's tight-lipped displeasure.

'And where in hades have you two been?' She gestured at the clock. 'Am I expected to sit here on my stern, twiddling my fingers, while you——' Then she saw my plaster and the state of our clothes. 'For God's sake don't tell me you and Kelly have been fighting? No, you wouldn't be living, Larry.'

'I guess not.' I liked Kelly far too much to take offence at that. 'I'm sorry, ma'am . . . you see . . .' I trailed off. Kelly, beaming and at his best, told the story. I thought Superintendent Laystall was going to fall off his chair.

'In Route des Sœurs?' His voice was shocked.

'Indeed it was, sir. The Little Tall Rabbits themselves.' Mrs. Pym's sigh was heavy.

'I'll be hanged if I know how it happens. First he's in a torture scene, then a war, then a gang fight. How in the name of God do you do it, boy?'

'Maybe I'm lucky, ma'am——'

'Lucky! Hell, you're natural worry for the police and a blessed gift to the *Daily News*. It beats me.'

'Perhaps it's the Pym personality, ma'am. I've a feeling neither the Cyanide Man nor the Dancers would have amounted to anything if you hadn't taken over and I'm in your reflection. By gosh, yes! Has it ever struck you that some people constitute sort of human lightning conductors—they draw all the concentrated uproar on themselves that, but for them, might be distributed over a lot of heads?' It was the first time it had ever occurred to me, and I was prophetic, for it was to apply right through Mrs. Pym's working life. Until she appeared on the scene Fate never really let rip. I could see the idea pleased her hugely.

'Well, there might be something in that . . .' Her words trailed off and I'm darned if our tame battle-axe didn't look down her nose, like a maiden with her first proposal.

Superintendent Laystall was worried about the realities.

'I don't like it one bit, Baker. The Little Tall Rabbits, for all that silly colloquial name, are a nasty crowd, professional thugs without a shred of pity. If these wretched Hop-Ley Dancers have sent them after you, it means trouble and danger. Perhaps you'd better take a holiday?'

'Me?' I paused, glancing at Mrs. Pym. Her grey-blue eyes were watching me like an impresario with a pupil. 'Why should I? I'm a reporter and I'm going to get the story. If I'm busted, then it's just too bad.'

Those watching eyes lightened; I'd said the right thing. There was a sound at the french windows; we all turned together.

A man had come in, a mild-looking little man with a

brown face bearing faint smallpox scars. His dark blue eyes were bleary and you could smell his load of liquor from where we stood. It was Toby Garnett, of the *Free Press*, completely and absolutely soused.

'Hi! Where'sh old Schyler?'

Mrs. Pym frowned at him; she recognized him all right.

'And what do you think you want to know for?'

'Shent for me pershonally.' Garnett giggled at us, clutching at the window frame. 'I borrowed ten dollarsh, and loaded up. "Toby," he shays on the tel-tel-telephone, "come round and shee me, my old friend Toby. Got newsh for you, To-To-*Toby*!" Yesh, newsh for me, the old kidder. "Laffin, funny old Laffin," thash wash he shays, "Laffin left you the lot—two hun'ed millionsh." Wash he kidding? Phoo!'

He waved jovially and fell flat on his face, out of this world.

CHAPTER XIV

GARNETT'S HOUSE

As a curtain to a drunken pass-out, it couldn't be beaten. I've never seen that stock novelist situation, too stunned to speak, in my whole life except that once.

None of us said a word, not even Mrs. Pym who took riots in her stride. Kelly moved first. He went to Garnett, picked him up as if he were a cushion, and dumped the old rumpot on the wall divan.

Mrs. Pym glowered at us as if we'd done something wrong, dug in her huge bag for a dark green bottle, sticking it under Garnett's nose. For a while he didn't react, then began to choke and splutter. When he was wriggling she sent Kelly off to the kitchen where, I imagined, he had confined the servants, for a bottle of Worcestershire sauce.

Garnett was given a liberal swig, and shaken till his head wobbled. Ten minutes later he was sitting up, probably aching for death. Worcestershire sauce and Mrs. Pym's smelling bottle would have brought an elephant out of a ten-day toot : Garnett smiled at us. It looked so like the *risus sardonicus* of lockjaw that I gaped at him.

' So you're awake ? ' Mrs. Pym's face helped to sober him a fraction more. ' What's all that roomaoo about you being Jacob Laffin's heir ? '

' Did I say that ? Lord, I must've been bad.' He waved. ' Hi, Larry. Superintendent ; Sergeant Kelly.' He shivered when he got back to Mrs. Pym, standing with her hands on her hips. ' First time I've ever tangled with you, ma'am. I don't like it.'

' That's not all you won't like if I don't have the truth out of you.'

' Yes'm. Where's Schyler ? '

'Never you mind. *What-is-all-this-about-Laffin?*'

'He rang me at the *Press* office—Schyler, I mean. Said I was to come round and see him at eight sharp. God, my *head*! Oh, yes, told me I was Laffin's heir.' For some reason Garnett's brown face lost all its colour and he looked scared.

'It just doesn't make sense, if it's true. Did you know Laffin?'

'Well, only in a manner of speaking, ma'am. I'd chatted with him off and on at the Ritz-Carlton. Nice old chap. I bought him his Vichy water half a dozen times. Didn't cost much and I got a kick out of it, him with all that cash.'

'You think Schyler was telling the truth?'

'He's a good liar if he wasn't. I believed him. It hit me so hard I borrowed ten dollars from my news editor and went out to get stinking before the nice feeling wore off—silly of me, wasn't it?'

'I'll say it was. Just what time did this happen?'

'You mean, Schyler? He telephoned at about six, and off I went.'

'Where?'

'Well . . . I started out in the Ningpo Inn. I had a few there. I don't remember anything after that, I'm afraid. Look here, is Schyler going to tell me what this is all about?'

'I'll come to that in a moment.' Mrs. Pym's eyes were suddenly implacable. 'Garnett, this thing stinks. You warned Larry Baker in Dinty Moore's to " keep out "— those were your words. You seemed to know a lot more than you said when you told him he was bucking the wrong crowd. Now you claim to be Laffin's heir; you don't know what you were doing between six o'clock or so and now; *and* you suddenly bust in like this. You didn't come in a car and I'd 've heard a rickshaw outside on that loose gravel surface. Schyler's been poisoned with cyanide, Garnett. See where it leaves you?'

Poor little Toby went green as a seasick man. He was

petrified with fright and so scared he couldn't even answer at first.

'But . . . I didn't do *that*, ma'am!'

'I hope you didn't. Garnett, just what do you know about the dangers threatening Larry?'

'Well, I know what I know. I'm not disclosing my sources, I promise you.' He looked at me appealingly. I knew what he meant. No reporter worth his salt would ever put a finger on the people who gave him under-cover news.

'He's right there, ma'am,' I suggested. 'It's a sort of unwritten law that we don't betray news-roots.'

'Faddle! I'm a cop, so's the superintendent, so's Kelly. Garnett, we're not going to pinch your sources, you poor fish.'

'I don't care.' He shook his head obstinately. 'I had it off the record and I'm keeping my mouth shut. All I know is that Larry was bucking the wrong mob. I don't know much about it except that he was playing with killers. Dash it, *you* ought to know that, going by this week's front pages.'

'Thank you; I learned to suck eggs as a girl. What do you say, Superintendent?'

He took off his uniform cap and pressed his white hair as though his head hurt.

'It's getting beyond me. Garnett, can't you tell us *anything*?'

'I've told you all I can, sir.' There was a touch of the old, light-hearted Toby in the next words: 'Perhaps, with all that money, Larry ought to go and 'phone for six high-class solicitors for me?'

'Don't go spending fool's-gold before you've got it, if it's true. Kelly, check on the 'phone with the hospital, will you? There should be news by now.'

We waited while he was gone, watching Toby Garnett, who sat holding his head. Kelly returned with a cheerful expression.

'Doc Fedor's still there, ma'am. I spoke to him. He's

searching the hospital library for a precedent, he says. Himself, he's in a tizzy. Schyler's going to pull through.'

' *What!* '

' It's true on my life's beat, ma'am. To-morrow he'll be shaken but on his feet, Fedor told me, and said he won't want to eat or drink for a week, but alive he is.'

' Can he tell us anything? '

' Asleep—doped. He needs rest. Because the throat showed something or other, or, maybe, didn't show it, the doc says it was a capsule, so it was.'

' Mr. Cyanide Man, *now* I've got an eye-witness! ' Mrs. Pym was suddenly jubilant. ' When Schyler talks we've got that killer, wherever he's hiding. Garnett, that makes things easier for you, but I'm still uncertain. You'd better sleep at Central Station to-night.'

' Am I under arrest? '

' You are not. Do you want me to recite the section of the Municipal Police Code that permits a twenty-four hour——'

' No, no! I'm sorry. Maybe any bed will do, long as I get some sleep.' Garnett stood up, sick and wretched.

Laystall and Kelly escorted him away, leaving me with Mrs. Pym. She prowled round the room, probing and digging as if she was looking for something. Then she whirled round.

' Larry, where's Irina's bag? '

' I'm sorry.' I hauled the thing from my pocket, handing it over.

Mrs. Pym undid it, turning it upside-down on a table. The litter was purely feminine, compact, lipstick, keys, perfume vial, cigarettes in a tortoise-shell case, matches, bits of material, and a little fold of grubby paper.

She teased it open, the carefully torn off portion of some typewritten message which read, in English : ' . . . and so promise your brothers to you.' Below it was stamped with a red-inked *hong*, a little carved signet of Chinese characters which was carried by every Chinese, his personal name, or synonym for a name—his signature.

She went at it as though she had the authority of a fire-bell to help her along. Since she had only the hooter, it was pounded at two-second intervals and, as usual, she did the impossible by going too fast, taking the wildest chances, which came off. On the other side of the Creek we really began to move. The air was stimulating, the moon bright, and the city its glamorous, faintly pungent self, the unfailing magic of night and a moon. I was too tired to care; my head was nodding when the jerk of the braked Bugatti woke me.

The house was one of a row, two-storied, narrow-fronted, a typical Hongkew home probably let at a reasonable rental. All the windows were dark.

Haining Road was quiet, almost deserted. Mrs. Pym studied it before going to the house.

'Homely, eh? Not a lot of street lamps, and fewer people. Tailor-made for trouble.' She shook her head. 'Not that it happens to you when I'm there. Pity, I like trouble as much as Kelly does. C'm on, we'll see what the house has to offer.'

I didn't venture to point out she had no search warrant, she was breaking Lord knows how many extra-territorial laws, and laying herself open for a million dollar suit if Garnett felt like it. You just don't point out things like that to Mrs. Pym—not then, or ever. She made her own rules as she went along, and since the god of luck considered her his favourite child, she always pulled off the risky trick she was playing.

I thought it was going to be all right, that we should be able to give the house a miss. There was a note pinned to the door: 'Toby. Taken children to stay night with my sister. She very sick. Back early the morning. Torö.' Garnett's wife, I remembered, was Japanese. I told Mrs. Pym.

'Um? That makes it fine. Now we can have a real look-see.'

'You mean, you're going to *break* in?'

She stared at me, in the dimness, with genuine surprise.

'No, I can't work out the characters. Wait a tick.'
Mrs. Pym went from the room and I heard her going along the passage, opening a door. There was a brief, noisy interlude in vernacular. No doubt she was telling the kitchen staff why it was to mind its own business, and demanding information. She came back, looking happier.
'It's a flowery one, Larry,' she put one finger on the *hong*, 'but it's Fong's, no doubt of it.'

'Then . . . yes, I remember Irina telling me on the way to the godown that she had two brothers.'

'That explains it, then. Fong has them, or knows who has them. It explains why she danced to his tune, I daresay.'

'And Fong's dead.'

'But Mr. 'Veh isn't—he's the one I want to find, him and the Cyanide Man, if they're not the same. Don't look so surprised. Somebody sent those gangsters after you, and Fong's dead. If it was the Cyanide Man who visited you, he could 've killed you then, couldn't he?'

'Yes. I never thought of that.'

'I thought as much! Larry, feel too tired to run out to West Hongkew with me?'

'Whyever?'

'According to the 'phone directory, Garnett lives in Haining Road. It struck me—well, well!'

'What, ma'am?'

'Haining Road, eh? A stone's throw from where the Ho brothers live, and not so far from the Hello Storage godown, either.'

'My God! You *don't* suspect Toby?'

'I'd suspect my sister Alice, if I had one, if she looked as suspicious as Garnett does to me. Well, are you coming?'

I drove all thoughts of bed from my mind, trailing out to Tracey Terrace and the Bugatti.

Mrs. Pym switched on the lights, started up and slid round the corner. At night the streets of Shanghai were less full of traffic, an absence made up by swarms of natives wandering all over the place. It didn't worry Mrs. Pym.

' Miss the chance of an empty house ? Oh, I see, you've gone all law-abiding. When you've been round with me long enough, son, you'll learn I obey the law so long as it suits me ; when it doesn't I make up my own. I'm doing so now. New Pym Law : when I suspect somebody and the house is empty, I do this.' She whipped a calling card from her pocket, bent it and leaned a shoulder against the door, snicking back the yale-type lock. ' Simple ? It's not my fault if they left the front door undone, is it ? "

There was nothing to do except follow. I admit my hair prickled at the roots when she switched on the electrics as she went. In the tiny, homely sitting-room her eyes were sardonic.

' Still queasy ? You poor mutt ! Is anybody going to suspect unauthorized entry when the lights are on ? Be your age, do.'

So I followed. It was a neat house, impeccably tidy. The tight, formal arrangements of the profuse flowers, the clean boards and few mats, the institution-like cleanliness, they were all eloquent of a Japanese hand in European surroundings, for your Japanese housewife can make her Dutch counterpart seem like a grubby slum-dweller by comparison.

It was so darned tidy that Mrs. Pym had to go carefully. The slightest carelessness in her search, and it would have shown up like a white man at a coloured peoples' convention.

We found Toby's room, a typical man's room, austere as the rest of the house, even to a wide-open window through which, I noticed when I peered, we might have crept with a bit more secrecy than by frontal entry.

Mrs. Pym delved there, taking her time. Once she paused over a drawer, then moved off to the other rooms. The only one she ignored was the minute nursery. She seemed satisfied and we headed back to the car, dousing the lights, and, to my relief, closing the door quietly. She sat in the Bugatti for a while, staring up at the house, then we started off.

'You want to go home to bed, Larry?'

'I'm a bit tired, ma'am.'

'What about your paper?'

'Oh, Lord!' I sat up in the rush of chill air. 'I'm going loco—you know, I'd completely forgotten all about it!'

'I thought as much. You're overtired, son, but duty's duty. I'll run you there.'

'Thank you, ma'am. Lanny'll never forgive me if I let him down on what's happened.' I looked at my watch. 'I'm safe for an hour, anyway. Gosh, Mrs. Pym, me forgetting my job.'

'Okay. You needn't weep in my car, or you'll rust the fittings.' She began to tear through the streets with her old zest, slowing down before the lighted pile of the *Daily News* building. 'Pym service.'

'Ma'am, it's very——'

'No goo.' She fumbled in her pocket and held something out to me. 'Found this in Toby Garnett's shirt drawer. Seen it before?'

I nearly flew in the air with shock.

'*No!*' I showed no manners at all, snatching at the thing to stare at it by her dash-board lights. 'My God, it *is*! It's the jade ring, the jade buffalo ring—the one I told you about. I'll swear it on a stack of Bibles!'

'No need to blow me out of the car,' She took the ring back, studying it. 'Cute little gimmick.'

'Does that mean Toby's the Cyanide Man?' I was so shaken I found it hard to speak.

'Maybe, or maybe he's Mr. 'Veh.' She waved, getting into bottom gear. 'I like dropping bombs. So long, son, see you to-morrow.' She drove off, leaving me there practically chewing my nails to the elbow.

How I got up to Lanny Coager I don't quite know. I was so dazed with tiredness and horror that I felt weak-kneed.

Lanny, a pink-shirted, red-bearded wet nurse, fed me brandy and bolstered up my ego and my spirits. He sat on the other side of the desk, tapping with a blue pencil, while I gave him every minute of my time since I went back to the house for my sleep, about a hundred years before.

'For crying out loud!' He opened his bright blue eyes at me. 'And you a reporter!'

'I'm sorry, Lanny. It's been like life on an all-out racing car with no stops.'

'Yes, I know. Still, you got to learn there's always a telephone with re-write at this end. Larry, I'm not beefing. It's your first big assignment, and you're bound to mis-step now and again. I'll have to replate; still, there's forty minutes in hand and we can do it.' He smiled suddenly. 'Thank the powers that be my foreman printer's Chinese; back home I'd have the union on my neck.

'Now, kid, I'll get Jessie and you can dictate. I'll clean it as it comes off the machine—no, don't get up. You're all in. Say it as it comes to your mind. I'll re-hash and shape it; you look like you're going to sleep where you are.'

He yelled for Jessie and in she came, a thin, bright-eyed, middle-aged Eurasian, his personal secretary. Jessie had a memory like ten elephants and she could typewrite a blue streak. She smiled at me, heard the orders, and went for her machine.

The three of us got down to it, Jessie's fingers burning up the keys as fast as I could talk. Lanny took the sheets, subbing, shaping, improving as he went, passing each finished page to waiting copy-boys. I was bug-eyed when it was done, yet done it was.

'*Swell!*' Lanny pounded my back. 'Nice going, kid. It's all there, except Schyler's telephone message to Toby, which might be nonsense, and that ring. It puts Pym in a bad light, quite apart from the court action Toby could spring on us if he happened to own a ringer, and don't grin, it's not a pun.'

'I'll swear it was the same——'

'Okay, okay, so it's the same ring. It still doesn't go

in the *News*. Now, you beat it home. I'll have one of the boys run you back in the office car. Be at the desk at ten. Can do?'

'Sure, Lanny, and thanks.'

'Thank me when you see the front page. You'll do, Larry, you've topped the last one—hold it a moment.' He picked up the ringing telephone. 'Yes? Well, he's here but he's going to bed. Sure, Coager. I'll take it— oh, Kelly. Hi, pal, got some news? Private stuff . . . *what!* The crazy goon. Why the hell didn't—okay, if you're in a hurry. Thanks a lot. I'll have Larry call you in the morning. 'Night.' He put down the receiver and looked at me. 'More coming up. Garnett. Called for some water half an hour ago, then beaned the guard with the detention room Bible, and ran for his life.'

'You mean . . . ?' I came practically awake.

'Sure. He's on the lam, and Laystall's dead sure he's the bogeyman. They've shoved a police guard on Schyler in hospital, and every available man is out looking for old Toby.'

'The silly damned fool! That's asking for trouble.'

'You're telling me——' Lanny paused again, as one of the junior reporters came in. 'What's biting you, Red?'

'Just came through, Lanny. The *tuchuns* are really mixing it now, and Wu's lot have gone crazy. They've been attacking the barriers and there's big trouble coming up. The warships are landing armed sailors. There's an emergency call for the Volunteer Corps, and I've got to run.'

'Okay—where the blazing hell are you going, Larry?'

'I'm an S.V.C. man in case you don't know. I've got to get my uniform, and——' I backed away from Lanny. 'What the heck?'

'You get right down on that couch over there and get a bit of shut-eye. I'll have you woken at six, and then you can do your stuff, but you'll sleep or I'll knock you for a loop. I'm not going to have my best man dead on his feet.'

I couldn't help it, I just fell on that lumpy, ancient

couch and went out nearly as fast as a light, coming awake again with a jerk when there was a queer *ther-ummp* near enough in the next room.

Young Red, half assembled in the uniform he kept in his locker, came streaking in, holding up his pants, maybe five minutes later.

Lanny, who had been watching me, waiting for proofs, glared at him.

'What now?'

'A shell, Lanny. My God, a real shell! Bang in the vacant lot back of Dinty Moore's. Betcha it's Wu.'

'Go and stop the bastard, then, and button up your pants, or you'll just shock him.' I began to pass out again; the devil with shells and the whole crazy business, but as I went I heard Lanny's voice on the inter-office 'phone, newspaper man before all else. 'Composing room? Coager. Hold me half a column. Copy coming up. International incident. Eighteen point Cheltenham head— Benchley? *Bench*-ley! Where's that bloody photographer —ah, Benchley, get out and take a pic of the shell-hole...'

CHAPTER XV

THE YELLOW RENAULT

LANNY COAGER was about everything a good mother could have been. Charlie Lee, the doorman, woke me at six to the minute, with hot coffee and a dish of ham and eggs. My uniform, even my shaving kit, had been brought from my room and were laid out on Lanny's tumbled desk. There was a note from him, too:

> Your station's Avenue Road. I've fixed with your C.O. that you won't be hung if you're there by seven. Get the war done with by noon; there's to-morrow's edition. Luck, boy. Lanny.

I tore at the food, nearly hacked my face off, then tumbled into my kit. I blessed Lanny to his big feet when I found a Willys Knight taxi on the door, waiting for me, and off I went to war the way it should be done, by car, and coddled like a moppet by the toughest city editor east of Suez.

The station was just beyond the Bubbling Well Police Station, the whole dreary view cold as a miser's heart in that bright, icy morning. My unit near enough kidded the pants off me when I fell out of the taxi and galloped up to the old man—Deadeye Larry Baker, just a few hours late for the war and due for a wall and an eye-bandage, had it been the real thing.

The old man's eyes twinkled suspiciously, though he tore my head off, just for the good of my immortal soul, then handed me over to the sergeant, Randy McCallum, but a bleak-eyed Quirk on the job.

He took me off at the double, cursing me out of the corner of his mouth.

'Sleeping off your excesses, you insubordinate sonofabitch. Wait till I get you at drill, you'll—oh, jump to it. Go up alongside Schlesinger and *pick up that musket* or I'll tear out your guts!'

Lew Schlesinger, perched behind a pile of sandbags, gave me a hand, and the story.

'Where you been, Larry? Heard you was out there. That so?'

'Sure. I was about dead on my feet—Lew, what's been going on?'

'Wu. Beating the pants off Chang. Got cocky when he started to run, and tried to go after us as well. There was three shells dropped back there in the city. Lookit, will you? Our lot, and the police. Over there—no, right of the old man—they're landing parties from the *Huron* and a coupla British warships are haring this way fast's they can make it.'

'Any trouble?'

'Naw, nothing much. Refugees. Coupla machine-guns beyond that house way over there. Randy cleaned them up. Lobbed over a coupla Mills' and they ran like scalded cats. Lookit, will you, and me with the nicest bed in town!'

It didn't look inviting. There were a lot of homes beyond the boundary where we stood, places I knew well, but their owners took the chance of living where they did. Some of them would be behind us, safe; the others—and there were plenty of them—probably said the hell with the soldiers and went back to sleep. It made things pretty hard for us if we had to use our guns.

I gave Lew some of my own adventures because there was nothing else to do. He was a nice little guy, with some sort of job on the Gasoline Landing Station. He'd been in Shanghai for years and, beyond his motor-bike, I don't think he had a thought in the world.

'You did all that out there? Chee, Larry, you was lucky, eh?'

'I thought so.'

' Say, didju——'

' Baker ? Baker—Bak-*er* ! ' It was Randy McCallum below me, red-faced with anger.

' Here, Sarge.'

' Keep your eyes out there, will you ? Been gabbing like an old woman at a hen feast. You're on duty, get it ? '

' Yes, Sarge. Sorry.' I winked at Lew and stared at the view ahead, feeling a bit better with the sun on the back of my neck. We went on talking out of the side of our mouths, like men in the penitentiary.

' You got yourself a slice of trouble in that godown, didn't you, Larry ? '

' The Hello Storage place ? Sure. Why, yes, it's right by you. I forgot that.'

' Yeah. We heard the firing, but we was on the job and couldn't get away.' Lew sucked a tooth. ' You're a lucky sonofabitch. I near enough had a smash-up there myself yesterday afternoon.'

' You did ? What happened ? '

Lew gave me a quick glance of pleasure ; he liked people to listen to him, though they seldom did.

' Aw, it wasn't nothing much. The manager sent me up to the head office for some papers. I was tooting back on my old Indian on Yangtzepoo Road, behind this car ahead of me. He pulls towards this Hello place, and starts slowing, so naturally I pulls out right to pass him. Then this native cop on the gate comes walking out to see who it was, and the filthy rat in the car swings round in a right-hand turn without so much as a signal. Get that, will you ? Just jerks round so's I near enough cracked into him.'

' Did he, dammit ? ' I forgot McCallum and stared at Lew. ' What then ? '

' Chee, you going to use it in your paper ? Why, I gives him the old home-town cussing and swings out of his way by inches. Why he skidded out when the cop appears got me beat, just when he was going to stop, too.'

' Lew, I think you've got something. Did you see the man driving ? '

'I never had a real look-see. Happened too fast, pal, but the car it was a lousy great Renault, bright yellow. I never saw the guy's face, me being in a fast wobble and spitting mad.'

'Thanks, Lew, maybe I'll make something of it—Lew, can you see some men down there? No, not that way, along the road, just beyond the white bungalow with the trees.'

'Yeah? Wait a minute. *Ye-ah!* Coupla dozen, lugging a machine-gun. Yeah, it's them!'

I jerked round, to see Randy watching me.

'Soldiers, Sarge. Moving up with a machine-gun. Golly, they're setting her up!'

Randy hauled himself up alongside us and stared, then dropped back, running to the empty shell-case we used as an alarm.

It rattled out and the American Company stood to; a whistle farther along told me the *Huron* gobs were also on their toes.

Then it came, the tinny *tatt-tatt-tatt*, aimed square at the post. We waited for the old man, standing there like a goon, watching. The machine-gun went on with some sporadic rifle fire to back it up. We were saying things under our breath, cautiously screening our bodies behind the sandbags, but the old man, being a lawyer himself, was nuts on the niceties of International Law.

He waited, ignoring the untidy fire, until one bullet took off the hat of a Chinese bystander beyond our rear barricade. That did it.

'Okay.' He glanced up and down. 'Aim for their legs. One round, *fire!*'

It went out sweetly, a volley in slick unison. I hoped the Field Artillery Battery and the Japanese Company were somewhere around; they were always calling us a bunch of gilded playboys. You couldn't have heard a volley torn off neater by the Brigade of Guards.

The machine-gun post disintegrated, leaving three of the

bunch on the ground. The old man came to me, as sharpshooter.

'Baker, can you blast that thing without hitting anyone?'

'I think so, sir.'

'Right.' He passed an order to Randy, then looked at me again. 'Empty your magazine, Baker, unless you do it before then. Now, slow-ly.'

I nuzzled against my gun—it was a British service issue —and studied the machine-gun. It looked like a Vickers .303 far as I could see. It was slightly turned away from me. I sighted on the breech and squeezed. The first shot was just a shade high, the second got her fair and square, jerking the whole contraption over. I gave it one more; it hit something; I couldn't see what.

The old man, standing beside me, nodded.

'Fine. Hold it, Baker. We'll wait and see.'

'Yes, sir.'

We watched while a couple of grey-uniformed men appeared and hauled their pals away, then we just went on waiting, through nine and ten to eleven o'clock, when a huddle of refugees appeared, pleading for admittance.

The old man, who spoke a dozen dialects, did some questioning himself, beckoning Sergeant McCallum.

Randy came out to front.

'Okay, you guys, break it up. Fall in; fall *in*!' When he was satisfied we didn't look any worse than usual the old man spoke to us.

'I'm informed there are no soldiers in the immediate vicinity. Sergeant McCallum will call you off. Every second man from the right rank will fall out. Go back to your work. Stay in uniform, but stack your arms.' He grinned. 'Thanks fellers.'

The roll was called; Lew was unlucky, but I wasn't. I followed the others to the waiting truck after Randy had told us the starting siren on the Bund boathouse would be sounded for five minutes when we were to report back. Anybody later than thirty minutes after the siren had stopped would be AWOL, and, he added, 'God help him.'

We sang all the way back to the Bund and I was in Lanny's office just as noon was sounding.

'Hullo, Larry. Okay?'

'Yes. Thanks for the arrangements. I made it on time. Some of us got stood down as they've sheered off somewhere.' I told him about the machine-gun. 'That's all that happened. By the way, that cyanide song of yours is a hit. We sang it on the way back in the truck, with suitable military variations we couldn't print in the *News*.'

'Nice work.' He looked pleased with himself. I've noticed that. You can compliment a man for building a bridge and he takes it for granted ; tell him he's clever when he's composed anything that remotely resembles poetry, and he'll lend you his bank-roll. 'Any news? No, I guess not.'

'Well, there is some.' I explained about the yellow Renault. 'Might be a lead?'

'Sure. Yes, sure. Larry, get out and find it, will you? It might be a hot tip.'

'Right. What's been happening here?'

'Quite a few things. They haven't found Toby Garnett yet. He's gone to earth like a fox.'

'And Schyler?'

'I spoke to Kelly. He's very cagey. Told me that when you turned up you'd better step round to Central Station. Get me a story, Larry?'

'Count it done. Do I spill the dope about the Renault?'

'I guess so.' His consent was reluctant. 'Yes, do that. You've been on the inside and the cops will find it quicker than you.'

Mrs. Pym was in front of the small mirror in her office, fixing her hat, when I was shown in. She studied me, turned round and rammed home a pin.

'Hi, General. Won the war, or have you come to save me from hordes of Chinese mercenaries?'

'Now, ma'am. The S.V.C.'s a pretty good organization.'

'Oh, sure. I like to see tired business men with adipose

tissue, all tricked out in their little uniforms. What's that ribbon for, kicking a top sergeant?'

'Sharpshooter, ma'am.'

'So you are! I'd forgotten that. Don't let my talk faze you. What's happened; war over?'

'They disappeared. I'm standing by, with a kick in the pants if I take this uniform off. I think I've got a lead.'

'Nice work, Larry. I need it.'

'One of our company told me about it.' I gave her Lew's motor-cycle incident verbatim. 'Does it strike you that the man was going to the godown and sheered off when he saw the cop?'

'Could be.' Her grey-blue eyes were pleased. 'I think we can use that, son. Nice front page on the *News* this morning—are you up in everything?'

'Well, no . . .'

'There isn't much. Garnett's still out of sight and we're having such a business tracing Irina Roberti that I think maybe she lived beyond the Settlement limits. Oh, yes, Schyler. Sitting up and taking bread and milk. He'll be out after lunch. Doc Fedor's over at the library, riffling through books to find out how the hades Schyler managed to live with all that cyanide in him. Schyler's going to fall on you and kiss you the moment he sees you.'

'Have a heart, Mrs. Pym. He saw the killer?'

'If you mean the Cyanide Man, he did not.' She sat on the edge of her desk, hands in her jacket pockets. 'There he was, working peacefully, wondering why you were so late. He was checking some documents, then somebody clunked him on the back of the head. He more or less passed out, but remembers something in his mouth, a nasty feeling, and he woke up in hospital. Helpful, ain't it?'

'Oh, Lord! What about Toby Garnett?'

'The McCoy. He's known Toby for years, and when he was getting ready to see you that evening he thought he'd give Toby a ring and raise his blood pressure—I never knew lawyers were that human.'

'You mean, Toby *is* the heir?'

'All signed, sealed, and delivered. I haven't seen the will yet. It's in Schyler's safe, but Laffin named him residuary legatee, which in English means sole heir—now, don't get excited. *I don't know why.*'

'It's incredible ! All that money, too.'

'Oh, sure, all that money. Maybe Toby knew and maybe Toby . . . ? ' she shrugged.

'I never thought of it like that. Do you think it ? '

'Why did he sock the guard and run ? '

'That's sense.' I rubbed my chin furiously. 'It's getting worse and worse.'

'It may do better yet.' She swung round and hooked up the inter-office telephone. 'Give me Traffic. Hullo, McIntyre ? Pym here. Tell me, do you know of a yellow Renault ? Yes, big, a saloon. Two ? Who owns them ? ' She made a note and thanked him, replacing the receiver. 'One belongs to Lorrie Bala, the oil man, and the other to the Yip Kee Garage, Bubbling Well Road. Bala ? H'm.'

'Lorrie ? I don't think so, ma'am. He's Armenian ; he's tricky——'

'I know ; I've met him on another case. I'll see him second and the Yip Kee place first. We can stop in at Böök's for some food if you're hungry ? '

'I haven't eaten since six.'

'Then come along. They'll think I've gone for a guy in uniform.' Mrs. Pym looked at me, sniffed, and led the way.

Böök's was fairly full, but there was a table for us. We saw Charlie Voucher on his way out and I called him over, introducing him to Mrs. Pym. She told him about the ring, describing it better than I had. Charlie indicted it as a fake instantly. I don't know how he knew ; I think it was something to do with the feel of the buffalo. It wasn't sharp or something, which made him dismiss it as a dollar imitation, probably from Tientsin, where the tourists were even bigger suckers than in Shanghai.

Mrs. Pym looked complacent after Charlie had gone.

'Coincidence, Larry ? '

'No, ma'am.' I chewed a piece of carraway-seed roll, looking back from the mixed crowd at the tables. 'No, I'll swear it isn't. There was a bit of black on the buffalo's muzzle. I remember it, and it's on the one you found in Toby's.'

'That's too bad for Toby if he was the man who came to see you.'

'Don't you think he was?'

'You said—least, you gave me the indication he was big.'

'Now, take it easy, ma'am! I couldn't see much of him, not in that light. He had on a Chinese gown, a black one. It gave me the impression of size; maybe it was only an impression.'

'That's too bad for Toby, then. Where did he get a thousand dollars—he's always broke, isn't he?'

'Well, he claims so.' I wriggled uneasily. 'You're making it like I want to trap him.'

'Go and jump in the creek; for a reporter you're too damn sensitive. C'm on, finish your mush and we'll get on.'

We stayed for coffee, just the same, then went into the sunshine, boarding the Bugatti. As we passed the Ritz-Carlton we saw sign-painters were busy blanking off Barbadoro's name from the permanent announcement boards where it said 'Personal Direction by.' There was one board, on the other side, finished. I nudged Mrs. Pym.

'See that, ma'am. They writing up "Enrico Santonelli." He's the new boss.'

'Who's he?'

'Rico? Nice little guy. Did all the real work. I'm glad to see the right guy getting his reward for a change.'

'Shanghai must be getting soft; it doesn't usually happen.' She gestured to an apartment block. 'Remember that? Where we went to see Nadia Sherbina, first singer in the cyanide chorus.' She stared at me, ignoring the crowded road. 'Gosh! And I thought it was twice as long since it happened.'

'Things move pretty fast here, ma'am.'

'Pym jogging Destiny's elbow, eh?' She gave me a leer, and headed for the kerb where a tinny sign announced it was fifty yards to the Yip Kee Garage.

It was a crowded place at the end of an alley, the usual chaotic Chinese garage, a combination of efficiency, muddle, and dirt. Somehow those places got things done, though now and again they might leave out a magneto or so when they repaired your car, but we Shanghailanders took it as it came.

There was an air of reasonably orderly bustle. The premises went back for quite a way, and real work was going on. We found the reason in a cramped little office, a big, red-faced, moustached man with massive arms.

Mrs. Pym seemed to like him because she spoke to him kindly.

'Mrs. Pym? I know your name well, ma'am. Mine's Holloway, Sam Holloway, from Bradford.'

'I thought this place was better than most. You work for Chinese owners?'

Holloway grinned.

'Ay, I'm a real Chinese from Yorkshire.' He grinned again. 'When folks see the name they think we're just a lot of ignorant heathens who'll do the work for next to nothing. We don't, and I see to it my shroff collects.'

'Fine.' Mrs. Pym almost beamed at him; it was just the sort of thing that appealed to her unreliable sense of humour. 'Holloway, have you got a yellow Renault?'

'The old hire car? Certainly. Want it?'

'No. We want to know who's used it recently.'

'It was as recent as yesterday afternoon——' He stared at her. 'Something oop, ma'am?'

Mrs. Pym's self-control was excellent.

'Maybe there is. Know the hirer?'

'Certainly, a native. Peculiar chap. Pays cash; doesn't like saying much. Dirty work, I wouldn't wonder. Want me to get him for you?'

'Can you?'

'My Number One knows where he hangs out. Just a

moment.' He put his head out of the little office and yelled, ' Fang—hey, Fang, come here a tick.'

A smiling little Chinese, in grease-soiled jeans, came in, carrying a big wrench in one oily hand.

' You wanchee, Mist' 'Olloway ? '

' That lad who hires the yellow Renault. You know where he hangs out, don't you ? '

' Yellow Renault ? Oh, yes, my savee. He catchee car lots times.'

' *That*'s him. You go and tell him I want to see him here, will you—no, better tell him . . . ? ' He raised his eyebrows at Mrs. Pym.

' The first one will do, thanks.'

' You tell this chap I want him, then.'

' Can do.' Fang nodded brightly, going to the door. ' My catchee Mr. 'Veh chop-chop ; my pay him this side.'

The silence, as he left, was so sulphurous that Holloway's eyebrows went up again in question.

' Did he do something wrong, ma'am ? '

Mrs. Pym's swallow was visible ; I sympathized with her.

' Did he say " Mr. 'Veh " ? '

' He did. That's the name the chap always uses. . . .' Poor Holloway's words trailed away. I didn't blame him. Mrs. Pym's eyes were ice-coated—I could just imagine her thinking how the whole city was being turned upside down for this darned Mr. 'Veh and she got him by just walking in a garage and asking.

I sat there, staring at the door, wondering what the blazing Harry was going to walk through it. Little cold shivers were running up and down the back of my neck and I think I had an attack of goose-pimples. Fascinated by Mrs. Pym's rigid gaze in the same direction, Holloway watched as well. I don't believe I breathed from then on.

CHAPTER XVI

THE MAN WHO WASN'T THERE

SMALL, unimportant sounds grew in dimension during the wait. A lathe whirred, and somewhere a Chinese voice was singing monotonously, the unconscious sound made by a man absorbed in some difficult mechanical task. I could hear Sam Holloway breathing—every third second he made a minor snuffle, as if he suffered from catarrh. Traffic rolled on Bubbling Well Road. Far away, above our heads, a gramophone was playing a slightly cracked record; I don't remember the tune—it irritated my taut nerves nearly beyond bearing.

Then it came, the busy shuffle of shoes, followed by a solid, clumping step. Holloway's eyes nearly fell out of his head when the Luger appeared in Mrs. Pym's hand and slid to her side, ready but hidden.

Ten thousand stretched violin strings in my head were twanging, I am sure of it. A trickle of perspiration ran down my nose; my uniform jacket became so tight under my arms that I felt as if I had stopped breathing. If anybody had touched me then, I should have jumped up, screaming like a girl.

Mrs. Pym's steady eyes watched the doorway. Her strong chin was set and she looked as if she had no lips at all. It was the first time I had ever seen her like that, with an eagle's watchfulness and poised, relentless, as the hammer of doom. Madly it struck me as being silly, for Mr. 'Veh might be a chance name; it might be anything; after all our efforts, it just *could not* happen that he, of all people in the Settlement, was going to walk in, just like that.

We heard little Fang's voice, politely requesting the visitor to step in. The doorway was filled with a huge, pock-marked Chinese in an elegant blue uniform, his cap politely carried under his arm, revealing his short shaven black hair.

Under my breath I whispered : ' The doorman at Nadia Sherbina's place ! '

Holloway, either to tag him or out of sheer reaction, said : ' Come in, Mr. 'Veh. . . .'

Mrs. Pym came to her feet, for there was no mistaking the hatred and anger in the doorman's brown eyes.

' 'Veh, I want you.'

He snapped something unprintable, saw the gun and threw himself back and sideways, through the door, bowling over poor Fang, at his heels. It was well done, too, without any betraying expression or unconscious look, a man who had been in tight corners before and whose reflexes were lightning quick.

Mrs. Pym was through the doorway and over the recumbent Fang while I was still getting to my feet. We followed her, Holloway and I, sticking in the doorway when we reached it together.

We broke free, half grinning, and into the garage. Mrs. Pym was streaking along between the wall and a row of cars, towards the rear. Beyond her, dodging like a scalded rabbit, went the doorman.

One of the native workmen at a bench saw him coming, squared up with a screwdriver, and went over backwards under a ramming fist which showed our man, so rare in China, knew what fists are for.

In vernacular I heard her shout to him to stop. He just speeded up, dropped round a half-dismantled Hudson when the Luger banged—every man in the shop went straight to earth—and he must have gone on his hands and knees to the back gate. I saw it burst open, a flash of blue, and he was gone.

The whole crowd of us were on Mrs. Pym's heels after that, pounding into the rear alley, fanning out excitedly when we could not see the quarry.

She stopped dead for perhaps three seconds, trying to get inside the doorman's psychology to judge his most likely direction. Off she went again, for a small doorway leading to the back yard of an apartment block.

I was right behind her. She got to the back door of the block and, inside, we could hear feet pounding on stone stairs. The chase went on and up, to the first floor, the second, the third, and through an open doorway to the roof. My heart was splitting wide open with effort, I swear it, but Mrs. Pym was absolutely on her toes. It struck me, like those things do, keeping up physical fitness paid off at such times and I saw why she was so rigid about it.

The roof was a vast expanse, dotted with chimney-stacks, broken up by intervening three-foot walls, and, worse still, connected with three other apartment blocks.

Up there the sun was warm, or it seemed warm, and there was a scuttering wind raising the fine dust of the asphalt. There was no sign of the man in blue.

He couldn't resist a target like us; pursued men never can. There was a zip and a crack from ahead of us. I nearly fell flat on my back. It felt as though somebody had hit my ear with a hard fist.

My searching hand came in front of me, bloodied. Mrs. Pym pushed me down, taking a quick glance as she followed me.

'Top of your ear, son. You won't die.' Off she went, towards the nearest wall, crouching there, waiting.

I lay on my stomach, dabbing my ear with a handkerchief, my eyes on that tweed-suited figure, the Luger poised. It came again, a second shot as a try-out. Almost as soon as I heard the crack the Luger answered. After that another wait.

Holloway appeared from a roof door on the far side of the place where the two shots had come from, his moustached face earnest and a tyre-lever in one large hand.

'Holloway! Run! He's got a gun, you *fool*!' I simply could not stop the warning. I saw a blue arm and part of a shoulder appear. I held my breath. Holloway was going to get his that very moment.

The Luger was first. Mrs. Pym came to her feet and fired in the same motion, the neatest, prettiest, most accurate shot I have ever seen in my life. The blue shoulder remained where it was, a patch of scarlet appeared and something metallic clattered on the roof. Holloway, breaking from his frozen stance, went leaping forward with the wrench, stopping at Mrs. Pym's strident :

' Don't kill him, man, leave him alone ! '

We both tore on our way. I know I was holding my bleeding ear with one hand and the other was tearing at the clasp of my mounted sharpshooter's ribbon. I had a silly desire to give it to the better shot.

The big doorman was on his knees, gripping his shoulder, moaning with pain. He tried to get his fallen gun when we appeared and had it kicked out of reach by one of Mrs. Pym's neat brogues. She jerked him to his feet, her eyes loving as slashing razor blades.

' Got you, my friend. You're coming downtown.'

' The hell I am ! ' He glared back.

' So you speak real English, eh ? ' She pushed him forward. ' On your way, lunkhead.' She thanked Holloway as she passed him, pushing the doorman in the back with the muzzle of the Luger. The Bugatti was left where it was and little Fang, in the excited crowd waiting in the back alley, was sent to fetch a car.

It was perhaps an ironic little footnote that we made for the Central Police Station in the yellow Renault. At Mrs. Pym's orders the Yip Kee Garage had already telephoned for Dr. Fedor to come running. He was in Laystall's office when we all trooped in.

The doorman's shoulder was dealt with, the slug extracted, and a dressing applied, then the big man was thrust in a chair while Fedor taped up my stinging ear. At last it was done.

Mrs. Pym told the baffled Laystall all that had happened, then switched to the doorman.

' Now you're going to talk.'

' Me ? Go climb a tree.' The man's face was evil and

his English, of all things, might have been learned on any American Main Street. 'I'll sue you——'

'Shut up! Super, every feminine twitch in my well-known woman's intuition tells me this is our bogeyman. Can I have him alone with Larry for ten minutes?'

In answer to Laystall's shocked: 'What are you going to do?' she whispered. He made an expression of distaste and walked out, Fedor following him.

She stood with hands on her hips.

'So you're not going to talk?'

'My, that's bright of you. How did you guess?'

'Cut out the funny stuff. Larry, do as I say or you can get out.' She swung round on me, giving me a tiny wink. 'Are you game?'

'Sure. My ear hurts.'

'Fine. Take the Luger and keep him covered. Shoot if he moves.'

I did as I was told, watching, and the porter watched her as well, suddenly uneasy.

She opened Fedor's little black bag, groped in it and pulled out a small towel. This was laid on Laystall's desk, then decorated with a scalpel, a steel probe, something that looked like long-nosed pliers, and a tiny saw. She delved some more and brought out a needle, a reel of catgut, a box of ampoules and another box containing a hypodermic.

This last was carefully assembled, filled from one of the ampoules—slowly and well in the doorman's eyes—and she advanced on him, the needle ready.

'This is where you get it, my friend.'

He looked scared to death for the first time.

'Take it easy. What's the big idea?'

'Oh, I'm not going to hurt you. This is a narcotic '—it nearly made me giggle because the box was labelled *Mercury ʒi*—' and you're going to sleep.'

'I don't wanna go to sleep.'

'How the hell do I cut off that arm while you're awake?'

'*What's that?*' His eyes went wide.

'Sure, you won't talk so you're going to feel it, later. Besides,' she added in a reasonable voice that did not fit in with her expression, ' you won't miss an arm and we can stick the thing in our central heating furnace while you're under the dope.'

The doorman's face was utterly petrified. I think he was tough enough even to losing an arm; he was also Chinese, whatever else had been grafted on him. You find me a Chinese who will face the idea of going to his grave with an incomplete body and you rate a medal. I've known a native carry his appendix in a spirit bottle for the rest of his days, rather than be buried without it and suffer hades on the other side.

That hypodermic needle was brought nearer, a patch on the man's arm rubbed with a piece of spirit-soaked cotton. He stared down in a curiously numbed fashion, as if it just couldn't happen to him. There was a faint red patch on Mrs. Pym's nearest cheek; I knew she was playing this one just as far as it would go, wondering who was going to quit first. That always has been her art, psychological trickery with physical torture to back it up; to my knowledge she's never actually had to carry out a threat yet.

Nor did it happen this time. The needle was on his skin when the doorman let out a hoot like a ship's siren and tore his arm away.

'No! *No!*' He gaped at the little saw. 'NO! I'll talk!'

She didn't move away, just calling out: ' Come in ' and remaining there. Laystall shot in with his secretary at his heels. He gaped, swallowed, and sat down, the secretary near him, his notebook open.

The doorman began to baulk, flinched from the moving needle with a spasmodic jerk; the words tumbled out, so fast I never thought that even shorthand would keep up with them.

It was a terrific tale. He was Mr. 'Veh all right, and he gave us more than I had ever expected, a newspaperman's golden dream come true. Every time he looked like quitting the needle hovered, and off he went again. Laystall's kind old face was a literal study in incredulous disbelief that this was happening, here in his tidy, law-abiding police station.

'Veh talked as a Chinese really can talk when the confessional bug bites ; I never took a note because it wouldn't have been wise. My memory, luckily enough, was good, so good, in fact, that I rather prided myself on never carrying a notebook.

That doorman told us he was thirty-four years old, that his name was Johnny Tee—I recalled it, the owner of the house where Irina had been held—and that his folks had been Tsingtao people, where he was born. The Germans had been ruling there then, and the Tees had become Methodist converts, probably because they hated Lutherism.

Johnny wanted the white barbarians thrown out, knowing he couldn't do much as a mere Chinese. So he shipped out as a seaman, lived all over the white man's world and ended, of all places, in Russia just after the Bolshevists had tossed out the Moderates.

He took to the new creed like a Malayan to liquor. The murder-drunk prophets of the new earth crammed him full of asinine theories. He met Lenin during his convalescence after the attempted assassination, and was in on the birth of the Communist International in 1919. He even gave a bit of advice on the initial blueprints of the New Economic Policy ; more than that, he knew *Materialism and Empirio-Criticism* like a good Christian knows his Bible. Marx, who would have spat in the eye of the Soviets, was Johnny Tee's god. When he drifted back to Shanghai he had amassed quite a pile of money, and almost instantly fell in with Albert Fong, another man with money, an intellectual who adored Communism but wasn't sure how to get into it.

Tee saw to that. He dug back and found the Jovial Hearts and picked on the Hop-Ley Dancers as a working title, founding a loose society with him as the boss and

Fong as the right-hand man, heading a bunch making quite a nucleus in the turmoil of China.

It was Tee's idea that he should work as a doorman. It gave him a focal point where anybody could approach him without comment, where he could come and go as he wished, and, which was more, the apartment block belonged to Fong and himself.

China was being chopped up by the militarists, the war-lords, and the Chinese Republic didn't amount to a damn. I think he saw himself as the coming *tuchun* of the whole works; he certainly had the Russians behind him, and all the help the Bolshevists could give him. The idea of four hundred million Chinese on their side was sending Lenin and his crowd crazy with excitement. Tee had his eyes, too, on the Kuomintang, a ready-made native revolutionary party.

However, when he talked to us he was mainly on his own. I think he might have led a real revolt if the dirty business of the Kiaochow restoration had already happened, instead of being a few weeks away, that being when the lords of Versailles kicked China in the face in handing back its own territory and making it pay for it, including even the Chinese-built railway—for what it is worth, a great deal of China's modern hatred for us stems from that graceless deal.

Johnny Tee cast his net wide and pulled in a lot of people, fools, grabbers, and half-comprehending admirers of Russia and what it was doing. Nadia Sherbina was an easy mark, a useful girl who, like all the Russians, was crazily patriotic even to enduring the idea of the Bolshevists *because* they were Russian. But Tee was working silently; he wasn't ready for publicity by a long way. Clever, shrewd, a born opportunist, he wanted to stay in the dark till whatever plans he had might mature.

He and Fong, the kingpins, nearly passed out when they learned of the paper Mrs. Pym found in Nadia Sherbina's apartment. No doubt, he suggested, she had written it down idly and tried translating the name into Russian, but it should never have been left around. In a panic he tackled Guido Barbadoro, in the game I thought and still do, for what he could get out of it. Barbadoro was a Royalist, but he wanted to make money and get home to Italy—Tee's crowd of visionaries obviously suggested pickings to him, and he got on the wagon.

Barbadoro, Johnny Tee told us, advised caution and a policy of wait and see. The message I got at the *News* office, telling me to keep away from the Hop-Ley Dancers, was his idea, to try and choke off newspaper publicity. Barbadoro even gave a private tip to Toby Garnett, whom he naturally knew well, asking him to see that I got told I was ' bucking the wrong crowd.'

Irina Roberti was raked in next. Poor kid, she had mentioned her two brothers. What she didn't tell me was that they were wanted by the Bolshevists and Johnny Tee had seen to it they were shipped to Vladivostok, where they were in a prison camp. He hauled in Irina as useful to him, and put her under Fong's orders. Fong kept her on a string, by which he held the fate of her brothers over her head. If she did as she was told they would eventually come back ; if not, his pals at Vladivostok would see they died quickly.

When it was decided to try and bribe me off, naturally Irina was the decoy to the godown she owned, which Fong used as a meeting-place. Mrs. Pym busted that end of it, and Irina was rushed to Johnny Tee's house until he decided what he would do about her. Then Barbadoro, who had all the natural Italian passion for cloak-and-dagger work, was quite prepared to scare the daylights out of me by that shot in Foochow Road. It wasn't meant to kill, and Barbadoro went because he was the only one who could shoot well—Tee said he paid over a thousand dollars for the business, but was frightened out of his wits when Barbadoro was run down and killed. The moment the news came he sent a man out to fire Barbadoro's house since he was scared the old boy might have records or diaries which, in his innocence, he regarded as the sort of thing all Europeans kept faithfully—something he had learned in his days in the States, where keeping diaries was and is something of a major industry.

Every single thing suddenly started going wrong for Johnny Tee. He had his society well in hand ; it was well known via the grapevine to a great many Chinese, and it had got a name for terror. Then Johnny's last two moves went wrong as well : he hired the yellow Renault to visit the godown to see that Fong had left nothing around, showing the curious blind spot so typical of the Chinese in casually letting the Yip Kee Garage know him as ' Mr. 'Veh.' When you know China that sort of thing isn't odd : they will plot like geniuses and nobody will know a thing, but some small and casual oversight will cause the business to stick out like a split nose. I could see Mrs. Pym blessing that native fault when she heard of it.

Tee never expected a cop would be at the godown, so naturally he sheered off, barely noticing poor old Lew Schlesinger on his motor-cycle.

I was the cause of all the trouble. If I hadn't gone to Nadia's, the Hop-Ley Dancers would never have got into the public eye. Tee tried to end it by hiring the Little White Rabbits to get me, and that, like all the rest, went wrong. If Lenin had run up against so many slips, I dare say he would have blown his mouth just as Tee did to us.

' Why,' Mrs. Pym demanded at that stage, ' have you been forcing things like this ? If you'd kept quiet about that bit of paper in Nadia Sherbina's, you could have been getting along nicely.'

Then it came out. All his spadework done and his society poised for the take-off in some direction, Johnny Tee was suddenly electrified by the advent of Dr. Wu Hsiung.

It was probably coincidence, but the Chinese themselves moved into Shanghai to start something in the Communist line. Wu Hsiung contacted Johnny Tee almost at once when he arrived ; big people had started to organize and

Johnny and his Dancers could come in if they got out of
the limelight. He passionately wanted to be in on this
new stunt ; and at five o'clock on the afternoon Mrs. Pym
had caught him, he was due to meet Dr. Wu Hsiung and
be taken to the big group that was getting down to brass
tacks. Then Johnny walked bang into Mrs. Pym's arms,
got shot himself, and she threatened to torture him. With
typical Chinese fatalism he gave up. All his failures since
I and my jinx popped out had culminated in his capture.
He shot us the works because he had lost heart, to say
nothing of 'face.' When a Chinese decides to throw in
his hand, he sinks plumb to the bottom.

'Um?' Mrs. Pym studied him. 'Where are you
meeting Wu Hsiung and his crowd?'

'Gosh, he's only introducing me.' Tee was horrified.
'It isn't his crowd ; he just the corner-boy. He talks big,
but he's only a front. They're lining up in the Chok Li
Hotel at five to-night, where I was going, to be looked over,
I guess, and given an in. From then on I figured I could
get control.'

'Who are you meeting ; do you know?'

'Oh, sure. I've heard about him, a little bookish guy,
peasant born,' Tee, the son of respectable parents, couldn't
hide a sniff of contempt, 'but an out-and-out Marxist.
He's busy organizing a Communist party right here in the
city, came here to do it, him and eleven other characters.
Name of Mao Tse-tung.'*

'Mao?' Mrs. Pym's eyes narrowed. 'I've heard that
name.' She glanced at Laystall, who nodded. 'I don't
care if he's the Czar of Russia, he's not going to plot
Communism here in the Settlement limits. Okay, Tee,
I'll deal with him.'

Without authority I voiced the main question, a bit
dramatically, but I was a well-brought-up kid.

'Johnny, I'm sorry I horned in, but you see how it is,

* The historically-minded will find Mao, present Communist boss
of China, was indeed in Shanghai then, doing just what Johnny Tee
said.

and it's not for me to pass comment. But you were scared about that arm business, so I figured you're a good Chinese. Do you swear on your ancestors' graves and your heavenly future you didn't kill Nadia Sherbina, Leslie Ho, Leslie Chow, and attempt to murder Nathan Schyler—in short, that you're not the Cyanide Man? I'm asking because you haven't touched on one single item of what I want to hear.'

Mrs. Pym was all set to stop me when I started to speak. She left it because she wanted to hear, too.

'The hell with that!' Johnny Tee glared at me. 'I'll swear on the hand of Lenin that I held, and the New China—I've no god-damned time for that ancient crap. Me, the Cyanide Man? Are you stark crazy? How the heck do you think I work, then? I've no time for that sort of nonsense.'

Mrs. Pym went at him, but at the end of fifteen minutes we were all prepared to go blind on the fact Tee certainly had nothing to do with the Cyanide Man. It didn't ring true in his case; it wasn't good sense, and, in the matter of the visit to my room, he offered to produce an alibi, four visitors who were talking to him in the doorway of the apartment block.

'And we can check it back and find it right,' Mrs. Pym said when Kelly had come in and taken Tee to the cells. 'The blazes with it—look at the time!'

I was invited and twenty minutes later we started out: Mrs. Pym, Laystall, Kelly, and, behind us, five cars filled with white, native, and Sikh police. We were headed for the Chok Li Hotel in Boone Road.

Mrs. Pym showed her efficiency the way she arranged the whole thing. The Chok Li Hotel was easy to cover, and cover it she did, so that a bug couldn't have crept out unseen. Of course half the district turned up to see it, and was held back.

I was behind her when she marched into the palm-and-lithograph-decorated foyer of that typical Chinese hotel. The clerk was frightened out of his wits. When he heard we wanted a group of men in one of his rooms, he gave the number and vanished under the counter.

I'll always remember that procession. Mrs. Pym heading up the brown-carpeted stairs, the Luger cocked. Me behind her, then Laystall and Kelly, both with guns. It was just a routine job to me, rounding up a bunch of conspirators. I was so well fed with dramatics that this was small stuff.

The room we wanted was right at the head of the stairs. Mrs. Pym didn't even knock, jerking round the handle and kicking open the door with one foot.

It was a big room, neat for a Chinese hotel and well furnished. There were newspapers, trays of cigarette butts, and an air of recent occupation. But there wasn't a soul there, only a wide-open window leading to a fire-escape.

Mrs. Pym sniffed, probing round.

'Grapevine warned them, or maybe Johnny Tee's capture frightened them away. It doesn't matter, I suppose. We'll throw out a drag-net, but probably the bunch and Wu Hsiung, for that matter, are legging it into Chinese territory. But I've heard of that Mao. Maybe he'll make a better job of it than the Hop-Ley Dancers.' Her grunt was loud. 'He couldn't make a worse hash of it, anyway. Let's get back. There's still the little matter of the Cyanide Man on our books.'

When I get around to thinking about it these days, I often wonder what the history of China might have been if Mrs. Pym had caught up with Mao Tse-tung and his eleven men. Like everything else, it would probably have been mundane ; he would have been fined and shoved out of the Settlement. But *if* he had been there and drawn a gun. I can just see that Luger blasting out a new future for China.

CHAPTER XVII

THE FRONT PAGE

In Laystall's office Mrs. Pym, the Superintendent, and I chewed the rag, chiefly, I think, because we were all conscious of a big let-down.

'What do we arrange about Tee?' Laystall, looking tired, leaned back in his chair. 'He hasn't been charged yet.'

'Let the police solicitor work it out.' Mrs. Pym, by the window, half turned to answer.

'What if he mentions your somewhat—ah—unorthodox method of extracting the confession?'

'Huh? Let him do it. If the magistrate gets argumentative, I can always say it was shadow-boxing and what does he want, the letter of the law or commies running loose all over the Settlement? That'll stop him. Magistrates are property owners and they hate commies worse than anything I know. Thing is, we're still stuck with the Cyanide Man.'

'You sound disturbed, ma'am. You regarded Tee and this poisoner as one and the same?'

'I took it for granted. It's a good lesson for me. We might get a lead if we could only get hands on Toby Garnett.'

'You know, I can't see why Toby should be mixed up in this.'

Mrs. Pym jerked right round at my remark.

'I can, two hundred million reasons.'

'But Toby's a nice little fellow——'

'Sure, Larry,' she named a string of poisoners, 'and so were they all nice little fellows. All they killed for was small potatoes. Garnett must've known he was heir from the beginning.'

'Then why *all* the murders?'

'Look, son, suppose you go and bowl your hoop. The discussion's full of holes and I'm tired of it. Don't you work on a newspaper?'

'Yes, ma'am.'

'Go and earn your pay'—her glance was friendly—'and tell Coager I think you're quite a boy.'

'Why, th——'

'Now!'

'Sorry, ma'am.' I smiled at Laystall, who smiled back. 'Maybe I'd better do some work before I'm hauled out to duty again. What can I print?'

'Nothing barred, is it, Superintendent?' She accepted Laystall's nod as consent, waving to me. 'Go on, spread me all over the front page.' She paused as Kelly came in, carrying something which he gave to her. 'Who took these?'

'Our photographer, ma'am. Since it was a raid and he was after thinking he would be needed, he exposed two plates just for exercise. Good, would you say?'

'Ver-ee nice.' She pushed one sheet to me, a full-plate photograph. It was good work, the frontage of the Chok Li Hotel, the police at their stations, and a first-class amount of detail showing Mrs. Pym striding in, Laystall, Kelly and I at her heels. We all looked on our toes, an action picture Lanny would go crazy about.

'Can I have this? It'll make the front page.'

She nodded.

'Told you I like publicity, didn't I? Now beat it, Larry. I'm in a mood and I'm liable to throw things at anyone handy. You're not official, so you'll do, if you're still here in five minutes.'

I was tempted to stick around. In the end I said goodbye and headed for the *News* building. Lanny Coager beamed on me as if I were his favourite child, putting power into the beam when I stuck the print on his desk.

'For pity's sake, you've done it again? This the raid?'

'You've heard about it?'

'This is a newspaper, in case you don't know. Pull up a chair and spill it.'

I told the story, down to its last detail.

'Like it?'

'*Swell!* Boy, we make another front page, bigger than ever! Can we print everything?'

'Mrs. Pym said so.'

'So Johnny Tee's the nigger in the woodpile? You know, I had an idea he was—or, I should say, that the boss of the Hop-Ley Dancers would turn out to be the Cyanide Man. Think there's a connection he hasn't spilled, or have they been running in parallel, unawares?'

'In parallel, for a guess.'

'Well, this time the Hop-Ley business is the news.' He crouched over a sheet of copy-paper, pencil in hand, with which he dug at his beard. His eyes lightened and he printed a rapid line in caps: MRS. PYM SMASHES GIANT RED PLOT. 'Like it, Larry?'

'*She* will.' It looked good to me, especially the use of 'Red' which was not really a commonplace word then. 'Isn't that building it a bit on the big side?'

'We'll recap. I've played down the Hop-Ley Dancers; now I can drag in the whole story, everything, and tag the lot on to-day's news. Being a natural culmination, it carries the early stuff, particularly that godown business, and, told that way, it's a giant plot right enough. It's mainly re-write. Mind if I write it myself?'

'Hell, you're the boss.'

'Thanks, Larry. The way I've got it is a scarehead across, drop in the cut underneath, then box three columns and run the lead to give the raid news and names. I'll get down to Johnny Tee's story and back to the earlier stuff. That way it'll read strongly, carry no byline and keep yours attached to the Cyanide Man.'

'Who hasn't done anything more.'

'Bless him. I don't want him to do anything till to-morrow, or he'll bust my front page. He won't, anyway.'

'Says who?'

'Me.' Lanny winked at me. 'Kid, when you've been in this racket a long time you get a feeling with a running case when it's climbing or when it's dropping. Right now I think the Cyanide Man's holding his hand, for the moment.'

'Well, if you say so. What shall I do?'

'Stick around. I'll use your spiked stuff and build with it. Like to watch? It's a type of story you don't often see in this business; it needs fitting together like precision tooling. You'll learn a few things.'

'I'll be glad to, Lanny.'

'Fine. By the way, Eddie Kafeldt was in an hour ago.'

'That's big of him.' I couldn't help grinning at Lanny's expression. Kafeldt was the editor of the *Daily News*, and its owner. He had a mania for Chinese pottery and we never saw him around the office more than once a year. His name was on the house plank heading our editorial page, but in effect he sat back and left everything to Lanny Coager.

'He's off some place after some Ming stuff he's heard about. He patted my head and was sorry to hear Laidler isn't coming back, and signed a cheque for him.'

'Why, what's happened?'

'This dysentry. Laidler's doc says he's to go back home to California and keep out of China. It doesn't suit him, so Eddie gave him a nice cheque; he said he could afford it after he'd spent thirty minutes with the counting-house and seen our sales over this Cyanide Man business.'

'Poor old Laidler. He's a good man.'

'Eh, sure.' Lanny's expression was baffling. 'Eddie also signed a cheque for two-fifty for you.'

'But I'm not owed any two dollars fifty——'

'Two *hundred* and fifty, you poor lunk. Bonus. Oh, yeah, I almost forgot, you take Laidler's desk, his rate of pay, byline, and you get a year's contract to go with it.'

It shook me so much I could think of only one thing— my gesture when I walked into the Californian-Oriental Bank and slapped that cheque on the manager's desk. It was such a beautiful vision I almost forgot to be civil.

'Lanny, that's the nicest thing——'

'Forget it, kid. You've earned it. What were you thinking of when I told you that, your overdraft?'

'How did you guess it?'

'I know one hell of a lot more than you think I do.' He cocked an ear, listening. In the basement the presses were running the early pages, already comped; from the rest of the building you could hear noises, voices, typewriters, the smooth, enchanting sound of a newspaper working towards its daily re-birth. Lanny nodded; that listening habit was his way of checking that the tempo of the place showed all was as it should be. 'Going to schedule. Grab a chair over here, and we'll get to work.'

It was fascinating watching the way it was done. With his portable in front of him, a cigarette in one corner of his mouth—where his red moustache and beard were nicotine yellow—and a scad of notes beside him, Lanny began to build his front page.

As a piece of journalism it was terrific. It eventually went right round the world and gave Mrs. Pym an international name, which was to take her to New Scotland Yard and an assistant commissionership. Normally it might have been ignored, Lanny's revelations, as troubles in Shanghai's backyard; but the United States newspapers picked up the story in a big way, pouncing on this new pulverizer of 'radicals and reds,' for, over there, they were still all worked up about Bart Vanzetti, the Tolstoyan liberal, and little Nick Sacco, the shoemaker, whose execution years later is something which makes me glad I wasn't born in Massachusetts.

But they were big news then, and the *News*' front page couldn't have happened at a better time; when the reverberations reached back to Shanghai weeks later Mrs. Pym was just about elevated to queen of the city.

When it had gone to the composing room, Lanny said he felt good.

'I certainly learned something. Mrs. Pym'll be glad to get you off any odd murder you may've overlooked, when she reads that.'

'Glad you like it. Maybe I'll take her up on it one of these days.' Lanny grinned at me and lit another cigarette. 'What's the next move?'

'I could eat, maybe, and then go and see Schyler. He might feel like talking?'

'Give him till to-morrow. You've done enough for the day. Beat it home after you've eaten. I'll call you if I want you. Don't forget your kit; you left it here this morning.'

After five minutes in the newsroom, where I took a certain amount of ribbing, I went over to my desk and gathered my razor and clothes together. I felt so pleased with myself that I felt somebody ought to share the news.

One of the two 'phone booths at the end of the room was vacant, the one bearing a big label: LOCAL CALLS. IF IT ISN'T 'NEWS' BUSINESS, KEEP THE HELL OUT OF HERE. My conscience accepted the suggestion that telling Mrs. Pym about my promotion was *News* business.

Kelly took the call. She'd gone back to her place in Bubbling Well Road, in something of a mood. It seemed the whole case from the beginning had been thoroughly chewed over after I left them.

Everything was re-examined and a few things came up I hadn't heard about. There was the routine on Nadia Sherbina; the door-to-door detectives, doing the chores Mrs. Pym wouldn't touch with a pole, had disinterred nothing we didn't know. All her letters had been read, and her diary. Most and probably all the people who ever knew her had been checked, without a single lead. Barbadoro had undergone the same treatment, his office being searched inside and out; it was a nil result, so was the check on Leslie Chow and Leslie Ho. Even Jacob Laffin's house had not yielded a thing, and since he had no friends or acquaintances of importance, the entire process of routine had failed to show results. As Kelly told me, whatever the Cyanide Man was doing and whoever he was, he came out of nowhere. There was no visible or possible connection with the dead people that tied to him in any way.

Usually, in murder cases, precise and patient searching turns up something, a connection, two people seen often together, a note, a letter, or even a witness who knows something—more cases are solved by that sort of enquiry than you would imagine, but here were five dead people whose lives didn't offer one small and remote lead. Either the killer was diabolically brilliant in cleaning up traces, or he had started out long ago with the plan of killing and had seen to it that nothing could ever be checked back. Motive, reason, suggestion, indication—just nothing had turned up. It was death out of nowhere, for no reason, that vanished from sight when the job was done. It beat the Central Police Station brains trust and it certainly beat me.

I went back to pick up my things from the desk, wondering how this case without a clue was going to be solved. I was so absorbed in it I had forgotten to tell Mike Kelly about my promotion, but I think he was gloomy himself. He hadn't even the joy of nabbing Dr. Wu Hsiung to his credit. He had gone personally to the Changs' house and found the doctor had high-tailed it out of the Settlement, probably with the Chok Li Hotel crowd; Paul Chang had been as red-faced as a Chinese could be, telling Kelly readily that the doctor had come to him with introductions from high-placed friends in Peking—that he had been entertaining a Red plotter shook poor old Paul so that, for weeks, I never saw him around the night spots. As Kelly said, the inside dope had naturally been passed to the government of the Republic, which was about as useful as writing on a scrap of paper and floating it down the Whangpoo.

I went to Böök's for some dinner, then felt I didn't want to go home at all. The Ritz-Carlton was nearest; I headed there to see how Rico Santonelli was making out in his new job.

Daisy Ting took my bundle, told me I looked 'handsome' in my uniform—it was worth the dollar I gave her—and went into the bar. The usual crowd was there, and poor old Wesley Ho behind the mahogany, smiling away as if he hadn't just lost his brother. I had a whisky sour just to keep him company and went down the steps to the reception area; Rico Santonelli was there with, it seemed, inches on his stature. He practically kissed me, gave me the best table on the floor, and the best whisky in the house. Come to think of it, I *had* shot his chief to death, but I don't suppose Rico saw it that way. He had climbed a big step and, in his eyes, I was the one who had fixed it.

Quite a lot of people in the busy room nodded to me, even Mrs. Erp, at her usual table with her usual crowd. I was a notoriety. In Shanghai it didn't matter much what you'd done; the fact you'd done it and you were being talked about made you important. It made me feel pretty miserable, just the same.

Highlo' Harry was right on the beam, giving me a wave you could see all over the room. I nearly ran when the spot picked me out, just before the cabaret was due, and Highlo' came to the edge of his platform.

'Ladies and gentlemen, we have here to-night Larry Baker, ace reporter of the *Daily News*, the man whose work has been exciting every one of us. A little bird whispered to me that Larry's stepping into the shoes of Bernie Laidler as Bernie's going back home. Larry Baker, the crime reporter of the *News*, the man we'll all be watching. Give him a great big hand, folks!'

They did, some of them standing up to see me. I felt the biggest damn fool on earth and I didn't know whether to bow, make a speech, or shake clasped hands like a victorious pug. I smiled like a sick cow instead, pretending I was trying to pour out some whisky. Thank the Lord the band, anxious to get backstage for its five minutes break, tore into the Ritz-Carlton girls' song, leaving me in the blessed dimness.

The cabaret was as slick as ever, and got the usual hand. After that the patrons sat around during the brief interval. When the dancing was resumed I saw Lydia Tschenko, the girl who had taken Nadia Sherbina's place, threading through the dancers, accepting their congratulations. She seemed to be coming my way so I gave her a polite smile. She kept on coming till she was at my table, standing there, blonde and lovely, the sort of girl George Petty was to immortalize in the future in *Esquire*.

I remembered my manners and stood up.

'Feel like joining me, Miss Tschenko?'

Her smile was friendly when she had sat down.

'Lydia, and I'll call you Larry. Can I have some of that whisky?'

'Sure.' I looked round for a glass and there it was, with a bottle of champagne and Santonelli hovering over us like a dark-eyed Bacchus.

'Something else I can get you, sare?'

'No, thanks, Rico—unless Miss Tschenko wants to eat?' She shook her head. 'Thanks, Rico.' He bowed and vanished.

'Larry,' she considered me, her English excellent and her eyes bright, 'you didn't mind me joining you?'

'I was feeling pretty down.'

'I thought so. Highlo' embarrassed you?'

'Let's say, made me feel I hadn't got any clothes on.'

'Well, you have, and that uniform looks very nice. We Russian people like men in uniform.'

'I'm just a Sunday afternoon soldier.'

'You *did* try to save Irina, didn't you, though?'

'You know about it?'

'Everybody does. You're famous, Larry. Irina was rather a pet.'

'You knew her?'

'I'd met her.' She drank some whisky as if she didn't much care for it. 'There was a nasty little woman from your paper up here to-day during rehearsal, trying to get me to tell her about Irina.'

'Oh, Matsy Stein.'

'That was the woman. Of course, I didn't tell her anything. I can look terribly stupid when I want to.' Her look was anything but stupid. 'Irina used to share a room at the consulate with a girl I know.'

'So *that's* where she was!' I might have guessed it. The White Russians still had a consulate there, headed by a staunch old czarist who wouldn't have any truck with the new government, maintaining the consulate out of his own pocket because he felt that if he could hold on long enough, the Bolshevists would be thrown out and his consulate would be re-accredited. It was a good place to hide.

'Yes. I'm sorry she was killed; but I suppose it's liable to happen to any of us.' There it was, that gloomy old Russian fatalism. She snapped out of it and had another drink. 'I didn't come to talk to you about that. Will you come back to my place with me? I've got something to show you and I think you may be able to do something about it.'

'Glad to. When shall I come?'

'There's an hour and a half before the next show. If you dance me over to the pass door, I can get out of these clothes and we'll go to my flat.'

It was like dancing with nobody, she was so darned light on her feet and, for which I blessed her, she didn't use *L'Origan* but some perfume that was more subtle. Quite a few people saw us vanish; the raised eyebrows didn't improve my temper.

Backstage the Ritz-Carlton was well equipped. There was plenty of room and you could hear the chorus in their place chattering away like a lot of schoolgirls.

I waited while Lydia changed behind a screen, then we went out the back way and flagged a waiting cab. It was not very far to Mohawk Road where her apartment was the second up in a big new block.

It was a garish place, Russian as an ikon, it was also comfortable and even homey. She switched on the electric fire in the big lounge, found me a drink and went out of the room, coming back with a box and some wrappings.

'Have a look, Larry.' She sat on the chesterfield at my side.

The wrapping was just brown paper, bearing her name and address in block letters. Inside was a box of chocolates, a famous American brand, expensive and widely known. There was one chocloate, bitten through, both pieces being still there.

'I don't get it.'

'No? Somebody sent those to me; they were left with the doorman after tea. Naturally all he remembers is that the person was a native boy. I thought some admirer might have sent them, and tried one. I'm rather cautious about chocolates; I mean, I hate eating them till I know what's inside, so I always bite off the edge first, just to look.' She picked up the bitten chocolate. 'It's a fudge centre.'

'Yeah?'

'I just didn't fancy eating it because I've been reading your paper. I washed out my mouth at once and I've been brooding about that box until I saw you and decided you could tell me what to do. It's baffling, Larry—I mean, *why?*'

I knew what was coming but I picked up the chocolate and smelled it.

'Cyanide! Lydia, don't tell me the Cyanide Man——'

'Yes.' Her voice was sharp, strained. 'Who else could it be? But why *me*? I haven't done anything.'

'You poor kid. That's just the trouble; he never seems to pick on anybody for a reason.' I jumped up. 'Hang on, I'll call Mrs. Pym. This is her pigeon. Oh, hell, so he's back again?'

I remember, as I headed for the 'phone, thinking that Lanny was unlucky. The Cyanide Man was at it again, spoiling our nice front page.

CHAPTER XVIII

SUSPICION

Mrs. Pym's place was only a short distance away, on the other side of the Recreation Ground. Ten minutes after I had called her, she came marching in wearing a different tweed suit, a hound's-tooth pattern, and a positively lunatic hat over which Lydia Tschenko crowed, the moment she saw it.

'Thanks.' The grey-blue eyes almost smiled at the girl. 'Most people jeer at my hats: the idea is to put 'em in a good humour for what they're going to see just below the brim.' She grimaced. 'Those the chocolates?'

'Yes, Mrs. Pym.' Lydia went to her side and stayed there. 'Did I do wrong, telling Larry and not you?'

'You did the right thing, honey'—that endearment shook me—'and I'm glad to hear you have sense enough to check what you're eating before you swallow it.' She sniffed at the bitten chocolate. 'I think I can smell it, this time. Got any ideas?'

Lydia shook her blonde head. Her liking for Mrs. Pym was so obvious that I think she was about the first woman to get into her good books.

'I'm nobody,' she told us frankly. 'I was tried out at the Ritz-Carlton after I was taken from the Astor. I made a hit, I suppose. I haven't been that for long enough to make anyone want to kill me.'

'The Cyanide Man kills like an elephant with *musth*. There's no damn sense in what he does. No clue to the sender?'

'The door porter didn't notice a thing.'

'He wouldn't.' Mrs. Pym was toying with the wrapping

and the box, staring at them. Suddenly she swung round, studying Lydia. ' Tell me, you're White Russian ? '

' Oh, yes. I was born in Moscow.'

' You speak English very well ? '

' I had an English governess. My father took mother and me to London several times when I was small.'

' Are they living ? '

' My mother and father ? No.' She sat down, stricken with that melancholy I had noticed before when many of those girls were asked about their past lives. ' We went to prison, all of us. They were taken away and I never saw them again. I was sent with a lot of other people to the Maritime Provinces, to another prison. But I got away, with two older women. It was awful. We walked for nine hundred miles in winter. . . . Mrs. Pym, I'd rather not talk about it.'

' I can guess the rest. Lydia,' Mrs. Pym's voice was more gentle than I'd ever heard it, ' are you tough enough to take a big chance, to help me ? '

' Of course. You mean, it would help Nadia ? '

' You're cute. You liked her ? '

' No, actually we detested each other, but she didn't deserve to die like that ; there wasn't any harm in her.'

' Um. I had an idea—tell me, what are you doing to-morrow ? '

' Nothing very important. There's a rehearsal of the full cabaret at ten. We've got to cut seven minutes. After lunch I was going riding. That's all.'

' Rehearsal ? That might fit.' Mrs. Pym knuckled her chin. ' Larry, keep this under your hat. I think I've got something. Lydia, here's my idea :

' When you go to rehearsal in the morning I want you to say somebody sent you some chocolates. Talk as though you're flattered by it and mention, casually, how silly it was of the person not to enclose a card.'

' Yes ? '

' When you've mentioned that, say the sender didn't really take care because he used a sheet of wrapping-paper with his name and address on the other side, that you're going to ring him up when you get home and thank him.'

' " He ? " '

Mrs. Pym beamed.

' Good thinking ! We'll stick to that, though, because if the visitor Larry Baker had is anything to go by, it's a man we're after.'

' Suppose he knows he used a blank sheet of paper ? '

' Go up another notch, but there we're safe, Lydia. He *knows* he used a clean sheet of paper, but, given enough time, he'll begin to wonder. Once that happens, I think he'll act.'

' You mean, the Cyanide Man would hear about it if I talk at rehearsal ? '

' If you make a point of seeing plenty of people know—yes, he'll hear about it, just like you hear everything in this city. The Ritz-Carlton crowd will chatter about it outside because it's gossip. Some of them probably envy you, having a solo, and will wish they had people send them things. They'll see that the chocolates are the first of a lot of free things I've no doubt you'll be offered.'

' And then what happens ? '

' Then it becomes tricky. If my reading of psychology is worth a nickel, the Cyanide Man will be round to get that name and address away from you.' Mrs. Pym turned when I made an exclamation. ' Hold it, will you, son ? I'm handling this.

' Now, Lydia, can you do it and stay away from this apartment till, say, four-thirty, and let it be known you're not coming home till then ? '

' I could, but I don't quite see why.'

' You're keeping him tensed up, waiting. You don't 'phone as you said you were going to. If he hears the news round tiffin-time, he's got over three hours to stew in. If he stews he'll worry ; if he worries he'll slip.

' *Now*, honey, if you spread those seeds well, you'll start something. When you come home at four-thirty, you'll do just what you always do when you get home. Chiefest of all, you'll come home alone and when you're here you won't bat a eyelid when you find me and a few others, neatly tucked away in various corners of this apartment. You won't speak or notice us. *If* you run into somebody you know well or casually—that is, when you're out or as you come into the doorway downstairs, hear him out. If you get pressed at all to invite him in, do so, and bring him up here. Got nerve enough to risk it?'

Lydia was frowning when the details had been explained.

'You mean, this Cyanide Man will want the wrapping paper back and then he'll try and . . . hurt me?'

'He certainly will! Your safe angle is this: put the chocolates away, in your bedroom. If he's the one we want, the first thing he'll get at, when you're alone, is the chocolates. That's your let-out. You've got to get them for him—he'll want that evidence, first. You're safe till you get them, but once you're on the way to the bedroom, he'll be nabbed.'

'I think I can do that. But two things have struck me: supposing I'm asked what the chocolates were like at rehearsal, and suppose he comes up to me outside, then he knows I know the name and address, but as I don't, how do I get over not knowing him and making natural thanks for the gift?'

Mrs. Pym nodded the queer hat vigorously.

'Lydia, you're a very smart girl. Luckily we can overcome both those angles. First, make it clear you didn't have time to try the chocolates, only to put them away before you went to rehearsal. The second is even easier: if he's the one we want and he accosts you outside, the subject of chocolates will come up pretty quickly. He'll let it be known he's the sender. Just act dumb. Explain that you didn't think *he* was the sender, that, if you know him already, you didn't realize he was so-and-so—and use his name. If he's somebody you don't know, you've nothing to worry about.'

I'd held my fire till then. After that I got mad.

' Hell, you can't stick the kid as a piece of bait in a trap, ma'am ! Why, he might shoot her down——'

' Larry ! ' Mrs. Pym's voice was ice-edged. ' Look, son, I've let you tag round with me because you've got a head on you. Don't spoil it by acting stupidly. Lydia's willing. I'll have this place sewed up tight. All we want to see is the Cyanide Man's face. The rest is easy. Go and read a book, will you ? '

They went over it again, like a couple of cold-blooded plotters. They tested every stitch and decided it would do ; it beat me that a pretty girl like Lydia Tschenko was willing to take a chance. I felt so annoyed I tried to throw a wrench in the works.

' And what about Lydia and I, disappearing into the back of the Ritz-Carlton ? If the Cyanide Man's in front, he'll be a damned fool if he doesn't guess what's going on.'

It went down the wrong way, naturally.

' Larry, you've got your brains back ! ' Mrs. Pym nodded affably at me. ' That's a good point. Lydia, is anybody likely to come into your dressing-room ? '

She glanced at her watch.

' Not for another thirty minutes, when my call is due. I don't know any of the people there very well yet. We're not on gossip terms.'

' Perfect ! Take Larry back, see nobody sees either of you, and take him into your dressing-room. When your call comes, open the door casually and leave it open after that. There'll be people passing and Larry will be noticed. When the show's over go out in front with Larry and sit with him at his table.' She made a face. ' A little goo wouldn't hurt. Larry, can you act as though you've got a crush on Lydia ? '

I looked at her.

' Easiest thing in the world.'

' Okay. There's your script. Any objections ? '

I had some, but I wasn't going to offer them. If Lydia was fool enough to take this risk, I wasn't going to say anything.

'One more thing.' Mrs. Pym halted us as we were getting ready to go. 'If anybody should join you to-night or talk to you, and the subject of anything being sent to you comes up—not that I think such a thing will happen— you can mention having received the package, but you've had no time to open it. That covers you.'

'Mrs. Pym . . .' I hesitated. 'Well, I was going to say you're sure nothing can slip, and can I be here at four-thirty to-morrow?'

Her expression was sardonic.

'Lydia, he won't have to put on a sloppy act with you to-night—he'll do it naturally. Beat it, Larry, and don't ask me damnfool questions.' She shook Lydia's hand. 'It's swell of you to help out like this; don't worry about us getting in to-morrow—that's an easy one. If the Cyanide Man's already here, we'll nab him for you. Now you run along. I'll go later, when I've checked how many of us can squash in here. Larry, I'll contact you to-morrow. And, Larry?'

'Yes, ma'am?'

'Go easy on the goo. Lydia's a nice girl. She probably likes it refined, not the Yank method of grab-'em-and-razzle. Okay?'

It was not surprising our journey back to the Ritz-Carlton was in a strained atmosphere. I sat in the dressing-room as the schedule demanded, and don't think I said a sensible word. Lydia glanced at me once or twice, but she didn't speak either. When the call-boy rapped, I had to sit before the open door with the giggling chorus peeking in as they passed, I felt Mrs. Pym could be just a bit rough at times.

It didn't get really rough till I went out with Lydia, who had changed into an evening gown, after the final cabaret. If I'd been hauled up on a rope and spot-lighted, I couldn't have felt more conspicuous, going through that pass-door behind her and moving to my table with, I swear, the entire room watching us. Highlo' was about the only one who wasn't staring: I figured he'd seen it all before, especially when I did my best to look like a smitten half-wit at my table with her. She stuck it gallantly till we were dancing.

'Larry,' she wasn't looking at me when she said it, 'I think your act's a very good one, but don't be quite so sloppy, there's a pet. I mean, you're almost drooling.'

'*Me?* I'm doing nothing——'

'There, there. How old are you?'

'Twenty-one and seven months.'

'Two years older than I am.'

'Eh?'

'That's very rude of you! What do you think I am—seventy odd?'

'No, I didn't mean that. I mean you're a bit old for your age.'

'It could be put in a nicer way, but I think I know what you mean.' Her smile was warm. 'I've had a few things happen to me, you know. It ages anybody.'

'I'm sorry; I'm being a crashing bore. It's just that business to-morrow—to-day. It's got under my skin.'

'I'm glad you're worried; you shouldn't be. Nothing will happen to me.'

'That's what you think. You're only a kid.'

'Thank you. You're getting awfully worried for a reporter and a mere acquaintance, aren't you?'

I glared at her, then we both chuckled together. I don't know how it happened, but, after it, we became natural and as if we'd known each other for years.

The music, the dance-floor, and the atmosphere became enjoyable instead of irritating. I began to enjoy myself, and it was nearly three before we realized we'd been talking and dancing without interruption, getting along in a way that startled the life out of me.

Lorrie Bala, biggest of the local oil-men, stopped to chat on his way home, just before we were leaving. I was cautious as I wondered why he did it, but his talk was entirely on the state of the Settlement. I had been so involved with my office and Mrs. Pym I had not realized, until Lorrie told us, the furore that had been going on since the first front page on the *News* had more or less set the place on fire. The murders; the Hop-Ley Dancers; the death of Jacob Laffin; the Cyanide Man—they were all anybody seemed to talk about. The inquest on Laffin the next day was being contested like a first night for favoured places. If you magnify the gossip in a small village when, say, a couple of murders take place there, you can get a shrewd idea of the prevailing excitement.

It seemed I had no sooner got into bed than Sung was there, waking me for breakfast. There was no call for me, nor any news, which meant the state of emergency still existed. I put on my uniform for safety.

The *News* had really gone to town with its front page. If Shanghai had been seething before, I expected Lanny Coager's latest layout on the Dancers would send the place sky-high with chatter. Mrs. MacNaughton was the first example, after breakfast, when she was in a shuddering state of horror at those 'awful Bolshevists,' convinced she was living on the edge of a live mine, torn between admiration for Mrs. Pym and awed horror that I was in the centre of all this business.

The rickshaw that turned up every morning to take me to the office was outside, waiting. The weather had changed to a raw dankness, with a hint of mist, almost an autumn day. I was glad I had my great-coat.

Just as the coolie was raising the shafts, I thought I'd take a chance and told him: '*Ngoo iau tau Tracey Terrace chi.*' It did no harm to make a casual call on Schyler; I might get myself some news before I started off to the office.

When I announced my name to Schyler's houseboy I heard him shout from inside the house: 'That Larry Baker? Come on in, and be welcome!'

He was in that well-remembered lounge, big, white-haired and affable as always, his pink nose less bright, his cheeks and kindly grey eyes dull, as if an inner light had nearly gone out. But there was no doubt of his welcome.

'Larry Baker, you old horse ! Come on and let's have a look at you.' He shook my hand till it hurt. 'I haven't thanked you for saving my life——'

'Take it easy, Mr. Schyler. I only——'

'Yeah ? ' He pushed me into a chair and beamed down at me. 'I've been trying for an hour to write the sort of letter you deserve. How the dickens do you thank a man for a thing like that ? Even my training as a lawyer doesn't help me.'

It made me wriggle uncomfortably.

'I'd been reading a medical book, and all I did was give you——'

He patted my shoulder warmly.

'Larry, I don't give a damn what you did or what you didn't do. Thing is, you hauled me back and used your bean. Otherwise, Nate Schyler would be a shade by now.'

'Do you feel all right ? '

'Horrible, just horrible. My knees are rocking and I'm all sick inside, but that'll pass. I'd give a lot to know who banged me on the head and gave me that muck.'

'Doc Fedor's nearly insane, I've heard, wondering how you got away with it.'

'Luck, and Larry Baker. Look, can I do anything? I mean, I can't just say " Thanks " and see you off. Aw, hell to Nebraska, you know what I mean ! '

'I don't want rewards for that. But I *am* a reporter ; if you have a story to give me on the Laffin will, that'd be something.'

'Larry, I'd like to do that, honestly I would, and I hate refusing anything you want. But I can't reveal the thing out of order. Wills are tricky things, and they have to be dealt with in the proper way—that's going ahead.'

'Is Toby Garnett really the heir, then ? '

'I shot off my mouth over that, man ! I can put it away right enough,' he added frankly, 'and I'd had quite a few when I got this crazy urge to spill the news to old Toby. Damned unethical, of course. It's true enough. He's the lucky guy, but don't quote me direct on that, will you?'

'Gosh! No, Mr. Schyler, I won't, but why Toby?'

'Old Jacob Laffin was his own master. I don't think he had any relatives, only the one who died—I told you about it, the business man at the Bund Club who paid the fare for him—remember? Maybe Toby did him a turn or two? Toby's a nice little chap; he's kind and generous; I think he and Laffin got along swell together.'

'There's an idea Toby's the Cyanide Man.'

'*Toby?*' Schyler gaped. 'Of all the damn-silly notions! Toby wouldn't hurt a soul.'

I didn't mention the jade buffalo ring because Mrs. Pym hadn't released the news. I asked where Toby had gone, if he was innocent.

'That's got me completely beaten. I've known Toby for years, and, knowing him, this stunt baffles me. I'm going to find him, even if Mrs. Pym can't. Maybe he lost his head when it looked black against him over me, and when he realized about the money. People do queer things.'

'You're telling me!'

'If you see Mrs. Pym you can tell her Toby never fed me that cyanide. I don't know why it was done, or who did it—it wasn't Toby. He's not the killing type.

'Larry, forgive me for seeming inhospitable. It's getting on and I have leeway to make up, dozens of people to see, and lunch at Böök's, an important date. Will you call me here this evening, and we'll fix a get-together?"'

'I'd like that. Thanks.'

'Good. I'll try and work out some sort of news for you. I'll be able to make a public statement after Laffin's inquest, and you shall have the news an hour before the others. Any good?'

'If you'll hold the news till late at night—yes.'

'I'll see what can be done.'

Schyler saw me to the door, grabbed my hand and near squeezed it flat again, telling me he didn't know how to thank me. I got in my rickshaw and headed for the office, feeling on top of the world.

Lanny Coager gave me his usual welcome, listening to all I had to say of things that had happened since I last saw him. I hated doing it, but Mrs. Pym had been clear on the point and I could see why, so I failed to tell him about the chocolates, or anything to do with them. He'd heard gossip, though.

'What's all this about you and Lydia Tschenko thick as a couple of young lovers, Larry?'

It made me feel darned silly.

'For pity's sake, can't a man have a few words with a girl and get away with it?'

'Not in Shanghai, you can't.' His eyes were amused. 'You spent the whole evening with her when I thought you'd gone home to bed.'

'Shucks! I looked in at the Ritz-Carlton because I felt flat. Highlo' Harry put a spot on me and gave us some free publicity. Lydia headed towards me as a celebrity, I imagine. She's a nice girl.'

It made me feel suddenly, gruesomely uneasy when Lanny said: 'For pity's sake, what kept you talking till all hours?' I remembered, with a flash of inner distress, that Lanny had never been around the office when the Cyanide Man was at work—it was such a revolutionary thought I had a job in hiding my feelings, especially when I remembered the prophecy in the Cyanide Song; I know I felt sick in my stomach. That's the sort of thing a mind keyed up to suspicion will do.

'I think we got along. She's—she's all right, Lanny.'

'Like that, eh?' He fingered his red beard, grinning. 'Seeing her to-day?'

'We didn't fix anything—look here, you trying to marry me off to the girl?'

'It'd be a story.' His wink was broad and friendly. 'Okay, son, I'll stop ribbing you. You say Schyler's eating out of your hand? Can't you get something from him to-day? There's a front page coming up.'

'No, he won't make a release till after the inquest.'

'Fair enough. Okay, Larry, you get busy and see what the world's got to offer. That's the trouble with exclusives, my boy. You can't sit down and preen. You have to follow up with more. Going to try and see what you can do?'

'It's in the bag.' I made a circle of my thumb and forefinger and went to my old desk, where I sat and felt uneasy inside. The more I thought about it the less I liked it. Lanny was my friend and I was fond of him; but suspicion is a rotten thing when it digs in between friendships. Just the same, the circumstantial evidence made my head spin, for the more I thought about it the more I hated what I was thinking.

It made me so depressed I headed from the newsroom, ignoring a certain amount of comment on my obviously gloomy face, and went round to the Central Police Station.

Mrs. Pym was out and so was Sergeant Kelly. I felt so down I asked if Superintendent Laystall could spare me a few minutes.

He was busy when I was shown in, with a pile of paper work in front of him. Just the same, his face was warm and welcoming.

'Hullo, Baker, sure you want to see me?'

'If you don't mind, sir.'

'I can give you fifteen minutes. Mrs. Pym's over in court, getting a postponement on John Tee so that we can build our case.'

'I see, sir. You've seen her this morning?'

'Certainly. What's bothering you? You look very worried to me.'

'I am, quite a bit. You know about the chocolates?'

Laystall frowned.

'I do. The method doesn't commend itself to me'—his smile was sudden—'but I don't think I can hide the fact from you that Mrs. Pym likes to—er—get her own way? And usually does.'

'That's right, sir.' I suddenly spilled out my fears and suspicions to him, his face becoming longer and longer as he listened.

'That's your trouble? Now, Baker, you've built it on circumstances. They're never entirely trustworthy; personally, I'm always very wary of circumstantial evidence. From the police point of view it can land one in trouble.'

'I know, sir, but he dug into me about Lydia Tschenko. I feel like a traitor, telling you all this. It's knocked me for a loop until I've a feeling I'm losing my judgment.'

'My dear fellow,' Laystall leaned forward, 'a great many things are told to me in confidence. I'm a police officer and an old man. You're not much more than a boy, and you're climbing very fast. You haven't experience to help you, and what is more natural than talking to me? There is one thing I will tell you: poisoning cases have a way of sowing evil suspicions. I was in the police at home before I came here, and, I can assure you, I saw poisoning cases in which the most manifestly innocent people came under my suspicion.

'Take my advice and forget about it. I'll talk to Mrs. Pym, of course, but I doubt if she'll take it seriously. She dislikes coincidences as much as I do.'

'You'll keep it in the office, sir?'

'My dear boy!'

'Sorry, sir. I feel better talking about it. I'm not quite as big as I thought I was.'

'The fact you think like that is a good sign. It never hurts to chasten yourself. Now, you——' he paused. A sound like a damned soul rang out, strident, shrill, and arresting. 'What on earth—good gracious, isn't that the starting siren on the Bund boathouse?'

'Oh, Lord, I'd forgotten about that——' I paused as Laystall's secretary came in.

'Excuse me, sir, will you take an urgent call under the emergency regulations?'

Laystall nodded, picking up the telephone. He listened, saying a word now and again while the siren went on and on. I fingered my damaged ear, nick though it was, wondering if more people would soon be shooting in my general direction.

' You'd better get along to your unit, Baker.' He stood up as he hooked the telephone receiver. ' There's a large-scale battle working in our direction. We're all going to be very busy—wait a minute, where is your station ? '

' Bubbling Well, by the police——'

He didn't wait for me to finish, picking up his cap and nodding to his secretary.

' I have to go there. Come along, young man, I'll give you a lift.'

I followed him into the gloomy street, sore as hell.

' Just my luck, sir. Something's probably going to break to-day and I'll be hanging round, waiting for a lot of coolies in uniforms to decide which way they're going to go.'

Laystall pushed me into the car, smiling.

' The Cyanide Man is a civic murderer, Baker, killing in ones. If those soldiers break in, it'll be mass slaughter. You should cultivate a sense of proportion.'

I daresay he was right. I sat back in comfort, consoling myself with the thought that, whatever else happened, you couldn't beat Baker's way of going to war. When I saw some of my unit toiling towards the station in rickshaws I began to get back my sense of humour again.

CHAPTER XIX

BOMBSHELL

In the mist and the dankness we seemed to be on our toes for hours. If there was a battle happening it was either happening a long way away, or both sides were lining up for the fight.

What we did have to contend with was refugees. The land beyond the Settlement had really got a scare in it —farmers, peasants, deserters, small merchants, riff-raff, they were all there in swarms, a tumbled litter of people with their personal possessions, household goods, livestock, wives and children—a screaming, moaning, shouting mass that was never still for a minute. They offered us prayers, money, and—some of them—their daughters, if we would only let them through.

It was tough, having to be tough. But what could we do? Shanghai wasn't a refugee camp; we had neither the space nor the resources to take them in, and the same tale would be repeated at every barrier. The sit-at-home humanitarian can easily think up nasty ones about us, but letting in that lot would not only stump us to feed them : disease would be brought in, insanitary conditions, and quite a few who were robbers with concealed arms. It just couldn't be done.

Those who wanted their kids taken care of could be helped to a limited extent. Quite a few moppets were handed over the barrier and passed back to the missions. I never thought much of missionaries, but when it came to children and medical aid, you couldn't beat them.

We forwarded the stream, where we could, round the border towards Nantao. They could huddle there in better part, for, unless the battle reached clean to the

Whangpoo, they were protected by the shoulder of the French Concession.

You could hear the noise in the distance, the faint rumbling, gunshots down corridors of air, and a dim shout or two. It was still quite a way back; it gave those people a chance to move on.

Some of the white dug-ins got scared and began to filter back after tiffin. Probably their servants spread the panic, and I was so busy helping in women and children, mostly American, that, after the rushed morning, I never had a chance to think of another drama that was getting ready for action behind me as tea-time approached.

A few minutes short of four o'clock Randy McCallum sent for me. He was in the front garden of a neighbouring house that was our acting headquarters.

'Baker, you're in the old man's good books so I've got a nice easy fatigue for you.'

I was suspicious; Randy's idea of that sort of thing was something a Chinese labourer wouldn't touch for big money: that's saying something.

He led me round the back of the house where our armoured car was parked. It was something we had bought by subscription to give us standing, a crazy old thing, a Dodge truck equipped with armour-plate. There were firing slats and a machine-gun in a movable turret. If you had to use it, you had head and shoulders exposed, which wouldn't have done much for you in a real fight; the armour-plate would have sat down and cried if you threw a ·45 bullet at it, but it *was* an armoured car. We were very proud of it.

'Lulu's got a spot of engine trouble.' Randy patted the old car affectionately. 'She goes like a dog on three legs. Lew's taking her down to Krug's Garage in Mohawk Road. You go with him and see him back, will you?'

'Okay.' I didn't question the order; the army, and that applied to the Shanghai Volunteer Corps, works on the principle that a private soldier isn't to be trusted alone with valuable property. Randy didn't imagine

Lew Schlesinger was going to snitch the car; just the same, rules are rules. ' Is Lew inside ? ' I added.

' Yeah. Where the hell did you think he was, pushing ? '

' Sorry, Sarge. If he'll open that door, I'll——'

' You won't. Are you nuts, Baker ? If that thing goes into the city, banging the way it is at present, you'll scare the natives into fits ; there'll be a panic, or something. You can take my car. Lead the way for Lew, about a car's length, and stay with him. Get it ? Have Krug's put it right and high-tail back here if you know what's good for you.'

' Okay, Sarge. It's in the bag.' I was jubilant ; I'd just remembered Lydia's apartment was in Mohawk Road. With a little bit of a blind eye on Lew's part, I might pop over and get the news, if there was any.

I didn't ask Randy why we shouldn't do the job ourselves. Quite apart from the fact Krug's had our repairing contract, nobody but a moron put ideas like that into the sergeant's head.

Randy's car was an old Stutz Bear-Cat, a bit undignified for him ; he'd brought it from the States when he came, and used it for knockabout work, having a slick new Cadillac for the showy stuff.

We started off, me leading and Lew at my tail. I could see what Randy meant. Old Lulu clanked along smoothly for about ten yards, then she'd spurt exhaust, let out a blazing bang and her armament would shudder and crash. It scared me, riding safely ahead.

When we reached Krug's there wasn't room in the garage, so we parked Lulu at the kerb, the old Stutz a few yards behind. A couple of grinning mechanics delved into the old tin's innards and said something about the ignorant blank volunteers. They were American kids, sassy as you please. Lew and I ignored them, and went inside to talk to Krug.

I had taken a look at Lydia's apartment house. It seemed quite normal and ordinary to me but I dared not go over. It was precisely four-thirty and I knew I should spoil Mrs. Pym's play if I appeared. I chatted instead, chewing my nails with nervousness. For a reporter to be within yards of breaking news that he dare not go near is a better torture than anything Albert Fong could have thought up.

The boys came back and asked us sneeringly if anybody had ever told us about spark-plugs and soot. They elaborated on it rudely, Krug grinning amiably. Lew retreated from the discussion explaining that he would be back in a few minutes because emergency or no emergency certain things were a darned sight more important than sergeants.

I was only dimly aware of running feet. We all looked round, but being behind the spares-room we couldn't see the street. I heard a crash, and started running, then came the unique sound of Lulu being started, a clanking and a shocking grind of gears.

Lulu was shuddering away from the kerb. A Chinese truck driver, either scared or petrified, had half turned in the roadway where his engine had stalled. I could hear Mrs. Pym's voice yelling something, and saw a group of people pouring out of Lydia's apartment block, and then Kelly's great voice from yards away.

'Larry! Jump, you fool! He's in that car—*quick!*'

I knew who 'he' was, and saw the Stutz was on the right side of the stalled truck in which the driver was trying to make the engine turn over. The little Stutz may have been old; she started first touch and went off like a bear-cat with a scalded tail.

It was terrific. Lulu was banging along ahead as if somebody was tumbling all the tin cans in the world, but her engine was all right. She was moving up fast, and I was a long way behind.

I hate to think of the uproar, even now. Crowds lined the pavements to watch, hooting and screaming. Traffic skidded to the kerbs to get out of the way, for you could hear Lulu coming for yards ahead. I did my best to hang on; it wasn't easy. I was chasing and using my head; the thing ahead just barged and didn't worry about anything, a runaway man scared to fits.

No matter how I tried, I could not get closer. People kept dodging across the street, between us. Opposing traffic got in my way, and a few well-intentioned, slightly insane Chinese on bicycles tried to trail along, got in the way, fell off, or hung on madly, whooping like a bunch of crazy folk. I think they imagined the armoured car was either running away, or it was another of the white barbarians' little jokes. No doubt quite a few of them had heard of that chariot race I ran with Randy in his buggy—whatever it was, I could not get closer or even level up. And you try and work out a way of stopping a man in an armoured car when he doesn't intend to stop.

We got round a couple of corners, landed in Sinza Road and there old Lulu was given her head. She snorted along like a berserk elephant in the ironmongery business. I remembered those mechanics of Krug's mentioned filling her up. If I knew anything about Lulu, she was good for a couple of hundred miles.

Then it came, the Sinza Road barrier. It was no more than a couple of coloured poles across the road with the Portuguese Volunteer Company in charge, good guys, maybe, but pure Latin when it came to the untoward. Lulu was crashing along in the fifties, and I expect they figured, seeing Lulu's pennants and her markings, that the war was on and the *Americanos* had either gone crazy or they were going to wipe out Wu Pei-fu and Chang Tso-lin for the hell of it.

The half-wits tore back the barriers, let Lulu through and when I followed, cursing them to blue blazes, they snapped to attention like Guardsmen while a lunkhead in the background ran up the Portuguese flag.

That was where I came in, so to speak. Chinese territory ahead of me, the Cyanide Man in the American Company's armoured car, and me in the sergeant's Stutz Bear-Cat. I had my rifle with me as a matter of course, but you try and tear off a shot with a military rifle, driving a bouncy two-seater over a road that steadily got worse. There was about twenty yards visibility, and it also began to rain.

I couldn't think where the fool ahead imagined he was going. To be literal, there was Jessfield Park somewhere on the road, not that it was going to help me.

We went on. The track was awful. I couldn't push the Stutz any faster, not without being shot from the seat. As we passed Jessfield Park, the best I could do was to keep the car in sight. I didn't even need to watch. It was a tin-plate factory in full blast: why the hades none of the armour had just fallen off I couldn't imagine.

We thundered past Tseu Ka Jau village, whirled round a corner on to an even worse native road and went rattling off into the unknown, with me watching my gasoline needle getting nearer and nearer to zero.

Of course it had to happen. The armoured car skidded off the road on a real slimy patch, shot half over a fallow field and stopped bang against one of those graves. I started to brake, skidded and near killed myself. While I was trying to keep on an even keel a handful of running Chinese soldiers burst out of the nearby houses. Then, timed to absolute perfection, everything in sight started to blow up. I think every soldier in the district had been lying quiet until that minute, then machine-guns, rifles, and revolvers began to blast hell out of the growing darkness.

It didn't make me feel any better to see the running men were carrying their wretched little paper umbrellas to keep off the drizzle. One of them sighted Lulu, let out a screech like a burned cat and went flat on his tummy. The others copied him and they lugged out their guns, firing at the stalled car. I actually fell out of the Stutz, dragging my rifle, and ducked behind, crawling round on my stomach with a proud feeling I had precisely twelve rounds of ammunition and that if I ever got out of this one, I'd retire to Regina and sit under an apple tree for the rest of my life.

Even Chinese marksmen were capable of hitting that hulking great armoured car, now and again. I heard the hollow *whang* as the bullets landed on Lulu's armour-plate. I was so astonished when it held together that I stared instead of firing. I'll be darned if whoever was inside didn't get up into the turret, fiddle with the machine-gun, nearly blow off Lulu's radiator with the first burst, and then the muzzle swung round. The belt must have been full and readied, for the gun stuttered angrily. I've never seen Chinese run quite as fast.

We must have started something, for a machine-gun to the north of the Stutz chattered back, rifles following and, within a minute, poor old Lulu was a target. I don't know how the man in the turret got away with it. He did, firing in bursts, which meant he had got the hang of the machine-gun, or he was conserving ammunition. I pulled off a couple of rounds; I don't think I hit anybody.

I just lay there on the wet road, wondering what the devil was going to happen to us—Cyanide Man or not, he was a white man, or, if he wasn't, I was going to be the most startled guy alive. The next moment I think I left my uniform behind me, took straight off into the murky, rainy sky and acquired a notable set of jitters, because somebody dug me in the ribs.

'Move over, son. This is my pigeon.'

And there she was, on her stomach in the mud, her crazy hat on one side, and the Luger in her right hand, the left holding about a dozen ammunition clips.

'Mrs. Pym! My God, you near frightened me green!'

'Sorry. Got the Bugatti after you soon as I could. I saw that thing skid off the road, and came to join you.'

I was still trying to drag back my normal self; it just wouldn't come. I was so plumb scarified it was minutes before my teeth stopped clacking.

The uproar was getting fierce. Guns were firing all over the place, men went running past, ignoring everything except getting away to somewhere. Lulu was still answering in little occasional bursts, and a few guns were still trying to silence her.

If I imagined lying on her stomach in the mud was Mrs. Pym's idea of police work, I was wrong. She suddenly said something that was probably as bad as it sounded, climbed to her feet and began shooting at everything in sight except Lulu. The Luger banged its great hollow bang, the new clips going in like clockwork, so I heaved up and let off my rifle here and there, cursing the dimness, the noise, the wet and every Chinese *tuchun* ever born.

There was a sudden yell from Lulu's direction and the machine-gun was silent.

Mrs. Pym dropped on her haunches, waddling forward that way round the grave.

'He's had it. C'm on, Larry. Can we get in that thing? Any ammunition?'

'Yeah. Can we do it?'

'Watch me.'

I didn't; I was waddling, too, dragging my gun, expecting something in my back any minute. But luck favours the insane and we reached the blind side of Lulu, still alive. I was never so pleased in my life as when I hauled open the nearside door, tumbled into the oily, cordite-reeking atmosphere that was Lulu's black interior at the heels of Mrs. Pym.

The damned old can was holding, too. It was better than I'd ever imagined, but was it dark!

'Get him out of that turret. Can you use the machine-gun, Larry?'

'Sure. Who——?'

'Shut up and get busy, son, or you won't be busy any more. It's hotting up.'

I crawled forward, felt somebody hanging, hauled a body to the floor and didn't even stop to help him, though he was groaning. Lulu was an open book to us all. I knew how she worked, what she was like, and, best of all, where the little racks at the turret-foot were, the racks containing the ammunition belts.

Lulu was well equipped because she came to us that way, and, beyond a few practice rounds, she had never been used in anger in her life.

I felt hideously exposed up there, the rain falling heavily, company for the shudders and clanks as a few questing guns shot at us and hit the armour. Down below, while I was readying the machine-gun, I could hear movements. Next minute there was real noise. Mrs. Pym had found a comfortable firing slot, and was blazing away with the Luger; happy, I'll swear, as a kid with unlimited mud and no inhibitions.

The machine-gun was a Vickers on a movable arm, a good enough job. I got it as I liked it, had my spare belts at my feet, then I got suddenly sore and began. I played the whole *1812 Overture* on that thing, firing at everything, only stopping long enough for new belts and hoping the water-jacket wouldn't bust and scald me to death.

Handling a machine-gun with some protection, and with a bunch of lousy shots lined up against you, is about the finest ego-builder on the face of this planet. I was having the old Harry of a time, blazing away, probably scaring everything within hearing distance that a whole squad of machine-guns was in action.

Something pulled at my foot, then I got a good swift sock on the ankle when I didn't stop.

'Larry! Larry! You young fool——'

'Sorry, ma'am.' I held the gun with my left hand and crouched. 'I was firing.'

'I'll say you were! Gosh, I'm stone deaf.'

'Sorry, ma'am.'

'You should be. Stand up and shout, will you? There's somebody yelling at us.'

I did as I was told, offering a nervous 'Who's that?' to the blackness, aware that the noise of firing had died away.

'Hi-yi, hi-yi! You are not Chinese, no?'

'No?' I stared into the blackness. 'Hell, no! Who's that?'

'You are an armoured car? Please, sir, are you English?'

'Canadian. Who's that?'

'Fourth Route Company. Lieutenant Ma Sing. I chase Wu Pei-fu's men. They have gone. Now I find you, please.'

'For God's sake! You Chang's men?'

'Very happy. Please, can you explain? Don't fire. We are friends of the English, please. My men don't like your machine-gun, sir.'

'What do I do?' I called down to Mrs. Pym.

'Tell him to come out with a light. If you don't like his face, blow it off.'

I grinned with reaction at the sheer, evil malignancy of the remark, but I did as I was told.

A small searchlight was switched on, hit the sky, the ground, then righted itself. Into the beam stepped a thin Chinese in uniform and shell-rimmed glasses, carrying a revolver in one hand. Behind him came four men so reluctantly that I wanted to shout with laughter.

I nearly doubled up at their transfixed shock when an undoubted female voice, suspicious but still female, snarled, from below my feet: 'Drop those guns before you come any further, unless you want trouble.'

They went into hasty, typically Chinese conference, but did as they were told and marched forward until they were below me, in line with the machine-gun.

It was a hysterical interval; I think I choked with joy inside while the five of them lined up before battered old Lulu and a completely invisible woman snapped out a rattle of questions in Mandarin, which, to his credit's sake, Ma Sing spoke.

Back and forth it went, question and answer, the Chinese soldiers staring blankly at Lulu's armoured side. Apparently it suited Mrs. Pym. I heard her grumbling, crashing about below me, then she attacked the door-handle and appeared round Lulu's bonnet, her face and tweed suit blackened with backfire. The searchlight wavered as if the operator was awed, then it righted and she glared at the uneasy five as though she hated them.

I don't know whether it was a woman appearing in the middle of that business, or the whole mad situation. Ma Sing began to chuckle and his men saw the joke. That weird sense of Chinese humour had taken over. You could hear echoing laughter from beyond the searchlight. Ma Sing said something of which I recognized only 'very bold' and 'woman.' Mrs. Pym grimaced, her face cleared and she added a harsh sound which became the ghost of a chuckle.

She looked up at me.

'Okay, Larry, it's all over. They're seeing us home. Come on down and we'll leave this thing—mind you don't tread on the Cyanide Man. I'm just arranging with the lieutenant to lend us stretcher-bearers—he's still alive.'

'Right, ma'am—eh? The Cyanide Man?' I had started to let myself down when I spoke.

'Yes. Get a wiggle on, boy.'

'But . . . look, I've got to know or I'll bust.'

'Did you—of course, you don't know, do you?' She glanced up at me again and I practically fell out of Lulu's turret when she said: 'Nathan Schyler. Hurry *up*, will you?'

CHAPTER XX

THE PARADOX

No matter how furious the uproar from which a man has emerged; no matter how soul-shaking the things he has gone through, going back to the office and getting together with the boss will cut an emotional jag down to size. Maybe it's the human inclination to feel, in some corner of the mind, a sneaking fear of the man who controls the pay envelope. No matter what it is, when you've had a good share in the impossible, got your nerves and imagination into a state of near psychosis, the answer is to go to the office. Not a psychiatrist in the country can beat it for getting back to normal at express speed.

That's how I found it. Mrs. Pym, Schyler, Lulu, the Stutz and I were all trundled to the Settlement barriers; I had a session with Mrs. Pym while a physician worked, in a first-aid tent, on Schyler, who talked his head off when he wasn't being hurt—he was so full of bullets he was convinced he was for the high jump. Then he went off to hospital under the personal guard of Sergeant Kelly. I had all the dope, and was given some more. With Mrs. Pym's influence I was granted the rest of the night off, as if I were an anxious maid-servant with a heavy date, and she shot me back to the *News*, telling me she would be along. I also had a free hand to spill everything I knew on the front page.

It was either the fact of being in Lanny Coager's office, or uneasiness at suspecting him. I know my scare fell away from me when I was sitting facing his friendly eyes.

'What the hell's been going on?' His demand was truculent. 'I've heard rumours, and why have I had a flatfoot on my tail all the time?'

'Have you . . . oh, Lord. . . .' I explained that, trying to sink through the chair with embarrassment.

'*Me?*' Lanny threw back his head and roared, drowning the basement presses. ' My God, you're one hell of a reporter, Larry, suspecting the boss ! '

' I'm sorry. You know how it is ? Look, will the biggest front page of all make up for me being a dope ? '

' Spill it, kid.'

I did, or most of it. Lanny's mouth was an orifice framed in his red beard.

' That's the mundane part so to speak.'

' Mundane ? My dear boy—look are you seriously telling me Nate Schyler's the Cyanide Man ? '

' Well, he turned up at Lydia's. He fell for that gag when he lunched at the Ritz-Carlton and heard about the chocolates and the address on the inside of the wrapping. Kelly jumped too soon when he sailed into Lydia's apartment, which is why he got away in old Lulu.'

' *Schyler ?* '

' Schyler. He figured he was going when the doc worked on him. The whole thing came out.'

' Give, Larry, give. It's crazy, but maybe you can make sense of it.'

' It's a simple story. I'll spill it the way I know it in my mind, then it can be whacked together for the front page.'

' It's released ? '

' Sure. Mrs. Pym said so.'

Lanny picked up his pencil, doodling on copy-paper ; I could see the headline forming : NOTED LAWYER CONFESSES, ' I AM THE CYANIDE MAN.'

' It stems back to Schyler's being Laffin's attorney. Schyler drinks like a fish and lives like a lord. He wanted money in a big way. But he was a generous guy and his friendship with Toby Garnett started all this.'

' Has Toby turned up ? '

' Not yet, Lanny. Schyler helped Toby time and again with cash, which Toby promptly drank up. It was only peanuts, but Schyler was a lawyer. Half in fun and half in earnest he made an agreement with Toby months ago that if Toby ever cleared any sum over and above ten thousand dollars, Schyler was to have two-thirds for services rendered. Toby needed a hundred dollars at the time and would have signed anything. He knew damned well he'd never make that much, so I guess it satisfied Schyler's instincts to have his paper on file.

' He forgot all about it till Jacob Laffin made a new will. He was a lonely old boy without relatives. The only two people he ever liked were Nadia Sherbina and Toby Garnett. Nadia used to try and dig Laffin for dough, not that he ever gave her any, and Toby was always ready to buy him his Vichy water.' It made me smile, when I saw Lanny's bright eyes staring. ' Yes, Laffin made Nadia heir to eighty per cent. of his estate and Toby heir to the rest. He considered the future by settling that, in event of either of them dying first in the meantime, the other became residuary legatee.'

' Golly ; that washed up Nadia. Is that it ? '

' Sure. Schyler saw the angle right away. If he got rid of Nadia, Tony would have it all, and of that Schyler would get two-thirds. It was made-to-measure for murder.

' Wait a moment. Yes, I've got it straight. Schyler got busy on his murder campaign because he saw the way to grabbing an outsize pile of money. The cyanide capsules he got made up easily—you know perfectly well, Lanny, a thing like that is easy in Shanghai. He never told us this, but Mrs. Pym said he probably bribed a Chinese druggist to get the things ready, and the Chinese don't talk.'

' I'll say they don't ! '

' Right—can I have one of your cigarettes ? Thanks. I needed it. Where was I ? Oh, yes, Schyler couldn't wait for Laffin to die. The old boy was ancient enough to live for ever, so Schyler rings for an appointment several days ahead, the usual custom, and Laffin leaves the front door open for him as he did on such occasions.

THE PARADOX 219

' Schyler went sailing in and found poor old Laffin on his desk, unconscious. He'd gone to murder him, wondering how he was going to make the man take one of his capsules and there he was, helpless. He jammed the filthy thing down the poor old duck's throat and beat it out of there.'

Lanny whistled.

' Wow ! And all the time Laffin was dying, and died before the cyanide got to work ? '

' That's it. Irony pure and simple. Schyler proceeded with the rest of his plan by going after Nadia Sherbina.'

' He didn't do the same thing there, for Pete's sake ? '

' He called on the poor kid at her apartment when she was asleep. He said he had a gun, and she was scared out of her wits. She swallowed the capsule because he told her it was only a sleeping draught. There was the gun, anyway. I don't know what she thought, but I figure that it being Schyler, the lawyer who had helped her over her contract with the Ritz-Carlton, then, maybe, it was some sort of a mad joke. The sonofabitch just watched her die, and shoved her in bed, tipping off the police from a call booth.'

' I'll be damned ! '

' You haven't heard anything yet, Lanny. Schyler wanted to get across the idea of a mad killer. A few lives didn't mean a thing when it came to all that money and seeing that suspicion didn't touch him. Poor old Leslie Chow got the same treatment. He was picked because his cousin worked in Schyler's office, and Schyler knew Leslie was a harmless little gink who'd make a real mystifying corpse. And Leslie Ho was even easier. He was another blind alley, picked because he mentioned once in the bar, to Schyler, about taking medicinal paraffin capsules every night. All Schyler had to do there was to bribe a coolie to let him into Leslie's Ho room, substitute a capsule and leave the rest to the law of averages. It spread any suspicion well away from him, if any of it ever stuck, just like that visit to me.

'That was ground-seed for a dumb reporter. Remember the " punishing evil " gag? That indicated a nut; he left it to me as a reporter to see the nonsense was spread.'

'And bribed you, or tried to, to lend sense to the gag. Is that it? But why the letter?'

'The one about Laffin? Because Schyler saw his plans being defeated by Laffin's solitary ways. Nobody had found his body. Until they did, the will couldn't go into process. Now you see why he wrote that letter so that the body *would* be discovered?'

Lanny Coager thrust back his chair, scratching his head with both hands.

'Kid, he sounds goofy to me.'

'Goofy, like a fox. He was so cute that when Toby lit out, he picked on another Ritz-Carlton lovely, Lydia Tschenko. He changed his tactics by sending cyanide-riddled chocolates because he wanted suspicion shifted on Toby. It was a good red herring and was up to Toby to wriggle out. Toby was on the lam, anyway, but Schyler said he would have defended him if he was found. He didn't know where Toby had run to, nor why he'd done it. But he guessed Mrs. Pym would investigate Toby.

'He wore that jade buffalo ring when he visited me to keep my attention away from getting too good an idea of him. Then it struck him, when Toby scrammed, that his spade work was good because he had already nipped in through Toby's bedroom window and planted the ring there. He said, at the time, he didn't know why he did it, but he had a sort of an idea at the back of his mind it would turn into something.

'It did. It clinched Mrs. Pym's mind that Toby was the nigger in the woodpile.'

'But she set that wrapping-paper trap, didn't she?'

'Because she never really considered Toby. She didn't know who it was. She just got an idea the moment I hauled her round to Lydia's. The trap was laid on that basis, that people, no matter how cute they are forget little things. What was more simple than the utterly ordinary trick of indicating that old wrapping-paper had been used on those chocolates, with the name and address inside? It's a thing one does automatically. Even if Schyler *knew* he had used clean paper, the perfectly normal reaction would be, when he heard Lydia was going to telephone and thank him, that he *had* used old paper. Mrs. Pym based her psychology on the fact that wrapping the chocolates was an unthinking action any person could do. By sowing the seed of doubt in his mind, the belief he'd slipped on a minor detail—darn it, she had him. Could you have resisted going to make sure you *hadn't* slipped up?'

'The clever old devil. Why didn't you give me that dope on Lydia when you knew it?'

'She said to keep it quiet—Mrs. Pym, I mean. She meant it for everybody. Before I told you what Schyler said, I gave you the chocolate stuff in my—well—mundane part of it. Now I've qualified it.'

'Larry! There's one big hole in this. Schyler was poisoned, wasn't he?'

'Gosh, I knew there was something!' I stared in dismay. 'So help me, I don't know. He didn't tell us, and it never came up.' I saw the whole thing tumbling into bits—wrecked on the most obvious rock of all. No matter what I thought of, there was no way round it. Either Schyler was lying from beginning to end, or we were clear up a gum-tree.

Lanny Coager tore up the copy-paper furiously.

'We're sunk, we're damn well sunk. It's a magnificent fairy story, but Schyler *is not the Cyanide Man*!'

CHAPTER XXI

FANTASTIC STORY

We sat like a couple of dummies, stuck and helpless. The story held together as if a genius had contrived it, yet it was the bunk. The facts I had acquired *could* have been true, but because no man can survive a lethal dose of cyanide Nathan Schyler was not in the picture. That he *had* survived was nothing to do with it. Maybe some mad prank of Fate had saved him, but not in this life did he take cyanide to divert suspicion. It was merely silly.

I was astounded that Mrs. Pym, usually needle-sharp, had let me walk away crammed full of nonsense, when, obviously, she must have known it was nonsense. In spite of it all, the thing dovetailed; Schyler had walked into the trap, he knew all the answers, but...

Lanny and I started to speak more than once. Each time the stumbling block stopped us. I wondered if Schyler was covering for someone. That one didn't ring true either. My mind scrabbled among the people I had met or heard about in the case, dismissing them all. There wasn't a soul who would fit.

Lanny said at last: 'It's no good, pal. We're right out on the end of a limb and any minute now we'll fall and break our stupid necks.'

'It's crazy, it's stark crazy, darn it all! Nobody but Schyler could have done it.'

'No? You tell me the one about the cyanide, and I'll trade you the one about a man taking cyanide and knowing he'll snap out of it, just like a hangover.' Lanny, scowled. 'He *did* have cyanide in him, I suppose?'

'What do you think? Doc Fedor's not a faker. Schyler didn't have a rubber stomach let in him; he didn't palm

the stuff—aw, nuts, he took cyanide or he was given it.
Get that in your head, will you?'

'And lived?'

'I'm not interested in that part of it. I just know he
did not take it himself——'

'No?' The door had opened silently and Mrs. Pym's
head, in that hat, was framed there. 'And just who the blazes
do you think you are? Dogmatic Dick or something?'

Lanny came to his feet, and so did I. Mrs. Pym threw
open the door and came marching in, a grimy, worried,
beat-looking Toby Garnett behind her. Backing up the
procession, beaming, balding, and full of himself, was little
Doc Fedor.

When we got ourselves sorted out and were reasonably
coherent, we were perched anywhere we could get. The
office about squeaked at the seams, giving the impression
it was strained fit to burst by Mrs. Pym, back to the fire-
place, standing there with her hands on her hips, affable,
cocky, personality plus, and looking like a woman with a
satchel full of bombs she was prepared to throw.

'Schyler died of wounds,' she said without preliminary.
'The Cyanide Man is dead right enough.'

'But——' I dwindled away, appalled at the malignant
glare in those grey-blue eyes.

'Still being dogmatic? We hauled in this creature
an hour ago.' She pointed to Garnett. 'He's been hiding
out in Lo-Pi's dosshouse, Chinese City-side. Maybe he
thought Central Station couldn't be worse than Chinese
bugs, so he handed himself over, and I brought him here.
I'm a great gal for knocking folks sideways with a really
big curtain.'

'You mean *he's* the one who did it?' Lanny Coager
said it before he thought.

Mrs. Pym glared at him, too, and waved down Toby's
yelp of protest.

'He did nothing of the sort. And you talk to him
politely. He's worth two hundred million dollars, Mex.
I don't know what it is in money; it's still a lot.'

'Toby,' my voice was anxious, ' spill it, will you ? '

' I'll have you know I work on the *Free Press*——' His voice was weak and indignant.

' I don't care a hoot if you do.' Mrs. Pym whirled round on him so that he flinched. 'You can buy the *Free Press* ten times if you want to. This is me talking. Coager, here, spread me over his front page this morning ; he's going to do it again to-morrow, bigger and better. I'm a hog for publicity and you're not going to spoil my play for one miserable little item so that the *Free Press* can have it. The *News* has the exclusive, son, so round it off.'

' Well, there isn't much to it,' Toby said meekly, a faint smile on his pock-marked face. ' When I was caught up by Mrs. Pym and detained, I got to thinking it over. I was in a spot and knew it, but I was more scared of Schyler.'

' You knew about him ? '

Toby looked at me.

' I didn't know anything, but I *did* know about that agreement to hand him any money over ten thousand that I made. It struck me nobody else *but* Schyler could have done the killings. I was so damned frightened I got out of the police station and went to earth. Don't ask me why I was frightened ; I just was. Gosh, for all I know he might've had me on the list.'

' Why ? ' Mrs. Pym demanded.

' I didn't stop to think it out. If you'd been through——'

' I know, I know.' She turned to me this time. ' So Schyler *did not* take cyanide ? '

' Well . . . now look, ma'am, it just isn't sense.'

' Clever little devil, aren't you ? Why do you suppose he 'phoned Garnett and gave him the news about the inheritance, and told him to be at Tracey Terrace by eight sharp ? '

' That doesn't seem to have much——'

' Larry, Larry ! You've been bright up till now. This minute you're being half-witted. Schyler wanted suspicion diverted. He took cyanide, knowing Toby would be there at eight to get help to him: he *knew* no man was going to miss an appointment that was to confirm he'd inherited that much money.

'And Garnett?' She glowered at him. 'Garnett did just what a man would do, just what Schyler, a toper himself, never thought of. Garnett got stinking to celebrate. And you turned up late as well, Larry, because you got mixed up in a war. Both Schyler's witnesses and both his rescuers let him down. He damn-near died, and he would have done if you hadn't read a book on cyanide and known what steps to take.'

'Thanks, ma'am.' I looked at Lanny's baffled face. I was groggy, but I came up for more. 'He couldn't *possibly* have taken cyanide.'

'Stubborn little stinker, aren't you? Larry, ever heard of Rasputin?'

'Naturally. He . . . ' I gaped. '*Rasputin!* The monk who brought down the Czar!'

'You're getting intelligent all of a sudden. You know about him, Coager?'

'Well, enough, Mrs. Pym.'

'Then you will be aware members of the Czar's court tried to kill Rasputin, and, later, succeeded. One thing they did was to give him wine laced with hydrocyanic acid, enough to kill a horse. He drank it and he was sick, but he recovered* and seemed well enough after it.

'Schyler was a lawyer. He never moved a step until he knew every inch of the way. Rasputin's death was old stuff to him, but knowing so many White Russians here, it wasn't long before he found out about that cyanide business. If you ask me, the whole of his slaughter

---

* All the medical facts explained by Mrs. Pym and Dr. Fedor are correct. Rasputin's immunity to the poison in his wine, which he was given in an assassination attempt, was due to the same stomach condition as Schyler's. Rasputin was an alcoholic, used to consuming great quantities of liquor. Taylor's *Medical Jurisprudence*, and other authorities, explain this immunity by suggesting the sugar in the wine, containing the hydrocyanic acid, inhibited its action. It was not this, but Rasputin's stomach condition which saved his life.

campaign was planned the moment he knew he would be immune to cyanide. I don't know who told him—betcha it was a medical man, like Dr. Fedor, who's bursting to tell you the news.'

Dr. Fedor was startled at being thrust forward. He stood helplessly until Mrs. Pym's face got him going.

'Why, yes. I simply could not believe that Schyler had been given cyanide in lethal strength. I knew it was so because I had the contents of the stomach pump, let alone other things, to prove it. I—um—I *had* to know the answer—as a medical man, quite apart from a very human curiosity—and I delved in libraries until I found it. Schyler was a lifelong alcoholic, a very heavy drinker indeed. He was suffering from a condition known as alcoholic gastritis.

'If you will bear with me for a moment,' he beamed at us all, proud of his centre of interest, 'I should explain that hydrocyanic acid was used, a somewhat swifter agent than potassium cyanide. It is a general protoplasmic poison, and is quickly absorbed from mucous membranes; it is even very toxic when inhaled.

'But Schyler ingested the poison in a gelatine capsule, which, of course, would not disintegrate until it reached the stomach. That, of course, means death, as we already know from the other victims.

'Now, here is the very big "but." A victim of alcoholic gastritis lacks the normal condition of hydrochloric acid in the stomach; the stomach's mucous membrane is thickened by alcoholic gastritis, and as the poisonous action of the substance is governed, to a large extent, by the presence of hydrochloric acid, the virtual effect would be to *null* the poison, either completely or, in any case, to delay its effect far beyond the greatest delay known to medical science. That—um—is what happened.'

'Schyler knew it,' Mrs. Pym added forthrightly. 'He played a bold hand, knowing perfectly well he was nearly as safe as houses. He didn't reckon on being left that long without help, though.'

I was thoroughly appalled.

'You mean he took a chance like that? The lunatic!'

'The fiction of the Cyanide Man depended on it. He knew very well that whatever suspicion might come, he would never be suspected because he had been a victim, saved by luck. Even his attempt on Lydia Tschenko was a safe bet; we could suspect everybody, but it would never include *him*.' Mrs. Pym nodded. 'I know he ran to get back the wrapping-paper; that was the frightened human being acting before the cold-booded lawyer had got to thinking it out. And was it such a risk? It was risking everything on one big throw, dammit. Men have done crazier things for a hell of a smaller sum of money.'

'I shall found a Society for the Abolition of Cyanide,' Toby Garnett said in a suddenly cheerful voice.

'Garnett! Of course!' Mrs. Pym actually beamed at him. She hauled out her cheque-book, tore off a cheque and waved it. 'Coager, got a photographer?'

'Eh? Why, yes, Benchley's probably outside. You mean you'd like a picture of Toby?'

'*And* me. It'll decorate the story you're going to write about the female man-eater. You're going to take a shot of me, handing Garnett his cheque for two hundred million. Garnett, you'd better grin like an ape—look pleased. Think of the hell-raising you'll be able to do with the money.'

'Ma'am.' I tried the voice of reason. 'You wouldn't be handing him the money; the will's not probated, and the law——'

'Larry Baker.' Her hands went on her hips, though there was real laughter in her eyes. 'Do you think I give a hoot about reality? I'm going to have that picture taken the way I want it. The public will know it's phoney; what does it matter? It's the gesture. I like making gestures. It's the Pym touch to make big gestures, high, wide and handsome ones, and I'll be a monkey's aunt if there's a bigger gesture in this world than me handing our down-trodden-looking friend here a cheque for two hundred million. Now, Coager, *jump to it* ! '

And he did. When Mrs. Pym wants a thing, she has it, which, I think is the way it should be, bless her crusted old heart.